ALL THE
LIES
WE TOLD

BOOKS BY JENNIFER HARVEY

Someone Else's Daughter

ALL THE LIES WE TOLD

JENNIFER HARVEY

bookouture

Published by Bookouture in 2020

An imprint of Storyfire Ltd.
Carmelite House
50 Victoria Embankment
London EC4Y 0DZ

www.bookouture.com

ISBN: 978-1-83888-727-8
eBook ISBN: 978-1-83888-726-1

Previously published as *No More Secrets*

For my sister, Elaine. Thank you for always being there for me.

CHAPTER ONE

March 2015

For the first couple of days, Evie thought nothing of it. She was used to him disappearing without warning or explanation. If she were being honest, she would even admit she enjoyed his absence. It was a relief not to have him around sometimes.

At least she'd seen it coming this time, had noticed the familiar descent into silence, the glazing over of his eyes. He was *away* again and there was no point in asking what was troubling him, he would never tell her. All she could do was wait for it to pass.

When he'd been gone three days, she texted him just to be sure—*Dad, where are you?*—and got no reply, but again, she didn't think too much about it. In a dark mood, his need for solitude could keep him away for days, and even when he returned, all she ever received was a grunt or a nod, by way of a reply, when she asked if he was okay.

It was only when she went around to his house that she started to worry. His cell phone was sitting on the table by the front door, the battery empty, so it had switched itself off. Even in the darkest of moods, he never left home without it. She felt the first trace of panic then because wherever he was, she'd not be able to contact him. When she checked the closet in the hall, and saw his overnight bag was still there, she was relieved; he always took it when he went away some place, so he couldn't have gone far.

Then he must be painting, she thought. Absorbed in some project and unaware that he hadn't seen anyone in days. But his studio was empty, and the painting he was working on was half-finished in its easel, the brushstrokes rough and unworked; the image too abstract and too unfinished to make any sense of it.

The scene left her with the impression that he could have left just moments before. Gone out to pick up a new tool, or paint color he decided was needed. The work stopped midway. It had that feel about it. Of something having been interrupted.

She asked around in town, at the post office and the grocery store. Had they seen him? But no one had.

"Has he wandered off again?" Donna asked her when she unloaded her groceries onto the counter. She'd been surprised at the question, by the "again"; though it shouldn't have surprised her. In a town this size, there wasn't much you could keep to yourself. Everyone knew her story, just as everyone knew her father was "never the same after all that business with Ethan."

"He'll be back when he's ready, I guess," she told Donna. And they both smiled and laughed, her father's disappearance just a quirky personality trait, as if it was understandable, endearing even, that he sometimes needed to take off without warning, and with no thought for other people.

But as the days went by, the worry became too great, and she picked up the phone and called Ryan at the police station, but he had the same reaction as Donna.

"He'll just be off somewhere, you know how he is," he told her.

Even when she mentioned the cell phone and the bag and explained that it wasn't like her father to go off without them, Ryan's concern was still muted.

"Okay, I tell you what. If he doesn't get in touch or turn up, call back in a couple of days." But she could tell from the tone of his voice that he wasn't expecting her to call.

So she had waited—just a day—then walked down to the station and insisted it was different this time. She could feel it. Though she didn't tell Ryan she'd been staring up at Mount Saxon, feeling the certainty take hold of her. *He's up there*, she thought, *I know he is.*

Though she tried to push it away, the certainty could not be shaken off so easily; he was dead and had been for days now. When they went up that mountainside it would be to retrieve a body, not to rescue a man.

No one questioned her when she suggested they head to Mount Saxon. "He sometimes takes a walk around there," she explained. "He says it keeps him fit in his old age."

And so, a small group of them, herself, Ryan, and some men from the town, had pulled on jackets and boots and headed up the trail in the early morning, just as the first blush of light brushed the mountainside.

It was cold still, crispy cold, and she listened to the sound of the frost underfoot as they walked, first across the grassy path then a long stretch through the dense pines, up to the rocky gravel road, before finally hitting the first snow as they gained altitude.

None of them spoke much. Just the guys up front chatting, then falling silent as the climb became steeper and the cold seeped into them.

But she could feel their nervousness and a tingle of intuition charged the air. She wasn't the only one who sensed Andrew was gone.

As they approached the first waypoint on the trail, Ryan stopped and waited for her to catch up with him.

"Listen, Evie," he said to her. "Are you sure you want to be out here with us?"

"You mean, if we find him, do I want to see it?"

He shuffled his feet and looked away, out over the lake and the valley, as if he needed to take in the scenery in order to work up the courage to reply.

"I guess that's what I mean, yes."

"I just need to know he's been found," she told him. "If I know that, I can walk back down without seeing him."

But before they could turn and walk on, one of the men shouted out, "He's here! He's here!"

Ryan reached out to her and placed his hand on her shoulder, as much to comfort her as to keep her from walking further. She wanted to lean on him; to let her head nestle in the folds of his jacket and feel protected.

It took only a few minutes for them to confirm he was dead. The unresponsive shape, crumpled in the rockfall at the base of a ledge, was something they'd witnessed before. The contorted shape of a faller, always the same, it seemed. Broken, bent, and silent.

She had done as she promised, nodded silently to Ryan and made her way back down, focusing on the sound of each step as she went, the initial scramble and scratch on the rocks becoming the hollow thud of feet meeting solid earth as she neared the bottom. Before she reached the road, she heard the *whump* of a helicopter making its way toward the summit. The rescue team come to recover her father, or what was left of him.

She stood and watched as it flew overhead and then out of sight, landing someplace over the ridge, just out of view, before she headed back home where she crawled into bed and tried to hide from the day, from the world, from the pain.

CHAPTER TWO

March 2015

When the doorbell rang, her instinct was to turn over and pull the covers up. Just wait until whoever it was went away. But they were persistent, and after a minute or so she heard Ashley calling out to her.

"Evie! Evie, are you okay?"

She would have to get up. Ashley knew she was at home, and she wouldn't leave until Evie let her inside.

"I know it's early," she said when Evie opened the door. "But when I heard what happened, I had to come over immediately. My God, are you all right?"

She was barely over the threshold when she pulled Evie to her in a firm embrace, and Evie could only stand there, limp and disoriented. There was a weight in her muscles that felt like flu, a heaviness that made movement difficult. Then she remembered: her father was dead. And she slumped a little deeper into Ashley's shoulder and allowed herself a moment of comfort.

When Ashley finally let go of her, they walked to the kitchen and Evie pulled up a chair at the table and sat there while Ashley took control.

"I'll make you some coffee," she said. "Have you eaten anything? You need to keep your strength up after a shock like that."

"I'm fine, Ashley," Evie replied. "Honestly, you don't need to go to any trouble."

"Hey, it's no trouble. It's what friends are for, isn't it, helping out in a crisis?"

"It's not a crisis. I'm just tired is all. I didn't sleep so well."

"I can imagine, I mean…"

She was glad Ashley couldn't bring herself to mention what had happened to Andrew. It helped a little, to know her grief and pain were shared and understood.

It had been a mistake not to see him. All night she had lain awake imagining him crumpled and broken on the mountainside. With every hour, his body seemed to contort into bloodier and ever more distorted forms. And the nightmare vision of him was still in the back of her mind as she tried to adjust to her first day without him.

"Would you like me to make breakfast?" Ashley asked.

"No, coffee's fine. Please, Ashley, don't fuss. I'm okay. I just need to take it all in."

But Ashley ignored her and set about preparing granola with fruit and yogurt. Ordinarily, Evie would have stopped her from taking over, but today she let herself be distracted by Ashley's busy efforts.

"Here you go," Ashley said as she placed cups of coffee and bowls of granola on the table for them both. The sight of them was more comforting than Evie anticipated, and she allowed herself a small smile of gratitude.

"Thanks," she said.

"No problem," Ashley replied, and sipped her coffee before continuing, "So tell me, what happened?"

"I don't know. They think he slipped and fell. There was a lot of ice up there."

"Oh God, poor Andrew," Ashley said. "What was he doing up there by himself, and at this time of year? That trail is so dangerous when it's icy, he must have known that."

"I'm sure he did, but he went up there all the time. He knew that trail better than anyone. I still can't believe he fell. It just doesn't make sense."

"Well, these things happen…"

"I guess, I just never thought it would happen to him. He could have walked it with his eyes closed. How…?"

"Don't torture yourself worrying about it, Evie. No good will come of it."

"I know, I just don't want to think about him up there alone, that his last minutes were…" But she couldn't finish. Imagining, even for one second, that her father had suffered, was too much for her.

"Have you spoken to your mom yet?"

"No, not yet. As soon as I came home yesterday after we found him, I collapsed. I think I've been asleep since seven o'clock last night."

"Would you like me to call her?"

Evie thought about it. It would be the easy option. The cowardly option. But she couldn't let her mother hear news like this from someone else. And besides, she would only be putting off the inevitable. As soon as her mom heard what had happened, she'd come over from Boulder and Evie would have to face her.

"No, I'll call her later. Maybe the police have already told her. I don't know. But she should hear it from me, don't you think?"

"Yeah, I guess. If you're okay with it. So what happens now?"

"I don't know, I couldn't take it in. Ryan said something about them having to confirm it was an accident before they can release the body. He said he'd let me know. But it should only take a few days apparently."

"Why would they think it was anything other than an accident?"

"I don't think they do, it's just a formality."

Ashley nodded. "So, when will you have the funeral? I can help, I can call the mortician if you like?"

Evie hadn't even thought of that. Her father's funeral. The very idea of it made her want to crawl back to bed and tell the world to carry on without her.

"Let's just wait until Ryan calls, I really don't know what's going on."

"Okay, but let me help you, Evie. Please?"

"Okay."

They sat there in silence for a moment, drinking their coffee, but she could see that Ashley was fidgety and wanted to say something. She didn't need to guess what it was: Ethan.

She wasn't sure she had the energy to talk about him yet, but Ashley gave her no choice.

"Listen, I know it's none of my business, but I suppose your brother will be coming home for the funeral?"

"I guess so," Evie replied. What else was there to say?

"Is that why you haven't called your mom yet? Are you afraid she'd tell Ethan what happened, and bring him back here?"

"To be honest," she said, "I can't even think about Ethan coming back here. It's all too much right now. I mean what am I supposed to say to him?"

"So what are you going to do, ignore him? He is your brother after all."

The question confused her. What could she do? Not tell her mom the news, or forbid her from bringing Ethan with her? Andrew was his father too. He had a right to attend his own father's funeral if he wanted to.

"I can't really do anything, can I?" Evie replied. "If he wants to come here then I can't stop him. Like you say, he's my brother—he has as much of a right to say his goodbyes as I do. Anyway, maybe he won't want to come back. I think he knows his presence wouldn't be appreciated."

"Well, that's one way of putting it. But sure, maybe he won't come. We can always hope,"

Ordinarily it was the sort of quip that would make her laugh, Ashley's sharp sense of humor something she appreciated. But today she could only tilt her head and raise her eyebrows.

"What? I'm only saying what you're thinking. Evie, I know you don't want him here either, so why pretend?"

She wondered if that was true though. She didn't want to face things alone, she was sure of that much at least. But she hadn't had the opportunity yet to think about her brother or her mom coming home.

"Listen I'm not going to stop him coming here if that's what he decides. Anyway, please can we stop talking about it? My dad just died and that's all I can deal with right now. Ethan, my mom, all that stuff… it can wait."

"Evie, you know everyone here is going to have an opinion about it. No one has forgotten what he did, and they'll never forgive him for it or accept him back."

"Not even for his father's funeral? No one's asking for forgiveness, but some compassion isn't too much to ask for, is it?"

She was expecting Ashley to look away, to feel a little ashamed at her lack of understanding, but when it came to Ethan, she had clearly underestimated the strength of Ashley's feelings, even after all this time.

"Just don't be surprised if people speak out if he does come back, that's all I'm saying. Be prepared for it."

"Dammit, Ashley. Then maybe they should all just keep their opinions to themselves. If he comes home, we'll deal with it. He'll be here and gone in a day. What harm will that do?"

"People have long memories, Evie. No one wants to be reminded of what he did, but if he comes back, they'll be forced to face it all again and—"

"Do you think I want to remember any of it?"

"No, of course not, I know you don't but—"

"Ashley, I've spent the last twenty years trying to put it all behind me, just talking about it again makes me—" But she couldn't finish what she wanted to say. She had no way of articulating what she felt. The fear, the old panic, all those feelings she had thought would never return.

"Listen," she heard Ashley saying, "maybe someone should talk to him, give him a call, tell him he won't be welcome…"

She was trying to sound reasonable, Evie realized. But the threat in those words was evident. *Not welcome*. Ethan didn't need someone to call him and tell him that. Twenty years ago, he knew what everyone here thought of him, and now, he still would. There were people who thought he should spend the rest of his life in prison. Or worse.

"I don't know if that's such a good idea," Evie replied.

Ashley leaned forward as if to make her point clearly. "All I'm saying is that maybe it would be better if he stayed away, for everyone. For you. Even if it is his dad's funeral, that doesn't give him the right—"

Ashley was trying hard to keep her tone reasonable, but Evie still caught the touch of irritation in her voice. She was determined to make her point. But there was no point in arguing—Ashley was not the type of person to back down easily—so Evie raised her palms. "Okay, okay. I get it."

"So I'll get Mason to give him a call then?"

"What?"

"Ethan. I'll get Mason to have a word with him."

She couldn't believe that Ashley seriously thought Mason should be the one to call. And she almost laughed at the suggestion because it was so preposterous.

"Listen, Ashley, can you just leave me alone for a while? I need to call my mom and I need to take a shower and I really need to get my head straight. What happened twenty years ago, I just… Just leave it for now, please?"

"Okay. For now. But this is what he's going to stir up if he comes back, Evie, all that viciousness and anger, and I just want to know you're prepared for it."

"I know. Do you seriously think I don't know that?"

"Right, well, I guess I should get going."

Ashley left her sitting in the kitchen, the day not quite bright yet and the bitter taste of coffee coating her tongue and leaving her nauseous.

All that viciousness and anger, Evie thought. The very idea that even a small flicker of it would be reignited was enough to make her feel sick.

*

She could still remember the number after all this time. When she heard her mom say "hello" at the end of the line, she hesitated before saying, "It's me, Evie," her voice shaking a little.

"Evie! Are you okay?"

"Yeah, I'm okay, but there's been an accident. It's Dad. He's gone."

If her mom heard the panic in Evie's voice as she announced the news, then she didn't acknowledge it. Just as Evie didn't acknowledge the little sigh her mom exhaled down the line, and the trace of disinterest it contained.

"Do you want me to drive over?" her mom asked.

"Could you? I'm not sure what I'm supposed to do…"

"Okay, I'll get an early start tomorrow and be with you for breakfast."

Evie was relieved to hear a hint of compassion in her mom's voice and she felt the tension in her neck and shoulders ease. "Thanks, Mom," she replied.

"Right, well then, I'll see you tomorrow. Oh, and Evie?"

"Yes?"

"Don't worry, everything will be okay."

Evie put down the receiver and stood in the hallway for a while, immobilized by the conversation. *Everything will be okay.* How certain her mother always was about things.

But nothing would be okay. She could feel it in every fiber of her body. Something was headed her way. Her dad's death was not the end of it—it was just the beginning.

And she closed her eyes and clenched her fists, bracing herself.

"Okay," she whispered, "I'm ready."

She chose to ignore the whispered reply that seemed to come from the mountain. That old, familiar voice.

Are you, Evie? Are you ready?

CHAPTER THREE

March 2015

Carole stood by the kitchen window, looking out over the lake. From the tilt of her head, Evie could see she was looking toward the mountains, and thinking about Andrew. Her mom gave a small shudder, then turned and approached the table where Evie sat drinking a cup of coffee. Without asking, Evie stood up, walked over to the coffee pot and poured her mom a cup, dribbling in a small amount of milk, then dropping in one cube of sugar, and set the coffee down on the table.

Her mom smiled as she lifted the cup to her lips and sipped. "Just as I like it. It's nice that you remember such a small detail. It makes this place feel like home again."

As Evie sat opposite her mom, she thought back to the last time they had been in the kitchen together like this. It was the day her mom had left for Boulder, about a year after the trial. Evie remembered her face, the way she had begged her one last time, "Come with me, Evie," and the sad resignation in her eyes when Evie had again said no.

It was still there, that distant look, as if the expression had fixed itself in place. The shock of the rejection had never really left her, and Evie wondered if her mother realized how distant it made her look, staring at the world with that world-weary stoicism.

But if her mom was aware of how nervous it made Evie to have her sitting in her kitchen drinking coffee after all these years, then she showed no sign of it. If anyone were to walk past the window and see them sitting together, they'd assume they were enjoying an everyday family breakfast, mom and daughter comfortable together in each other's presence.

But Evie had long ago learned how to mimic the inscrutable gaze her mother possessed, and she soon fell back into that habit of hiding her own feelings from the one person she should have been able to confide in.

"It must be hard for you too, I guess," Evie said, "to be back here now Dad's gone, I mean."

"It is…" her mom replied. "And knowing that he died alone up there, the thought of that…" She paused, as if she needed to check her emotions before she could continue.

Evie wondered if she should comfort her in some way, but she felt paralyzed as to how.

"It's not just his death," her mom continued. "It's everything else too. The past. It's not easy being back here. I had good reasons for leaving after all…"

Her voice trailed off, but she didn't need to finish what she was saying. Evie knew what her mother was thinking without her having to say it out loud. The memories. All that trauma and sadness. The way their once happy family had disintegrated. And the one thing they hadn't mentioned yet: Ethan.

Neither of them had spoken of him or even dared to say his name.

"Would it help if I said there were happy days as well, back then, in the past?" Evie asked.

"Were there? I seem to have forgotten."

"Yes. Before everything. Before, well, you know… We laughed a lot. Don't you remember?"

She could see her mom pause as she tried to remember the happier times as a family, the sounds of them together as a family, laughing, joking, teasing each other.

Typical, Evie thought, *never remembering the good things. Forgetting how much laughter filled the house, accompanying so many small, insignificant moments.*

She could think of a hundred happy moments off the top of her head. Pulling a fish from the lake and cooking it on an open fire by the shore. Hiking to the top of Mount Saxon in summer. Her father teaching her how to paint the wildflowers in spring. They had enjoyed every one of these things. And so many more. Why could her mom never give herself over to remembering small moments like this?

After a minute or so, her mom shook her head. "It's strange, isn't it?" she said. "You can remember someone's face, the way they stood or walked. But the sound of them? Their voice, the way they laughed. I tried to recall your dad's laugh just then, but I couldn't. How can that be?"

Evie tried herself. She assumed she could conjure up the sound of her dad's laughter at will. But nothing came. Her mom was right, the sound of him was gone. A significant, yet intangible piece of him had evaporated before she'd had a chance to lock it away safely in her mind. And she felt the jolt of grief rush over her again.

To Evie's surprise, Carole sensed it, and stretching an arm across the table, she took hold of Evie's hand, and they sat there quietly lost in their thoughts, their coffee turning cold, forgotten and unwanted.

How would Ethan feel about this? Evie thought. *If he saw them sitting here together comforting one another?* And she was struck by the realization that he might need to be comforted too.

They were about to bury Andrew, and it felt wrong that Ethan would be absent. Even a long-lost son had the right to say a final farewell to their own father, did he not?

She was going to ask Carole if they had made a mistake when the doorbell rang.

*

When Evie opened the door, she was groggy still with grief, and she blinked to be sure that what she saw was not some sort of hallucination.

"Ethan?" she whispered.

And he nodded, swallowed down some emotion she couldn't quite decipher, then whispered back, "Hey there."

If he hadn't been standing at her front door, she wouldn't have recognized him. Something about the set of his shoulders, the confidence in his stance, would have fooled her. She'd have walked right past him on the street without even looking in his direction.

But up close like this, there could be no mistaking him. Her brother. Those eyes of his, so crystalline blue and striking, and offset by a full head of dark chestnut hair, no gray or bald spots yet. He looked younger than she expected, and his freckles were still visible along the bridge of his nose. Though his smile was no longer as small and shy as it was, and his teeth were more yellow, more cigarette-stained than she remembered.

She tried to stop the trembling in her legs as she struggled to think of something to say, but she was too dumbfounded by his unexpected appearance.

"So can I come in?" he asked her.

And she nodded, gestured with her arm, and stepped aside behind the door—too nervous to stand too close to him, she needed to have something between them. He stood in the hallway, waiting for her to show him where to go, as if the house was unfamiliar to him, the way to the living room forgotten after twenty years away.

"Sorry if I woke you up," he said.

And it was only then she remembered her disheveled appearance. The tousled hair, the grainy sleep-encrusted eyes, the slightly musty smell of her dressing gown.

She spoke without thinking, "I thought you were the mortician. For Dad, I mean." The words had slipped out and there was no way to take them back now, so all she could do was stutter. "Dad… He… fell… He… he's dead."

She felt the weight of her grief mingle with the shock of seeing him, and it made her feel limp and confused as to how she should react.

"I know," he said. "That's why I'm here."

"You know? How? Who told you?"

He just smiled at her and headed down the hallway toward the kitchen, the way familiar to him still, after all.

"Is Mom here?" he asked. But Evie didn't need to answer. Their mom was standing in the doorway of the kitchen, and when he walked up to her, she drew him in for a hug and said, "So you made it."

So that was it, Evie thought. She had told him. Of course she had. She would hardly keep him from his own father's funeral.

She watched them walk into the kitchen arm in arm, their easy intimacy surprising her with a pang of resentment. Ethan pulled out a chair from under the table, sat down and looked around the room, taking in the ways it had changed, the ways it had stayed the same. Evie could see that the familiarity of it all surprised him. He ran his fingers over the grain in the wood, trying to find the scratches he had left there when he was a kid. Yes, it was the same table. Did he realize, she wondered, that he had pulled out the chair he always sat in? That he had taken his seat as if it was the most natural thing in the world, the place at the table his still.

"It's been a long time," Evie said, her voice dreamy, the words slow and slightly slurred. "Such a very long time." She could feel the world turning to syrup, the air in the room thickening as she tried to figure out what was happening. A trickle of sweat slid down her spine and the palms of her hands turned clammy. She was scared of him, she realized. Her own brother.

"Listen, Evie," her mom said. "Why don't you go straighten yourself up, then we can talk?"

She nodded, glad to have her thoughts interrupted. As she went upstairs to her bedroom, the weakness in her legs grew with every step, as the shock of seeing Ethan finally hit her. He had come home for the funeral after all. Why hadn't Mom warned her that he was coming? She could have prepared for his arrival. And it made her teeth clench to think that her mom still didn't trust her when it came to Ethan.

When she closed the bedroom door behind her, she flopped onto the bed and lay there for a minute or two, as the shaking took hold of her, a mixture of emotions flooding through her. Her dad was gone. Ethan was here. And her mom. After all this time.

She showered and dressed in a daze, pulling a brush through her hair and trying to think about what it meant, because it was obvious he wasn't only here for the funeral. There was a glint in his eyes which suggested as much, but she wasn't sure she was ready to confront him—or if she really wanted him back here.

And she wouldn't be the only one. There was a town full of people who would not be pleased to see him and would demand to know what he was doing here. There were still people here who thought he should never have been released. "Let him rot in prison." How often had she heard them say that? And their anger had not diminished over the years. If anything, it had hardened.

"Dammit," she whispered. "Why didn't Mom tell me you were coming home?"

*

When she came back into the kitchen, Ethan was making fresh coffee and the comforting smell of it filled the room. The machine sputtered away as if the world was exactly as it had been yesterday morning. As if Ethan making coffee in her kitchen was nothing out of the ordinary.

"I hope it's okay?" he asked her as he gestured to the coffee pot.

She nodded, then sat at the table and asked him to pour her a cup. She would remain composed, she had decided. She would not allow herself to be overwhelmed or intimidated.

"I hope you made it strong," she told him, relieved that her voice was steady, her tone straightforward.

He walked over to the table and set down three cups, before looking around for sugar and milk.

"The sugar's right there, by the machine," Carole told him. "And the milk's in the fridge."

Evie felt like she should do something. Take control. This was her home now, after all. But her mom's assertive presence left her feeling hopeless and incapable of action. Better to let her mom resume her old role, she thought. Even if it was annoying, it was easier that way.

Evie watched Ethan and took in the changes in him again. The way he walked was so unfamiliar to her now, she realized. And again, it was his confidence which struck her. The way he moved so easily around the kitchen, so loose and relaxed. Not arrogant exactly, but purposeful, as if he didn't question his right to fill this space.

That quiet kid she used to know, that awkward boy, was long gone. The man in her kitchen was her brother, yes, but not the one she knew, not the one she remembered. This was a man who had been in prison for twenty years, and it showed. Things had clearly happened to him in that time and they had changed him; it would take months of watching him before she could figure out how he got from that boy, to this man.

She thought about herself. How she must look to him, sitting there at the kitchen table cradling a cup of coffee and staring at him, her composure regained after the shock of opening the door to him, but her confusion still evident.

Did she seem like a woman to him? Or was she still his sixteen-year-old little sister, as fragile and dreamy as ever?

"So," he said as he sat down opposite her and stirred his coffee. He was trying not to look at her, unsure, she supposed, as to how he should begin.

She preferred this shyness—it was more familiar to her—but his presence still put her on edge and before realizing it, she asked the one question she had wondered about since he arrived on her doorstep: "What are you doing here, Ethan?" Immediately she regretted the confrontational tone in her voice, because it sounded as though she was telling him he had no right to be here.

"He's just here for the funeral, Evie," Carole intervened.

"Really, is that all?" she said, keeping her gaze fixed on her brother. She hoped she looked more confident than she felt.

"I've a right to be here for that, surely? He was my father too," Ethan replied.

"I'm not saying you don't, but there's more to it than that, isn't there? You might have been in prison for twenty years, but I can still tell when you're not telling me everything."

He smiled at her, as if hearing this pleased him for some reason. As if what she had really said was that she recognized him still, remembered him still, knew who he was at some intimate, filial level.

"Right," he said, "I forgot. There never was any fooling you, was there?"

His voice contained a sharpness Evie did not recognize—and something defensive that made her catch her breath.

"Ethan, that's enough," Carole interrupted.

"Just tell me what you're doing here," she asked him again. "That's all I want to know."

Carole answered again on his behalf, as if he was a child who could not stand up for himself. "There are a few things he needs to clear up."

"Sorry, what?" Evie asked, and she couldn't contain her agitation now. "*Clear up*? What the hell does that mean?"

"Michael," Ethan said. And he looked at her, the concern in his eyes leaving her in no doubt he was serious.

"Michael?" she said. "There's nothing that needs to be cleared up about Michael. Shit, Ethan, come on—"

"I just want everyone to know the truth. I want everyone to know what really happened to him!" His voice wavered as he spoke, because he knew the impact such a statement would have.

Evie could see that his loss of self-control made Carole nervous. "Ethan, please," Carole said, "let's just take things one step at a time. That's what we agreed. And besides, we've a funeral to get through first."

Evie turned to face her, imploring her to explain. "Mom, we know what happened to Michael. He spent twenty years in prison for what he did to him. Dammit, Ethan, you even admitted it in court."

"Stop, please," Carole said. "Let's just start again."

"Huh? Mom, did you hear what he just said? He basically just walked into my home after more than twenty years and announced he's innocent. I mean, that's what he means, doesn't he? What the hell is going on?"

"No, Evie, that's not what he said. What he means is—"

"I meant what I said," Ethan interrupted. "I just want everyone to know the truth."

And Evie looked at him, sitting straight backed and confident in his chair and she knew that he meant it.

She should have told him to leave right then. She should have stood up and opened the door and said, "Just go." Because she knew what it meant. *Michael.* Surely he knew it would only cause trouble. There could be no clearing things up, only an opening of deep wounds that had never healed. That name, Michael; she never mentioned him out loud. It was like scar tissue. If you picked it open, it would rupture and let all the old poison ooze out.

"Don't say his name," Evie whispered. "Please, don't talk about him."

And Ethan looked at her, open mouthed and uncertain whether he had heard her correctly. He tried to say something, but Carole reached out and laid her hand on his arm.

"No, not yet, Ethan," she said. "Okay? Not yet. We agreed."

But it was too late.

Michael, Evie thought. *Michael.*

And she closed her eyes but could not escape it. That fiery red, glowing and burning behind her eyes and the sweet warm taste of something rising in her throat and making her retch. The iron taste of blood she had tried so long to forget.

*

Michael Deacon. For more than twenty years, he had been the one person she needed to forget. Because whenever she remembered him, she risked falling into a spiral of trauma. Forgetting him had been a matter of survival. Ever since her father found her in the forest, disoriented and mute with fear, she had struggled to come to terms with what had happened to him. With what Ethan did to him.

She learned to keep a picture of Michael in her mind, as he had been: laughing and singing and goofing about. Michael, beautiful Michael. "Fix that image in your mind." That was what her therapist taught her. "Keep that piece of him with you. Create a bright, beautiful memory."

But just hearing his name on her brother's lips now caused her to slip already. Those other images, the ones she learned to push away, resurfacing before she could have a chance to fight them. As if they were waiting to sabotage her all along.

And she knew the danger of it. The way these memories could force her back into that deep, impenetrable darkness. The same dark hole her father pulled her from more than twenty years ago. He had gathered her up from the forest floor, and carried her home, away from the forest, away from the burning cabin and back to safety. But there was something hidden in those trees, something dangerous. She could feel it still, and she feared it.

But Michael Deacon was gone. Michael Deacon was dead. And she understood she must forget him if she was to survive. *Make no mystery of it*—that was what she learned over the years. *Ask no questions.* As painful as it had been to accept, her brother was guilty. There was nothing else she needed to know.

So why bring it all back now? she wondered. *What purpose did it serve?*

No, she was not going to be forced to remember these things. She had tried too long to forget. Michael Deacon was dead and buried, and that was how he should remain. And besides, her mother was right. They had a funeral to get through.

CHAPTER FOUR

March 2015

It was a quiet, understated ceremony. Efficient and with no fuss, just as Andrew would have wanted it. Prayers were said, but there were no tears, no hymns, and just a simple sermon. Though her mother had insisted on flowers for the casket. "No need for the whole thing to be spartan and miserable." Then the slow walk to the grave. The respectful mutterings of condolence.

As the ceremony progressed, Evie hoped they would get through it without incident. Ethan's presence in the church, next to her, had elicited gasps as the mourners entered, but she turned to watch as people took their seats, and made eye contact with each of them and nodded, in the hope they would see the desperate plea in her eyes: *Please, don't say anything. Please, don't leave. Stay here, for my father.*

Maybe the presence of the casket subdued them. It was for Andrew that they had come to say goodbye. There was enough respect for him to hold their tongues. And if they refused to acknowledge Ethan's presence, if they refused to look at him or shake his hand and offer their condolences, well, she could understand that.

At the graveside, Evie watched as the casket was lowered into the earth and felt an unexpected dread. Her father had been the one who had steadied her all these years. The one who had saved her from going under. He could always see when she was beginning to flounder and had known how to steer her to shore before she hit the rocks. Now she feared his death would bring it all crashing down again and she didn't trust herself to stay on an even keel.

The dread left her praying at the graveside and she sent a wish down with her father into the ground, where she hoped it would take root.

Help me, she asked him, as she took a handful of soil and threw it into the grave. *Please help me.*

And the sound of the earth as it thumped on the casket was an answer of sorts, as if her father was standing right beside her, squeezing her hand and whispering in her ear: *Just remember what I always told you, Evie. If you need to forget what happened, for your own peace of mind, then that's what you need to do. Push it all away and you'll come to no harm.*

They walked through the churchyard in silence, each of them lost in contemplation, and with every step Evie felt her resolve strengthen.

She would stay calm and keep her distance. She would leave Ethan to do whatever it was he needed to do—his *clearing up*—and then, when it was done, she would ask them both to leave. They would carry on with their separate lives and Evie would learn, somehow, to live without her father. She would come to no harm, just as her father had promised.

It seemed so easy thinking it in that moment. Attainable, even. And if she needed to pretend, if she needed to keep a lid on things and appear to be in control, she could do, she was sure of it.

At the cemetery gates, Ashley approached her and wrapped her arms around her. "If you need anything then call me okay?" she said. And Evie nodded and promised she would.

She could see Mason hovering behind his sister, his face somber and firm. The difference between them always surprised her—Mason's meanness something Ashley always seemed to be trying to balance out with kindness.

But when Mason pulled her aside as they walked back home, she understood the coiled-up anger in his voice as he whispered in her ear. "He had better be gone by tomorrow, Evie. You make sure that he is, okay?"

He didn't wait for a reply. That wasn't Mason's style. He had made his demand and he expected it to be granted. She had neither the will nor the energy to worry about him. Mason might want Ethan gone quickly, but she would find a way to appease him. What choice did she have?

*

When they got home, they shuffled around the house not knowing what to do or what to say. They had buried a father, a husband, a man only one of them could still claim to love, and the weight of their grief—their different experiences of it—had become apparent now that the practicalities of the funeral were no longer there to distract them.

Later that evening, when she had time for the weight of the day to lift a little, she went looking for Ethan and found him in the living room. She could barely make him out sitting on the sofa in the dark, staring out of the window.

"Hey," she called out to him as she turned on the light. "Are you okay?"

When he looked up at her, she hadn't expected to see tears—the sight of him crying disarmed her and she didn't know what to do. She'd come to tell him that he could only stay for a few days at most. She needed to get back to normal, he'd understand that. And if he didn't, then she'd tell him about Mason and explain that there were too many people who wanted him gone as soon as possible. She had to make him see the strength of feeling—and respect it.

But when he let out a sob, and she saw his shoulders shudder, she was overcome with an unexpected need to comfort him, and she sat beside him and held him as he cried.

It was strange to touch him again. After all this time, the intimacy of it felt so unfamiliar but she gave herself over to her instinct to console him.

Years ago he had helped her in the same way. He had held her and rocked her and told her she was safe. But she didn't want to think about that. Not today, not so soon after they had buried their father. She pushed the memory away, but felt it try to rise to the surface again almost immediately.

From the kitchen she could hear her mom rattling around as she made a start on dinner. Keeping busy was her reaction to every problem—distracting herself by being practical her only coping mechanism. Evie had to smile at that. It was the one thing they had in common. A need to do things in order to keep their thoughts at bay.

It felt unexpectedly comforting to know her mom was there, and Ethan seemed to sense it too.

"It's just like when we were kids, this, isn't it?" he said.

When he smiled at her, it really did feel like they were kids again. As if time had started traveling in the opposite direction, taking her back to days she had spent a lifetime trying to forget. But this only made her aware of the ways that childhood had been ruined—and the reasons she had worked so hard to forget it.

"I guess," she said. "But that was all a long time ago and it's not something we can ever get back."

He pulled himself away from her and wiped his eyes. "I know I can't just come home and expect things to be as they were, Evie. Not when I've been so thoroughly erased."

"Erased? That's a bit much, don't you think? You weren't *erased*, Ethan."

"No?"

"No, I mean—"

But he didn't let her finish. "I was looking for traces of myself last night, up in my room—my *old* room, I guess I should say."

She knew what he was going to say then. She had given him the room he had when he was a kid, and he had smiled when she told him she had made it ready for him. But she had noticed his disappointment when he opened the door and looked inside and saw how much it had changed. It was just a room now and had been for years. One of those anonymous, bland pastel-colored rooms, the type for guests, not a childhood room filled with memories. There was nothing left of him up there. If he looked, he wouldn't find the initials he'd scraped into the windowsill, or the cigarette burn he'd singed into the rug, or the tin box he'd kept hidden under the bedside cabinet. Andrew had been sure to eliminate every trace of Ethan, right down to peeling off the old NFL stickers Ethan had stuck on the inside of the closet one year.

"Twenty years is a very long time, Ethan," she said. "Things change. But that doesn't mean they're erased."

"Maybe… I just hoped—"

It was her turn to interrupt now. "No, Ethan," she said. "Don't hope for anything. Whatever you do, don't hope."

Then she stood and headed to the kitchen, the intimacy of the moment broken. She'd hurt him just then, by saying that, she knew she had. But it was the truth and he might as well acknowledge it. Whatever hope he had coming back here, whatever it was he was trying to achieve, he had to understand that it was pointless. Because he had not been erased. No one here had forgotten him, and he'd be a fool to think they had. It would be dangerous even, for him to think that people didn't look at him with suspicion still. It might have happened twenty years ago, but Michael's death was still raw. Death. She still thought of it that way. It had been the only way she could get through it. To think of it as a death like any other. But it had never been that.

And now Ethan's presence was forcing her to confront the truth. Michael had been murdered and that was the word she should use when she thought of him. It was the word everyone else used when they spoke about him. The word she always avoided, because it caused her too much pain. But she needed to confront it now, just as Ethan needed to understand the fear that was contained in that word too. He had murdered Michael, and that fact alone made people scared of him. They had good reasons for wanting Ethan to leave as soon as possible. She found Carole rummaging around in the kitchen trying to see what she could throw together for dinner. If Evie had been alone, she'd have settled for something simple and easy, grilled cheese perhaps, but her mother apparently thought a more substantial meal was needed. Not celebratory exactly, but food that acknowledged the uniqueness of the day.

She watched Carole as she stood by the sink taking in the sad little pile of ingredients she'd laid out.

"You don't need to go to any trouble," Evie said.

And Carole motioned to the ingredients and laughed.

"It's all a bit paltry. I can probably manage a bowl of pasta, but that's about it. Honestly, Evie, I wonder if you know how to look after yourself properly, you've got no decent food in the house."

Evie ignored the criticism and walked over to the counter to examine the things her mother had laid out. A bag of pasta and some tins of tomatoes. A few dried herbs. An onion.

"Hey, that's not so bad," Evie told her. "C'mon, let me give you a hand."

"No, no need. It's good to have something to do, especially after a day like today."

It was funny that her own mom didn't recognize that they shared the same trait, and Evie needed to keep busy too.

"I'll lay the table then," Evie offered.

"Why don't you get Ethan to help?" Carole suggested.

"I think he just needs time alone. It's been a long day."

Carole was chopping the onion, and she stopped what she was doing, laid the knife on the chopping board and wiped her hands on a tea towel.

"Oh, is he okay?" she asked, and started to head to the door. "I'll check on him."

"No, Mom, leave him, he needs to be by himself for a bit."

"No, I can't leave him, he—"

"Mom, trust me. He's okay. Just let him be."

Evie saw Carole hesitate, before relenting and heading back to her task. "I just worry about him," she said. "It's not easy for him, all of this."

"No, it's not," Evie agreed. "You know, I'm struggling too."

She hoped her mom would recognize how difficult it was for her to open up like this and ask for some understanding. And it hurt when her mom chose to ignore it. Ethan's problems taking precedent, as always.

"He was hoping to come up here before all this, did he tell you that?" Carole asked her.

"Who, Ethan?"

"Yes. I think he hoped they'd be able to talk, that maybe they'd make their peace. And then—"

"You mean with Dad? Did he really think he'd be able to talk to Dad? That they'd be able to 'make their peace'? Seriously?" Evie said.

"Yes, that's what he wanted. And, I think it would have been worth a try. Now we'll never know."

"Know what?"

"If they'd have been able to talk it through. To make their peace."

Evie knew the answer, but she said nothing as she laid the table and tried to ignore the knot of irritation that was tightening her stomach. She'd forgotten the way her mother could get under her skin so easily. *Just stick it out for a few days*, she thought. *They'll be gone soon.* And that thought was enough to settle her and get her through the meal.

But during dinner, a strange numbness came over her. It was more than grief, she knew that, but what it was, she couldn't say, only that it seemed to be slowly surrounding her. They had eaten pretty much in silence, none of them able to talk, as if her lethargy was contagious, and afterward they'd sat together in the living room, the television on, but with the volume down low, and no one really watching it.

"Was that Mason Cardew I saw you talking to?" her mom asked.

"Yes," Evie replied. She hoped her mom would hear the exhaustion in her voice and leave it at that, but she failed to pick up on her weariness and simply carried on.

"What did he want?"

"He was just offering his condolences."

"Oh," Carole replied. "He looked a bit agitated, I thought."

Why did she need to bring it up at all? If she had noticed Mason's agitation at the cemetery then there was no need to discuss it further. They all knew how moody Mason could be and that it was always better to ignore him.

"It was just a shock for everyone, seeing Ethan there. That's not so surprising, is it? And, you know, Mason is still Mason."

"I guess he suggested you tell me to leave?" Ethan said.

There was no point denying it. Her brother may have been in prison for twenty years, but he was still smart when it came to figuring people out. He still watched people and picked up on the slightest emotional signal.

"Yes… You know a lot of people aren't happy about you being around. They're not going to change—you need to stop getting your hopes up."

"My hopes up? My hopes up for what?" There was a tinge of frustration in his voice and she didn't want to have an argument with him, but she had to tell him the truth. He had to at least understand the reality of the situation.

"I don't know," she said. "That you can come back here and *clear a few things up*? What makes you think anyone will listen to what you have to say? And why the great need to suddenly talk about it?"

Right away he seemed deflated. She saw his shoulders droop, not defeated exactly, but more as if he thought it was impossible to explain things to her.

"I hope you'll listen at least… that would be enough for me."

Their mom interrupted, "Ethan… I told you to just leave it be."

And Evie felt it then, the throbbing in her temples, the palpitation behind her eyelids—the old fear and panic inching closer, coming back again, and she wasn't sure she could keep it at bay. She tried to focus on her father's voice. On those imagined words he had uttered at the graveside: *If you need to forget what happened, for your own peace of mind, then that's what you need to do.*

"I'm too tired for this right now. I need to get some sleep."

She left them in the room with the television flickering and as she headed upstairs, she made a wish: *Let me wake in the morning and find them gone.*

*

The bedroom was dark, but she couldn't sleep. So she listened for a while to the unfamiliar sounds of Ethan and her mom getting ready for bed. Their presence should have comforted her—they were family after all. But listening to them made her realize she had missed being this close to others. For years, she refused to think of herself as lonely. *Solitary,* that was the word she used to describe herself. But now, she wondered if it was simply a convenient lie she told herself. Something she could use to keep people at bay. Ever since Michael died, she had avoided getting too close to anyone. She didn't want to feel that pain again, the pain of losing someone you love.

That name again, filling her head. Taunting her, haunting her. *Michael, Michael.*

She pulled her pillow up around her ears and closed her eyes, trying to block out the sounds and her thoughts. But it was no use. She couldn't stop it. He was there again, after all these years. Ethan had made sure of that.

She tried to remember Michael as she had been told to. Happy and laughing and alive. She tried to remember that brief happy summer they had spent together. But no sooner had she fixed on Michael's smiling face than another image appeared. The terrible end to that summer. Her face in the mirror, dirty and messed up. The bruises on her arms and legs. And Michael, gone. Spirited away in a haze of smoke and flames.

"Remember a happier time with him," Dr. Newton had told her. "When you feel yourself panic, remember something good that happened."

Okay then, Evie, she thought. *Let it come, just let it come.*

As she drifted back in time, she felt the heat of that day on her skin again, and heard the ripple of the water lapping the shore of the lake and his laughter, bright and sunny and filling her with joy.

"Michael," she whispered. "Michael."

CHAPTER FIVE

July 1994

That fateful summer of 1994, the heat had been relentless. Everyone moved slowly, the air so thick they could barely breathe. Ethan had reveled in it, as if his energy and enthusiasm for everything were charged by the shimmering heat. The temperatures soared, and they began to spend their days down by the lakeshore. Evie would take a book, a backpack full of snacks, a portable radio, and a picnic blanket to lie down, and read, while Ethan would cool off.

"Are you coming in for a swim?"

Every morning he would ask her, and every morning she would say no. It irritated her that he couldn't resist teasing her. He knew she would never go swimming in that lake again. He knew, too, that her fears were real and not imagined. But that summer, for some reason, he wouldn't let her be.

"You know you shouldn't be asking me that," she would tell him.

And he would laugh and whip his towel at her in a playful way that annoyed her even more.

"Hey! Quit that, will you?" she'd yell at him.

"Ah, come on, Evie. One day you're going to have to face it. One day you're going to have to get back in there."

"Stop it, already. Please."

"Why? It's just water. You need to stop imagining there's something in there. It's a lake. It's just a stupid lake."

And then, as if to prove his point, he ran to the water and dived below the surface, reappearing a few meters further out and turning to wave at her and yell, "You see?" before flipping over and gliding through the water with smooth, effortless strokes.

She'd watched him and wondered why he had to go and spoil things by bringing it up. It was easy for him to laugh, but he wasn't the one who had almost drowned. Perhaps it was just the heat that was getting to him.

She stared at the lake and thought back to that day when she was six years old. *Just a lake.* That wasn't what it was to her and he knew it. It had been Ethan who had brought her to the surface after all, her arms wrapped around his neck, clinging to him in terror at the water's depths. For years she had been unable to shake the belief that what she had felt there in the water was real. She had not imagined it, she had felt it dragging her down, a force that pulled at her legs and wouldn't let her go.

But she had been just a kid, too young to be capable of explaining how it felt to be pulled under by a hidden current and dragged deeper and deeper, knowing for certain that she was going to die. She had no words to describe how it felt to turn in the water and look upward at the light falling through in great sheaths of glistening yellow. She had reached up to it and felt the weight of water on her chest and understood how far she was from the surface, from the light, from safety, from air.

That was when she felt the panic overwhelm her, and the sour contraction of cramps in her legs grow heavier as her arms fell to her side, the weight of her limbs pulling her under. She was drowning, and she knew it but felt powerless, and strangely unwilling, to stop it. Then, something broke the surface and shattered the light into a million tiny pieces. She had blinked and almost gasped, almost filling her lungs with the dark cold water as the swirling water and the bubbles of air enveloped her. For the longest moment, they floated, suspended in the water, and when she looked at him, when she saw it was Ethan, she felt her body relax.

Together, they had looked up at the surface, at that beautiful glistening light. Then she felt an arm grabbing her and pulling her upward. Ethan tugging and tugging until she thought her shoulder would be torn from its socket. They reached the surface, gasping, neither of them able to speak, while from the shore someone waded toward them and helped them back to safety. Her father.

He was yelling at Ethan and shaking him. "You were supposed to be looking after her! What the hell was she doing in the water? She can't swim, Goddammit!"

She had never blamed him. Because he had been down there with her. He had looked her in the eye, and seen how close she was to giving up. And he had known what to do to save her. He had held her gaze and pulled her to the surface in defiance of the water, in defiance of fate.

Since that day, she always felt safer with him by her side. She needed his guidance, his energy, his courage. Her brother, a talisman. Without him beside her, something bad would happen, that was what she believed.

She always felt she owed him for saving her, and she hoped that one day, she would be able to do the same for him. She would save him too if he ever needed her.

But just water? Just a lake? No, it could never be just that, and Ethan knew it. Maybe one day, when she was ready, she would confront it. Maybe one day she would get back in, take a swim. One day... but for now, all she could do was try to ignore his taunts and pretend his words didn't matter.

And so the days rolled by at the start of that fateful summer. Reading her book on the shore, she would watch Ethan every time he emerged from the lake shivering, his skin all bluish gray and goosebumps all over.

"You see!" she shouted out, "it can't be good for you to swim in water that cold." And he would sneer at her and joke that she was a coward.

She thought that was how they would fill the days—each day the same as the last, just another long and forgettable summer fighting the boredom and wishing they were someplace else.

Then Michael arrived, and everything changed.

It was as if her heart anticipated something was coming and had kept her alert and twitching with some inexplicable excitement. Sometimes you can feel people nearing you.

Every moment, every feeling of that first day was imprinted in her mind, the smallest of details sharp and clear.

She was idly thumbing through her book when she heard Ashley calling out to them, "Hey, you guys!"

When Evie looked up, she saw Ashley emerge from the heat rippled air, beside her someone she had never seen before. And for a moment, she thought she was dreaming. It felt as though time had slowed down, her heart beating in time with the seconds as they ticked by, the pressure in her chest expanding as she held her breath in anticipation.

She had never seen anyone like him. The flop of dark hair that fell across his face highlighted the ocean blue of his eyes. He was squinting into the sunlight and the little frown on his forehead was irresistibly intriguing. He had a slightly detached air about him, as if he was someplace else, as if he existed on some other level. He looked ethereal.

When he smiled a quiet *hello* as Ashley introduced him, Evie felt a ripple of energy surge through her. She wanted to stand up and walk over to him and touch him, just to see if he was real, but all she could manage was a nod, her ability to speak completely disrupted by the effect his presence had on her.

Oh my God, she thought. *Oh my God.*

She watched, enthralled by the way he moved as he sauntered over to the lake and looked out over the water and toward the mountains. There was a grace to him she'd never seen before in a boy. He moved like a cat, instinctively aware of every placement of foot and hand, of arm and leg, without having to think. Feline, languid, but still masculine. Still strong and muscular.

How can a boy be so perfect? she thought, as Ashley sat down beside her.

"Michael's here from San Francisco," she explained. "He's working at the hotel for the summer."

Evie had smiled and said "hello," too afraid to say any more and Ashley had teased her a little.

"Don't worry," Ashley said to Michael. "She's not usually this quiet, trust me. The sun must have got to her. Anyway, is Ethan around?"

Evie pointed to the lake and said, "He's in the water cooling off."

Ashley stood up and walked to the shoreline, held her hand above her eyes to shade them from the sun, and scanned the lake, waving and yelling when she spotted Ethan bobbing about in the glistening water. "Hey, Ethan! How is it in there?"

"Freezing!" came his reply.

Evie sat up, leaned on her elbows and watched Ethan swim to shore, glad of the distraction. He was fast, cutting through the ripples with clean, strong strokes. Head in the water, then up to the side to breathe on the third stroke—his confidence in the water was something she envied.

She watched as he stumbled out of the lake and scrambled to get his footing on the pebbles that formed the shoreline and she heard Michael laugh. When she turned to look at him, she saw him smiling and felt a quiver of excitement when he asked her, "Is *that* your brother?" his voice filled with mock incredulity. And she dared to speak now, because she could feel it, some small connection had been made. The ice broken with a smile and a lighthearted joke at her brother's expense.

"Yeah," she said. "I can't believe it either sometimes." He laughed and came and sat beside her and they watched as Ashley walked over to Ethan with a towel and draped it over his shoulders before pulling it tight around him, her actions so thoughtful, it made Evie squirm to watch them together. Her brother and her best friend. It still felt wrong for some reason, and she figured she would never get used to it.

"You've been in there too long," Ashley said as she rubbed Ethan dry. "Look at all the goosebumps!"

And Ethan laughed. "A bit of cold water won't kill me."

He sat down beside Michael and fidgeted a little, getting comfortable on the grassy bank and fumbling around amid a pile of clothes to find his T-shirt.

Evie laughed at him, glad she had the opportunity to tease him at last. "Hey, I thought you said you could handle the cold."

"Well, if you're feeling so brave," Ethan replied, "then why don't you go in yourself? See how it feels."

Then he turned to Michael before she had a chance to react and held out his hand. "Hi, I'm Ethan," he said. "Ashley says you're here for the summer season."

When Michael beamed that charming smile, she thought she saw Ethan shiver. But it was not with cold. It was excitement. Michael's energy was so powerful it put a spell on everyone, it seemed.

"I can't believe you guys go swimming in there," Michael said. "It looks as if it's about to freeze over."

"Only Ethan's stupid enough to go in," Evie said. "No one else wants to get pneumonia."

And Michael laughed. "I hear you."

"Oh, come on, Evie," Ethan said. "It's not the cold you're scared of, is it?"

Michael turned to face her and smiled. "Oh no?" he said. "Don't tell me there's some monster of the deep down there or something?"

She could only stare at him and blink in desperation as she tried to think of a suitable answer. But before she could speak, Ethan was talking again.

"Yeah," he said. "She swears there are water sprites lurking down there. She's scared they'll pull her under again."

Michael looked at her and tilted his head, and she wasn't sure if he was appraising her sanity or if what he had just heard was simply intriguing. *Oh God*, she thought. *He's thinks I'm a weirdo.* And she had wanted to grab Ethan and drag him toward the lake and throw him into the water.

She looked Ethan straight in the eye and asked, "If you'd almost drowned in there, then you'd be scared to go in too."

"Hey, relax already, I'm just joking. Let's just forget about it. No one wants to be hearing your stories."

And Michael replied, "I'd want to hear about it. Sounds pretty scary, though, that you almost drowned."

She smiled at him and said, "I would have if Ethan hadn't saved me."

"Oh, right! So he's actually the hero in all of this? I didn't realize!"

She laughed while Ethan flexed his muscles and joked, "I sure am, can't you tell?"

Then Michael touched her leg and said, "You guys are just like me and my sister, Beth. We're always messing with each other."

"Yeah?" was all she could say as she tried to calm the shiver that ran down her spine in response to his touch.

"She loves me really," Michael added. "Anyway, you guys gonna show me all the fun things to do here? I didn't come here just to work."

When he smiled at her, she smiled back and saw him inch a little closer, the energy magnetic, as if there was a force drawing them to one another. Behind him, she could see Ethan watching them. Or watching her. The ever-alert brother always making sure his little sister stayed out of trouble and never strayed. And so she inched a little closer and told him in a low, soft voice, so that Ethan couldn't hear, "There's not so much to do here. It's nature stuff mostly, hiking, kayaking, swimming, that kind of thing. Just hanging out, you know?"

He raised an eyebrow and replied, "Are you telling me no one here likes to party?"

"Hey!" Ashley joined in. "We sure can party. I don't know where you think you've come to, but Georgetown is no backwater."

"Did someone say party?"

No one saw him arrive. He just appeared and sat down next to her, and she felt his leg brush against hers and his arm touch her as he said, "Hey there, Evie." His touch was possessive, as if he was claiming her, and she saw Michael move away and realized the look in his eyes was surprise and disappointment. She hoped that Michael would see it was not what he thought. She had to shake him off. Mason Cardew might try to claim her, but she was never going to allow it.

"Hey, Mason," Ethan said. "Michael was just wondering what we all do for fun around here."

"Well, I don't know what these guys have told you, but we don't party much if that's what you're thinking," Mason said as he stripped down to his swimming shorts and laid out a towel to lie on. "Or were you planning on organizing one?"

"Shit!" Ashley said, laughing. "If you do, Michael, don't go inviting my kid brother. He can kill a party stone dead in seconds."

"Oh, fuck off, Ashley," Mason sulked. "Did it even occur to you that maybe you wouldn't be invited? Huh?"

Michael interrupted, "Hey! Everyone's welcome. Isn't that right, Evie?"

And she smiled and shrugged and said, "Sure, why not?" and figured that as the days went by, he'd soon understand why Mason should never be invited to a party.

As the afternoon wore on, the heat started to wear them down and they did little more than lounge and listen to the radio, too tired to swim or talk. Mason, the odd one out as usual, sitting there between them, needy for attention. When he turned up the dial on the radio Evie got a shock as a jangly guitar tune blasted through the speakers, by some band she wasn't cool enough to know. But Michael nodded along and seemed to know them. She cringed as she saw Mason joining in, slapping his hands on his thighs, out of step with the beat.

"What band is this?" he asked.

Ethan was the one who replied, "God, Mason. The Lemonheads? You haven't heard of The Lemonheads? Seriously?"

It wasn't the Ethan she knew, putting people down like that, but he seemed to want to impress Michael. *Asshole*, she thought. *You know he's going to make you pay for that.*

She could see Mason's throat tightening, and his eyes blink at the sting of the put down. It wasn't just the embarrassment, he had never been the cool kid and he'd grown used to it—she thought he even liked it sometimes, to always be the odd one out, always on the sidelines watching. But this time the disappointment cut him.

"I was just asking," Mason mumbled.

When Michael looked across at him and said, "You like it? I have the CD back at the hotel—you can listen to it if you want," she knew everything she had felt about him when she first saw him was right. He was the guy who was kind to the kid no one liked and everyone laughed at. If she'd had the guts, she'd have leaned over and kissed him right then.

But she wasn't brave enough and instead she rolled onto her stomach and picked up her book and pretended to read. But the words blurred on the page. It was impossible to concentrate, and she knew it was more than just the heat. She could feel Michael's energy as he lay beside her, as if he was transferring some of his excitement to her. She looked over at Ashley and wondered if she wanted to head home for a cool shower and a drink, but she was taking snacks out of her bag—treats leftover from the breakfast bar and lunch buffet. The perks of being a hotel owner's daughter.

Evie saw Ashley pass around a tray of strawberries—deep-red little wild berries. A local delicacy.

"These are crazy sweet, I've never had any like this!" Michael was saying. "Where the hell did you get them?"

Evie thought to tell him they were wild strawberries. Stephen Harrison picked them every summer from a secret spot in the forest to sell in his store. She'd tried looking for them, wandering for miles through the forest, but all she ever found was a scattering of tiny fruits on the forest floor.

Instead, she simply asked, "Can I have one?"

"Sure!" Michael picked out a berry, leaned over her and dangled it tantalizingly over her lips. "Here you go." His gaze made her tingle. She opened her mouth slightly and he dropped it in, and she relished the little smile there on his lips, as the strawberry burst on her tongue, the sweetness of the strawberry and the moment, otherworldly.

"Delicious," she said, as she held his gaze.

Then Mason broke the spell. "Hey, what about the rest of us?"

She looked over and saw a flash of jealousy in his eyes. And something else too. Anger. As if accepting strawberries from beautiful Californian boys was forbidden.

When Ashley laughed and plucked a strawberry from the tray and dangled it over Ethan's lips, she heard Mason curse under his breath.

She had never seen Ethan act this way before. He was always so careful, so aware of who was watching him. Always so conscious of people's expectations. He was the responsible brother who had saved his sister and who always looked out for her. He wasn't the type of boy who sat by a lake, and allowed someone to drop strawberries into his mouth as if those responsibilities had fallen away. And yet, there he was, seemingly transformed by Michael's presence.

He turned his gaze to Michael and smiled as he swallowed his strawberry, the look in his eyes bright and a little wild, as if he had just been freed from something. Just like that, with one small gesture, Michael had given Ethan a reason to lose his self-consciousness and inhibitions.

It was as if Michael had sat down by the lakeshore that afternoon and flicked a switch, the old Ethan transformed into this new version. And she felt a small shiver of fear, something thrilling. Because she knew then, they all did, that Michael had the power to change them.

She had felt the same shift occur within her the moment she set eyes on him. It was as if he had put a spell on them. But they had been willing to succumb, had wanted it even—to be charmed and mesmerized and led astray.

She found herself falling into a haze of daydreams as the afternoon wore on. She thought about the world Michael came from, a world beyond the mountains and insularity of Georgetown. She imagined them on some cross-country road trip, sun-kissed and happy, driving along a meandering coastal road above the crashing frothy sea, or heading to the beach to surf and dance and laugh.

It was a cliché, she knew that, and the chances of it ever happening were almost zilch. But that didn't diminish the power of the dream, and the small, growing longing that maybe, just maybe, in this other, golden world, a boy like Michael would smile at her and lean in for a kiss, and with it, a new life would start. *Such stupid, impossible dreams,* she thought.

And yet she kept on dreaming, kept imagining the Californian coastline. The breaking waves on the rocky shore, the sun, golden and energizing. The orange trees fragrant and ripe. It was just a daydream, like in the movies. California was a different world. A world that produced boys like this. Boys like Michael who dropped strawberries into your mouth and made it seem like the most natural thing in the world. Boys who offered a tantalizing glimpse of a life she had never dared to dream of before. Boys who could turn your life upside down. Because that was what he did, in the end, he turned their lives inside out and upside down without them even noticing.

CHAPTER SIX

March 2015

When she woke, Evie could still feel the trace of Michael. His death was still something her body refused to contemplate, even after all these years. It was why she never thought of him. Even to imagine him that summer, to remember those happy moments, was too painful. Because in her heart, she knew it was a lie. That happy image she conjured up as an act of self-preservation was an illusion. But her body could not be fooled for long. The weight of memory was too heavy to bear. It was why she had learned to forget him. To push him so far into the corner of her memory, he had ceased to exist. And until now it had worked. She was able to carry on. She was able to live. She survived.

But now Ethan and Carole were here, insisting she say his name. Insisting she remember. Jeopardizing everything she had fought so hard for. *And for what?* she wondered. *What reason could they possibly have to turn her life upside down like this?*

She thought back to their conversation the previous day, and Ethan's insistence that he had something to "clear up." His unfounded suggestion that some truth had yet to be revealed. It made no sense to her and she couldn't accept or believe it. *No,* she thought, *whatever reason he had for coming back, it couldn't be to try and undo the facts of the last twenty years.*

She lay in bed and as she watched a new day begin and the light slowly filter through the curtain, she thought of her mother and brother asleep in the rooms beside her. Their proximity should have been a comfort, but instead all she felt was anxiety and the increasing wish for them to be gone.

I need to get away from them, she thought. *Just long enough to pull myself together and figure out what it is they want.*

She could already see from the color of the light that the day would be crisp and cold, but bright and dry enough for a walk. Good weather for getting outside and shaking off unwanted memories.

She pulled back the bedcovers and lowered herself to the floor, and felt the wobble in her legs still as she walked over to the window, the weight of her dreams still pulling at her every fiber, as if her body wanted to keep her pinned to the bed and tucked safely away from the world. But when she opened the curtains, she could see the first slivers of light brushing the mountainside, a blush of pink and orange, the ground still hardened white with frost, a smattering of snow on the peaks, and the sight energized her.

A walk would help her to get her head around everything that was unsettling her. It wasn't only Ethan's sudden reappearance that had rattled her. There was something else that had been niggling at her. The calm he had about him. She had first noticed it when they talked about Andrew's accident. Despite everything that had happened between them, she had expected Ethan to be upset when she told him the details of Andrew's death. But he had sat there, sipping his coffee and listening to her story and had responded with nothing more than the smallest of nods, and the quietest of mumbled responses. It was as if nothing she said mattered. As if their father falling from a mountainside was not something sad or horrific.

She couldn't quite fathom it. She had told him the sad, terrible truth of how their father had died, and he hadn't even flinched. It was as if she had been talking about a stranger, someone he didn't care about at all. Someone whose death didn't matter.

They both remembered their father in different ways, she knew that, and she wasn't naïve enough to assume Ethan would have found a way to forgive Andrew for the things he had said and done years ago. But she still felt the need to defend her father. To tell Ethan about the ways he had helped her recover after Michael. She would never have survived if it hadn't been for him. He was the one who had pulled her back from the brink, no one else. And in those moments when her father had needed her, she had been there for him too, sharing the burden of all they had experienced.

She could show Ethan who their father truly was—his compassion, his care, everything he had done for her. And hadn't there been so many happy times as a family to remember? There was so much more to their family history than Michael's death.

But the disinterested way Ethan had reacted when she told him about Andrew's accident suggested he wasn't ready to listen and it had left her feeling uneasy.

She dressed quickly and grabbed an apple for breakfast, then carefully pulled the door shut behind her so as not to wake them.

She had the feeling as she cut across the lawn and headed down to the road that if Ethan heard her, he would follow her, so she looked up at his bedroom window just to be sure he wasn't watching. When she turned to look up, there was no one there. The curtains were drawn, the lights out. *Good*, she thought. Then she slipped out of the gate and started to walk, not noticing where her feet were carrying her.

She crossed the bridge over the river and began to follow the narrow trail up to the forest. The soft thud of her feet on the ground, muffled by the layer of pine needles and the astringent smell of the trees as the night-time frost began to thaw in the early sunlight, left her feeling dreamy and slow.

She'd been tiptoeing around Ethan ever since he arrived, and it had not been easy to hide her unease. It had taken hold the minute she saw the look in Mason's eyes. It was that old way people had of looking at her. She had become the other Evie again. The girl who had learned, in the cruelest possible way, that people were capable of terrible things, even people you loved and thought you knew. And she didn't want to be that girl again, the girl who elicited such pitiful stares.

Ethan seemed to have no idea the way the events of that fateful summer had come to define her for so long. It was this that troubled her most. He had sat at the kitchen table drinking his coffee, as if all those years he had been away had never happened. As if time could wash it all away. To look at him, you would never have believed he had committed such a terrible crime.

The way he had so easily made himself at home made her nervous. There was something too confident about it, as if he knew she would be too scared to challenge him. He was still her brother even after all these years and he seemed to know that she would always feel some sort of responsibility toward him. She owed him. That had always been the understanding between them. But if her mom had not been there she was sure she would have told him to leave. That she would have let him see how uncomfortable he made her. She was a little scared of him even. She wondered if he really believed you could scrub away the past simply by walking through the door. That you could breezily announce you were home to "clear things up" and that somehow everyone would accept it.

She walked on, lost in her thoughts.

Relax, try and push it away.

But she felt the tension in her limbs, and there was a stiffness in her neck that she couldn't massage away. She used to have a calming technique for moments such as this. *What was it again?* she wondered.

Until last night, she hadn't thought of Dr. Newton in years, but she found herself remembering her now, and trying to recall the advice she had once given her. An image of the sea she could focus on, synchronizing her breath with the back and forth of the waves on the shore. And she stood still for a moment and allowed herself to breathe and waited until she felt a little of her strength return before walking on.

At a bend in the track she pulled off the trail and scrambled over the forest floor, picking her way through tree roots and boulders and over fallen branches until she came to the clearing. Just behind the cluster of pines lay the blackened foundations of the cabins, all that was left of that summer being slowly reclaimed by moss, fern and lichen. She felt a little shiver of grief ripple through her. She had been drawn to this place as if she had no control over her own movements. The forest pulling her inside, almost as though she had been hypnotized.

At the edge of the clearing, the large granite block sat between two old growth pines, solid and familiar, and she walked toward it and pulled herself up into the nook that had been weathered there over the years. The cold of the stone penetrated her jeans, and she had to pull her jacket down under her to prevent the chill from seeping deep inside.

For a couple of minutes, all she could hear was her own breath and the crackle and crumple of her raincoat. Then slowly a rustling somewhere. A bird no doubt, rooting in the undergrowth. In the distance, from below, she could just make out the screech of a buzzard. But apart from that there was nothing. No sound.

She sat there, calm at last, and waited for it to come. The thought that had kept her awake last night. The niggling idea that was at the root of everything.

Not Michael, or Ethan, but her father.

It was all connected to him in some way. Even his death. The timing of it all. None of it was a coincidence. Even this, coming back to this forest, to this rock, was no coincidence. It was her father who had brought her back here, back to this place she had avoided for so long.

The horror of what happened in this forest could never be removed. It was like a stain in the ground, in the trees, in the rocks, in the air. The trauma she had endured was captured and held there, waiting for her to return. She could feel it still. She knew she would have to give herself over to her memories because she didn't have the energy to fight.

And slowly, slowly an old feeling returned. Like pins and needles. She felt her limbs tingle and knew that if she were to try and stand, she would tumble and fall. Her eyes fluttered and her breath quickened as she sat on the rock and watched as the scene before her rippled and expanded, then contracted as it pulled her back in time.

Back to that day she wished had never happened.

CHAPTER SEVEN

August 1994

Her dad had found her alone in the clearing, barely conscious and curled up tight, her face buried in her hands as if she couldn't bear to look at the world. When he lifted her from the forest floor, he saw she was scratched and bloodied and bruised. He had cupped her face in his hands, and she had looked at him with a vacant stare as if she didn't know who he was or how she came to be there.

"Evie," he whispered. "Evie are you okay? What happened to you, did you fall?"

But she didn't say a word. She could barely focus on him as he stroked her face and tried to calm her before wrapping his arms around her. Her mouth felt swollen and heavy, as if it was filled with soil, and she shivered with cold and fear as she remembered crashing through the trees and stumbling and falling over roots and branches. She had run from something. *But what?* she wondered.

"Evie," Andrew said again, his voice louder this time. When she finally opened her eyes, she saw he was pale and looked worried, and she wondered if he had seen it too, whatever it was that was lurking there in the woods.

She tried to tell him about it, but her mouth was numb. And then the images came again. Something on the forest floor, bloodied and battered. Its shape twisted and bent out of form in a hideous contortion of pain. She had approached it slowly, not sure if she could help, but the sight of the blood had left her faint and shaking, and she had run from it.

"What was it?" she asked her father.

"What?" he replied.

She pointed to the dense trees beyond the granite boulder.

"There, on the ground. Something… I don't know what… it was on the ground… there was blood… I tried to help, but…"

Then she leaned against him and grew limp. It took her a moment to understand that the sobs she heard were her own.

When he held her closer, she shivered as he tried to calm and reassure her.

"Everything will be okay, Evie. Everything will be okay."

"No… Michael, where's Michael? He needs help," she told him.

Her father shook his head and said, "Shh, shh. Don't worry about him, don't worry about him. Come on, let's get you home."

But she didn't want to go. She wanted to stay in the clearing, hidden and protected by the trees. She wanted to take shelter from whatever it was she had run from.

"Evie," Andrew said again. "Evie, are you alright?"

Through the forest she could hear voices echoing through the valley. Shouting and yelling. Then something else. A smell of smoke, acrid and dry and dangerous, followed by a scream.

"Ethan?" she asked. "Was that Ethan?"

"It must be the fire team," Andrew told her. "Come on now, Evie. It's too dangerous here. We need to get out of here. We need to get home."

"No, I heard a scream. Not them. That other sound. Did you not hear it? Someone screamed!"

He took hold of her shoulders and looked at her, holding her gaze and making sure she didn't look away. There was something threatening about the way he held her, even as he tried to calm her and convince her she was mistaken. The strength of his grip hinted at something close to panic, something close to fear.

"No," he told her. "There was no scream. I told you, it's the fire team making sure no one's in here. They need to clear this place out." And he let out a whistle and shouted out to them. "It's okay. I've found her! We're going!" Then held out his hand to her. "Come on now, let's go."

"But what about Michael?" she asked.

"Michael?"

"Did you see him?" she said. "He was here. Please, you have to check on him. He needs to get out of here too."

Andrew looked around the clearing and shook his head and pulled on her arm trying to force her to stand up.

"No, there's no one else here, Evie. Now come on!"

But she pointed through the trees.

"No, not here," she said. "Over there. He's over there, past the clearing."

Andrew looked through the pines but saw only darkness and shade and the orange glow of flames just beyond, as they licked the cabins.

"What are you talking about, Evie?" he asked her. "There's no one there. I just came that way."

And she held up her hands, then ran a finger down her father's cheek, leaving a wet smear of red on his skin.

"Oh, look," she said. "Blood." And held out her hands to him.

Andrew looked at her hands. They were smudged with dirt and the unmistakable red of blood.

"Where did it come from?" she asked him. "Is it my blood? Am I bleeding?"

"It's going to be okay, Evie," he told her again. "It's going to be okay."

But she didn't believe him. She could feel his fear, and there was an insistence to his voice that made her nervous.

"We need to get you home, Evie," he said. "Let the doctor take a look at you."

But she was staring at the blood and the dirt on her hands and thought she caught a flash of something. The briefest shape of a memory. She had leaned over the shape on the forest floor and touched it. Felt its warmth, then saw the blood. Then the image was gone as quickly as it came.

"I touched it," she said. "I touched it because it didn't look real, you see, it looked—"

"Evie, what are you talking about?"

"Michael," she said again. "Is he dead? Where is he? I thought I saw him there. I know I saw him there."

And again she pointed back into the forest "There," she said. "Did you see?"

But he was already running. Running toward the shape in the darkness. And she was about to call out to him when she saw him freeze and stand still.

"Did you see him?" she asked. "Is it Michael? Did you see him?"

"It's just a deer, Evie. Looks like a cougar made a kill."

Such a strange thing to say, she thought. *That's no deer.*

"A deer?" she said. "No, it's not a deer."

And he looked at her and then beckoned her. When she didn't come to him, he walked back and took her by the arm and walked her over to the shape that lay on the forest floor.

"Evie, what are you talking about? Look, it's a deer. It's just a deer. A cougar's been hunting. The fire must have frightened it away."

And she caught the flash of an eye. Big and brown and unblinking. Dead. *But that can't be right*, she thought. *It can't be.*

"Michael," she muttered. "Where is Michael?"

"Okay, enough," he said, his voice firmer, agitated. "We need to get you out of here."

And when he took her arm, she did not resist. The dead black of that eye had weakened and confused her. *Because the eye was blue,* she thought. *His eyes were blue.* Arm in arm, they walked back down the trail to the house.

*

Back home, Ethan was sitting in the kitchen. He was shaking and making a sad, pitiful sound—a whimpering noise, like a scared dog. He was looking at his hands and shaking his head in disbelief. And she saw the blood again. On his hands, his jacket, his jeans. A smear of it under his eye. Traces of blood all over him, and the smell of smoke on his clothes. Smoke and gasoline.

"I tried to help her," he mumbled when he saw his father. "I tried to get her to come home with me, but… that deer, she wouldn't leave it. She just kept saying his name, and then…"

He lifted his bloodied hands and stared at the red of his shirt and the darkening stain on his trousers, and she watched as he started to shake his head, as if he didn't understand what he was looking at. Then he stood up and quickly stripped down to his underwear and walked over to the sink where he began to wash his hands and face, bending under the faucet to rinse out his hair.

"What are you doing?" she asked him.

"That smell, I can't get rid of that smell," he said, his voice quivering and filled with a nervous energy that unsettled her.

When Andrew saw him, he walked over to the sink and turned off the water, and then guided Ethan back to the table and sat him down on the chair and told Carole to go and fetch him some clean clothes.

And Evie sat beside him, confused and shocked. But no one was looking at her or listening to her. She watched Ethan dress himself in the clean clothes Carole brought for him and wondered why he had needed to undress. Why he had needed to wash those traces away. Why he had needed to scrub himself, when Michael was gone. She wanted to tell them that something terrible had happened, but when she tried to explain what it was, she couldn't find the right words. The more she tried to concentrate, the more nebulous it became. The words and thoughts ebbing away from her.

"Michael's gone," was all she managed to say. "Michael's gone…"

But no one paid her any attention. They were hovering over Ethan and asking him what he had seen, what he had done. But he just sat there in stony silence and refused to look at them.

All she remembered was Ethan crying and her dad asking him over and over again, "What happened, Ethan? What happened?" while Mom stood there, pale and shaking and staring at her son as if she didn't recognize him.

And Ethan turned to face her and looked at her with a gaze that was filled with pity and horror, and that was when the world turned black.

CHAPTER EIGHT

March 2015

The walk home from the forest took her twice as long as usual, her legs barely able to carry her home, every step heavy and slow. Everything felt out of focus, as if she was walking through a fine mist. She had to concentrate on every step and bring herself slowly back into the world. It felt as if two worlds existed—the forest which held the past, and this blue-sky morning which held reality.

When she walked off the trailhead and onto the dirt road, she saw Donna walking toward her, on her way home from her early morning shift at the store and Evie muttered a quiet, "damn" when she realized she could not avoid her.

"Hey," Donna called to her. "You're out early."

Evie tried to smile a hello but could not hide her weariness and exhaustion. "Shit, are you okay?" Donna asked her.

"I'm fine," she lied. "I took a walk up around the trail, but I guess I was more tired than I thought."

And she saw Donna look up the road to the spot where the trailhead started.

"You went up the trail?" she asked. "To the old cabins? Shit, Evie, should you be doing that?"

Small towns—there was no escape. People knew every intimate detail of your life. There was no need for Donna to say more, they both knew what she meant. The whole of the last twenty years was wrapped up in that question.

"I guess not," Evie replied. But it was enough to set Donna off.

"Dammit, Ethan got you doing this, didn't he?" she said. "I knew as soon as I heard he was planning on sticking around, I just knew that it would come to no good. Evie, seriously, don't make yourself ill again because of him, do you hear me? Please don't let him do that to you. I mean, you haven't gone up in those woods for years, and—"

"I just went for a walk… That's all. Please don't worry about me."

"Of course I do, we all do. You're not okay and I can see it in your eyes. Trust me, people here just want to look out for you. You know that, don't you? We'll do whatever it takes to make sure you're safe."

"I'm fine, okay? I promise you. So please, don't worry about me. Everything's fine," she said.

As she walked away, she could hear them already, the whispers that would now spread around town. *She's been walking in the forest alone again. She came off that trailhead looking like a ghost. Barely able to walk. It's because Ethan's home. He's trouble, always has been.* She picked up the pace, Donna's final words ringing in her ears.

"We've got your back, okay? We've got your back."

*

Ethan was in the kitchen and he mumbled a good morning as she walked in and asked her where she'd been.

"Oh nowhere. I woke early so thought I'd take a walk to clear my head," she told him. "Did you sleep okay?"

"Not really," he admitted.

She poured herself a coffee and pulled up a chair at the kitchen table and they sat there sipping their coffees in silence. She could feel he had things to say, questions to ask. The way he licked his lips, that small furtive action he had had since he was a kid, it was always a giveaway that something was worrying him. She was glad he still did it. That small nervous tick helped her pay attention. Because with

Ethan, it was always about the things he didn't say. You had to look for the signs and then figure out what it was he was withholding. The problem was, he'd been gone for more than twenty years and she wasn't sure if she could read him so well anymore. He could lie to her now and she might miss it—and that put her on edge.

"You know," he said. "I've wondered about this for years. What it would be like to come back here, I mean. To sit in this kitchen with my family again."

"I suppose you didn't imagine this, though? Dad gone, and just me here."

"That's true, I didn't. It's a shame I didn't get the chance to talk to him. I'd have liked that, y'know? To see if…"

He couldn't finish and got up and poured himself another cup of coffee from the pot and allowed himself a few seconds to pull himself together.

"What did you want to say to him?" she asked.

But he shook his head as he sat back down and didn't look at her. And again, she could tell he was holding something back, and that he wasn't going to tell her what it was.

"I don't know, really," he said. "I just needed to talk to him. Though whether he would have wanted to talk to me…"

"Well, he wasn't an easy man to talk to. Sometimes I never knew what to say to him. Talking wasn't really his thing."

He smiled, happy they at least shared this impression of him.

"Evie," he said. "Can I ask you something?"

"Sure."

"I know you don't want me here—" he said.

He would catch the lie, she knew he would, but she interrupted him anyway. "It's fine," she said. "I'll make sure there's no trouble, from Mason or anyone else for that matter."

He looked at her for a moment, licked his lips again and swallowed.

"Most people would be nervous," he said. "Having their brother back after all this time. I mean, when's the last time we spoke? I can't even remember it."

She tried to think back but drew a blank. That last trip to Cañon City to visit him in prison, perhaps?

"It was long ago," she told him, "that's all I know."

"You know," he said, "when I stood outside that front door, I wasn't expecting you to let me in. I thought you'd slam it shut in my face when you saw me standing there."

"So why didn't I? Is that what you want to know?"

He nodded.

"Shock, I guess. I wasn't expecting to see you there and Mom had given me no warning."

"So he didn't tell you?"

"Who?"

"Dad. He didn't tell you that I called him, the week before he died, and asked if I could visit?"

It took her a few seconds to process what he had said, and she struggled to remember if Andrew had ever mentioned it. But he couldn't have. She would never have forgotten something so momentous. Yet it seemed impossible that he would have spoken to Ethan and not mentioned it.

"You spoke to Dad?" she asked him.

"Yeah. The week before he died."

It explained her father's agitation that week, she realized. And immediately she wondered if that was the reason he had walked up Mount Saxon. He would have needed to think long and hard about any conversation he had had with Ethan. She felt her stomach clench as she tried to imagine what they had talked about. It was clearly something serious enough to have sent her father out into the cold and the danger of that mountainside. And she remembered what Ethan had told her yesterday about wanting to "clear things up." The more she thought about that, the more anxious she became.

"What did you talk about?" she asked him.

"Not much as it happens. He was very wary, asked me why I was calling, what it was I wanted. I don't think it occurred to him that I just wanted to see you all again. To talk to you. He still thought I had no right to want that, or to ask for it."

It was strange, she thought, that he didn't think Andrew had a right to be wary. It was as if he never even considered that they might not want to see him again. And his casualness, his strange assumption that he could somehow pick up the phone and talk to them as if the past didn't exist, made her wonder if it had even occurred to him what such a call might do to them.

"So why did you call him?" she asked.

"Sorry?"

"Why Dad? Why call *him*? You could have called me."

"Come on, Evie, do you think he'd have been okay if I'd just wandered in here and told him you said it was all okay?"

"I don't know. I guess not. But still, you could have called me. We could have met someplace else maybe, or—"

He looked at her and raised his eyebrows to let her know he thought she was being ridiculous. And she felt herself blush. They both knew that if he had called her out of the blue, she would have reacted the same way as her father.

"Yeah, well, it's weird when you speak to someone again after so many years," Ethan continued. "I don't know why I thought I would be able to call him like that, with no warning, and expect him to be open to what I had to say. I guess I was too naïve."

She couldn't help but smile when he said that, and she had to fight to contain it. Naïve was not a word anyone would use to describe her brother, and he knew it. But she knew too that Ethan could not have been surprised by Andrew's reticence.

"So what did you want to talk to him about?"

"I just wanted to finish a conversation we started years ago. Or one I wanted to finish, at least. For my own peace of mind if nothing else. But Dad had other ideas, so…"

She didn't mean to raise her voice, but the fact that he was seeing things from his own perspective again irritated her. "And what about our peace of mind, Ethan? What about Dad's peace of mind? Do you think he would have wandered up that mountain if you hadn't called him?"

"Oh please, Evie, don't. Don't blame me for something I could never have anticipated."

"Okay, I'm sorry. That came out wrong. I just meant you could have thought it through, thought about what calling him would do to him. It's just a shame it came too late."

"What did?"

"I mean that it's too late now to make things good with him." And she thought she saw a little spark of hope in his eyes, as if she had just suggested that, given time, given the opportunity, their father would have sought out some sort of reconciliation.

"Do you think it was possible?" he asked.

No, was the truthful answer, but it would be cruel to tell him that.

"Well, we'll never know now, will we?"

"No, I guess not. But, Evie?"

"Yeah?"

"Is it possible? With you I mean. Can we make things good?"

She had to ask him now. No hesitation. No fear. Just words. Simple and clear and easier to say than she had imagined they would be.

"That depends," she told him.

He waited for her to carry on, and she could see in his eyes that he knew what was coming. *So just come out with it,* she thought. *Just ask him. He can handle it.*

"I need to know what you mean when you say you're here to clear things up? I mean, there's nothing to clear up, is there? So why say a thing like that? It's like a proclamation of innocence. But you're not, though, are you, you're not innocent?"

He turned away and looked down at the table and bit his lip. That little tick again. He was nervous, and unsure of what to say. And she was almost at the point of coming to a decision. If he had reason to pause, if he needed to think of what to say, to form his response, then it wasn't a good sign.

And she could almost hear her father warning her. *Tell him to go, Evie. Tell him to go before he does you any harm.*

When Ethan replied, she listened, but she had already decided that whatever he said could be truth or lie. His hesitation had made it clear. He wasn't sure how much he could trust her.

"The last few years, I've been thinking about Michael a lot," he began. "The idea that you might know something about what happened to him, what *really* happened to him, I mean, it just—"

"No, Ethan please, don't say any more."

"Please, just hear me out—"

"No, Ethan. I've spent years trying to put all that behind me. Trying not to think about what happened to him. Because it won't do any good. The only thing that comes from obsessing about it is more pain. Trust me, Ethan, if you go down that route, you'll ruin yourself. Michael, he's…"

But she could not think about him. Just the mention of his name was enough for the shaking to take hold of her again. A small, tingling feeling for now, but if she let it grow, it would consume her, she knew that.

Don't let him in, Evie. Don't see it. Forget it all. Forget Michael. Forget it, forget it, forget it.

That was what her father had told her. And it was good advice. It had protected her over the years. But there was no way she could keep it at bay now. And there was the memory again. The full horror of it. Her father was no longer here to hold her steady; Dr. Newton was just a distant memory.

"Please, Evie," she heard Ethan say. "I just want to talk to you…"

But all she saw was red. All she saw was blood and fire and smoke. And she tried to find those words that Dr. Newton told her. *Breathe. Nice and slow. Think of the sea.* But the fire and the smoke pushed it all away.

And once again, the blackness came.

CHAPTER NINE

First Therapy Session, January 1995

The room was more clinical than she had imagined it would be, the walls painted a bland cream color. On one wall there were photographs of pleasant landscapes. Flowering meadows at the foot of a mountain range. Waves breaking on a pebble beach. A forest in summertime, the light shining through the canopy in golden cathedral rays. It was clichéd to the point of embarrassment and Evie smiled when she looked at them, because their intention seemed too obvious. She wondered how uncomfortable the discussions were going to be, if such visual calming techniques were considered necessary.

The therapist herself was unobtrusive—after every session Evie struggled to recall her face. All she could remember was her soothing manner, and her calm voice as she asked those strange matter-of-fact questions, as if all she had to say was, "Here, why don't you tell me what happened," for Evie to open up. It left her feeling she was being led, but she was never quite sure where to.

At that first session, the therapist had motioned to her to take a seat. There were two chairs in the room, both upholstered in pale blue fabric, facing one another in the nook by the window. No couch, but there was a large oak desk, tidy, almost sterile, with only a phone, a closed notebook and a pot filled with pencils and pens. No computer, which pleased her for some reason, as if it somehow signified that whatever was discussed in the room would not be documented. That the notes scratched onto paper as they spoke were somehow impermanent and not necessarily a record of what she thought or felt, or who she was. Of what was *wrong* with her.

"Good morning," the therapist had said. "I'm Doctor Newton." Her voice was too cheery. Like an operator at some call center who was trying to sell you insurance.

Evie nodded but didn't offer her name in return. She could see it was right there on the papers which sat on a small table beside Dr. Newton's chair.

"I just wanted to start off today by explaining a little about how things work," Dr. Newton continued, as if silence was not uncommon, as if reticent and surly teenage girls were nothing to worry about. She knew how to deal with such situations.

"Don't we just talk?" Evie interrupted.

"Well, yes, we do, but first I wanted to explain how it works and discuss why you're here and—"

"I know why I'm here."

Dr. Newton smiled and nodded. "You do? Okay, that's good. Perhaps you can tell me then?"

It was disconcerting, the way she seemed so unphased, and the straightforward question left Evie feeling she had no place to hide.

"Do you know why you're here?" the doctor asked her again.

"My dad wants to see if you can help me remember what happened," I replied.

"And what about you?"

"Me?"

"Yes. Why are you here, do *you* want to remember?"

"It's not really a question of whether I want to or not. It's more that I can't. I've tried. So many times. But I can't. There's no point to it."

"So why are you here then?"

"I told you. My dad wants to see if you can help me, and my mom, she thinks maybe if I remember something then…"

Dr. Newton said nothing and waited for her to continue. She took no notes, made no attempt to speak, she simply sat and waited until Evie could endure the silence no longer.

"I really don't remember anything. I'm not lying when I say that. And I wish everyone would believe me. I know you all want me to try just one more time, and I'll do it, but there's nothing there. I swear. It's a black hole. And there must be a reason for that, right? I mean, there's a reason I wiped it out, there has to be."

"Is that possible do you think? To wipe something out completely?"

"I don't know. I thought that was what you were going to help me with. That's what you do, isn't it? Help people forget, wipe out their memories, and make them normal again?"

"No, Evie, that's not what I do. I can't *erase* your memories. But I can help you cope with them. Stop them overwhelming you."

"I just want to forget him. I can't…"

"Who, Evie? Who do you need to forget?"

And the question caused a fleeting shadow to flit before her. She felt as if her lungs had been pinched together and the flow of air to her brain had been stopped. If she had been standing, she would have fallen. And she tried to contain it, but his name spilled out before she could stop it.

"Michael," she whispered.

"And who is Michael?"

Evie shook her head and gripped the sides of the chair and tried to silence that word, that name, because she didn't want to hear it. She never wanted to hear or speak that name again. Why did they not understand that?

"No one. He's dead," was all she could say. As if the fact of his death rendered him unimportant.

"Can you tell me a little about him? If you want to, that is."

"There's nothing to tell, he's dead."

"Okay, then why don't you tell me what he meant to you? You seemed upset, when you mentioned his name. Why is that?"

Dr. Newton looked at her with an impassive expression. It was impossible to guess what she was thinking. No doubt her neutral expression was meant to make Evie feel calm; that vacant, non-judgmental gaze was not meant to provoke, rather it was meant to tease out the truth, little by little. *Trust me*, she seemed to be saying. Trust my professionalism and understand that you can talk to me, that you can tell me anything.

But Evie wasn't so sure. *No*, she thought. *Don't tell her anything, not yet. Listen to her questions and wait before answering. Just keep your thoughts to yourself. Then tell her what she wants to hear.*

"Are you okay, Evie?" Dr. Newton interrupted.

"I was just thinking."

"About Michael?"

No, I don't want to think about him anymore. I can't.

"Is it not all there in the file, what happened to him? Do I really need to tell you about all that?"

"It is in the file, yes. But I'd prefer it if you told me yourself who he was, what he meant to you."

What he meant to me? Do you think I can put that into words? What do you want me to say, that I loved him? In a file, they would say something clinical. Just a basic fact. They would say...

"He's just this boy... he died. It was terrible, what happened to him, but... I..."

"It's okay, Evie, take your time."

But I have nothing to say. Nothing to tell. Time won't matter. Just help me to forget. Just help me to push it all away.

She looked down at the file on the table—it would all be in there, surely? The police report, her statement.

"You don't need me to tell you about it. It's all in there," Evie told her, and she pointed to the folder.

Dr. Newton lifted the file from the table and flipped through to one of the pages and read it while Evie watched her, looking for signs. *What was she reading? What was she thinking? What would the next question be?*

When Dr. Newton put the folder down, she looked up and said, "I read this earlier today and it all seems pretty straightforward. The statement you provided to the police is very clear."

Somehow, they made sense of it. All the things I told them. The things I could remember. It was all jumbled up, but they straightened it out.

"It's as clear as we could make it," she replied. "They helped me get things straight. My head was a mess after it. I didn't know what was remembered and what was imagined. And I'm still not sure if it happened exactly that way. But that's as good as we could make it, so…"

"Which is why I asked you why you thought you were here."

You know why. They must have told you. Or written it down there in the notes. My "funny turns" as my dad calls them. There's no need to be so delicate about it.

"Because my parents are worried about me."

"Why are they worried about you?"

"You know why. The blackouts."

"You don't sound too comfortable saying that."

"I'm not."

"Why is that?"

"Because… because of him. It all started because of him."

"Do you mean Michael?"

"Yes"

"Okay, let's pause for a while. I don't want you to feel you have to talk or that it's necessary to answer every question. Especially not during this first session."

"But I thought that was the point of all this. To talk."

"It is. But only if you feel comfortable talking. And I'm not sure you want to talk to me about it. Not just yet."

"So is this it then? I just stop coming, I just give up?"

"No, not quite. Here, wait a second."

She watched as Dr. Newton stood up and walked over to a cabinet in the corner of the room and opened it and took out some notebooks and pens, then walked back to her chair and sat down.

She handed her the notebooks and pens and said, "Sometimes it helps to write things down."

Evie took them and stared at them, unsure what she was supposed to do. "What, so you want me to write a journal or something?"

"Yes, something like that."

Evie set the notebooks and pens on the floor beside her chair and sighed, "I don't know—"

"They'll just be for you," Dr. Newton explained. "Everything you write down is for you. You don't have to share them with me, though if you want to, you can. I always suggest to clients that it's better to do so, if they feel able to that is."

Evie looked at the notebooks lying at her feet and tried to imagine herself sitting at the small table in her bedroom writing. The whole idea terrified her.

"I'll leave it up to you to decide what to do," Dr. Newton continued. "Please, don't feel you have to. All I'll say is that some clients feel it helps to go back over things when it's quiet and they've had a chance to think and absorb the conversations we have. Sometimes it can take a while before these things are processed and writing it down can help bring things into focus."

"And I don't have to show them to you if I don't want to?" Evie asked.

"No," Dr. Newton replied.

"Okay… maybe… I'll think about it."

"Good. Good."

"Right, okay, I guess—"

"I'll see you next week."

*

As her dad drove her home, she felt the weight of the notebooks in her bag on her lap and thought about what she could write there. What part of their conversation did she need to think about? What did she need to process? But no sooner had she thought it than the question came to her. Something Dr. Newton had said, something she had recoiled from immediately, because it went to the heart of the matter and unless she worked through it, she would never be over it. That terrible summer, Michael's death, it would linger forever.

Okay, then why don't you tell me what he meant to you? You seemed upset, when you mentioned his name. Why is that?

And the car swerved as she cried out, "Oh God. Oh God," and startled her father.

CHAPTER TEN

March 2015

He had forgotten what it was like to live in this town, that was what she thought when he suggested it. He had forgotten the unspoken rules of a close-knit community. You traded some of your privacy in return for support. That was that deal, that was how it worked. Everyone knew one another, looked out for one another and kept a close watch on everything. And anyone who broke that trust was never allowed back in. Because trust was the thing that held it all together. And Ethan had broken that trust, so how could he forget that?

When he told her he was heading out for a walk around town, she had stared at him in disbelief and asked him if he was sure. Had given him the chance to change his mind.

"I don't think that's a good idea…" she told him. And when he asked her why not, she had hesitated, because she didn't think it was something she needed to explain.

He seemed to think her caution was an over-reaction, but Evie had no difficulty imagining the commotion; the shocked faces, the whispering voices. Or perhaps he simply didn't care? Twenty-years away had left him impervious to the opinion of others. As far as Ethan was concerned, he had already been judged, and had served his time, so what people thought of him now didn't matter. There was nothing more anyone could throw at him. He'd been through it all and come out the other side. And now he was a free man again.

But that thought made her even more nervous. If he walked around town and looked everyone squarely in the eye with a confidence they did not expect, it would antagonize people and mean they would come to her, in the end. Ask her what he was doing there. Ask her what she was going to do about it. Ask her when she was going to send him away.

You need to tell him he's not welcome here, Evie, she could imagine Ashley telling her. *Or would you like Mason to come around and remind him?*

But, in the end, she didn't have the energy to explain it to him, she had seen the confidence and determination in his eyes and the certainty he possessed that he had every right to be here. She might think that confidence was misplaced but she knew it would be difficult to convince him. All she could do was let him go. If he wanted to go about things this way, then it was up to him to face the consequences.

She'd deal with anyone demanding she do something about it—especially Mason. *What do you want me to do, send him away? My own brother?* That would silence them, for a while at least.

In the meantime, she had a call to make. If Ethan was planning on sticking around, then she wasn't going to try and defend him on her own.

Ryan was off duty when she called, out and about some place. She could hear the traffic and the rustle of his jacket as he walked down the street interfering with the connection, so she had needed to tell him twice.

"Ethan's planning on staying for a while," she told him.

She heard Ryan catch his breath and imagined him standing in the middle of the street, brought to a sudden standstill by the unexpected news. People bumping into him and tutting their annoyance while he blocked their way.

"What? Why?" he eventually asked.

"He told me he had some things he needed to clear up."

There was another moment's silence while Ryan absorbed the news.

"Wait, you mean he's staying with you and Carole?" he asked. It was only when she heard the panic and incredulity in Ryan's voice that she realized there was so much more to his staying than just what others thought. That perhaps she'd been naïve letting Ethan stay with her, despite how uncomfortable it made her. As if it was normal. As if he posed no threat.

"Are you okay?" Ryan asked her, the silence down the line worrying him.

"Sorry," she replied. "I'm fine. I was just wondering if you could come over. I don't think I can manage this on my own."

"Is Carole not there with you?"

"She is, yes, but I can't talk to her about a lot of things, you know how she is, especially when it comes to Ethan."

"Listen, Evie, tell him to leave. It's your home and it's your life and you have a right to feel safe."

This was why she had called him, she realized. She knew he would be clear and decisive. That he would tell her what she needed to hear and give her the confidence to act. She just wasn't sure if she was able to tell her own brother to leave. It felt impossible.

"You make it sound easy," she said.

"Sorry, that's not what I meant. I just want you to look out for yourself…"

"He won't do anything to hurt me, Ryan, if that's what you're thinking."

"Can you blame me?"

And it left her feeling hesitant and unsure to hear him say that. As if he thought it really was a possibility that Ethan was a threat to her. A physical threat. And what had felt vague and unlikely now seemed realistic. And she knew she couldn't face that on her own.

"Just come over when you get the chance, is that okay? We can talk about it later."

"Okay. But listen, I'm in Denver right now."

"Denver?"

"Yeah, on a training course. I'll be here until tomorrow, sorry."

"No, that's okay. What can you do about it?"

"I mean it, though, Evie. You don't need to let him stay with you. Not if it makes you uncomfortable."

"Where else is he supposed to go? I can't send him to some hotel, can I?"

He paused, needing time to think, and in that instant she wished he was with her and she had to fight the urge to tell him so, to ask him to come back immediately.

If his solution hadn't been so simple, she knew the panic would have started to rise and she wasn't sure if she would have been able to control it once it took hold: "Then give him the key to Andrew's house. He can stay there for now."

"You think so?"

"Why not?"

It made sense, she knew it did, but she was worried about what people would think if they knew Ethan was staying in Andrew's home so soon after his death. It would look so disrespectful.

"I'll think about it," she told Ryan. "I mean, I'm not sure I like the idea of him being alone, for his own safety."

"Well, it's up to you, but if it was me—"

"Listen, just come over when you get back from Denver, will you?"

"Okay. But call me, if you need me. I can send someone over if you need help."

"I don't think that'll be necessary, Ryan."

"It's just as a precaution, Evie, that's all."

She wanted to say something to put him at ease, to let him know that any doubts she had were due to nerves and exhaustion. She knew he was right, she knew what he had said made sense, she just needed a chance to think about how she was going to do it on her own.

"Yeah, I know, but listen… don't worry, I'll be fine."

"You sure?"

"Yeah, honestly."

But when she hung up, she started to worry. *I'll be fine. Really?* She thought. *Then why did you call Ryan?*

*

Half an hour after she spoke to Ryan, the doorbell rang and she opened it to find Ashley standing there, pale with rage.

"I just saw Ethan," she said as she pushed Evie aside and walked into the hallway.

"Hey Ashley, why don't you come on in."

"Evie, did you hear me? Your brother. I just saw your brother in the grocery store. I thought he'd gone back to Boulder. I mean, the funeral's over so what the hell is he doing here?"

They walked down the hallway and into the kitchen and Ashley took a seat at the table, talking all the while, commanding the space as if it was her own home.

"I couldn't believe my eyes when I saw him," she continued. "He walked in as if it was the most normal thing in the world. Just took some things from the shelves, put them in his basket, and then walked up to the cashier and smiled when he saw me. And do you know what he said? "Oh, hello there, Ashley," as if we were best friends and had met up for a coffee and a friendly chat only yesterday. I mean, can you believe that?"

Evie thought back to the moment she had opened the door to see Ethan standing on her doorstep smiling and waiting for her to let him in. The hope that he would be welcome in his eyes. And now she found herself defending him, despite her instinct not to.

"Yeah well, when you've been away so long," she told Ashley. "It makes you lose track of time. Maybe to him it does feel like he only spoke to you yesterday."

Ashley had looked back at her, her face blank. It made Evie smile to see her caught off guard, her busybody energy sapped for an instant.

"I have no clue what you're talking about, Evie," Ashley replied. "Twenty years ago is not yesterday. And he was not *away*. He spent twenty years in prison for murder, or have you forgotten? He was punished for a damn good reason."

"Please, Ashley," Evie said. "We just buried Andrew, and all he wants to do is stay here for a while with his family while we get over it. You can understand that, can't you? I mean, if you were in his position, you'd want a bit of time to adjust, wouldn't you?"

Ashley was about to reply when the kitchen door opened, and Ethan walked in.

"Oh, sorry," he said when he saw Ashley sitting at the table. "I didn't realize you had company."

She hoped that Ashley wouldn't say anything, but the sight of Ethan standing there, his small bag of groceries dangling at his side, seemed to provoke her.

"What are you doing here?" she asked him. "Shouldn't you be back in Boulder by now?"

Evie tried to intervene when she saw Ashley push the chair back and stand up, her movements defensive, as if she needed to ready herself for what she imagined was coming.

But Ethan simply smiled and held up his hand to pacify her and show Ashley he was harmless. "I just have a few things to talk about with Evie. I'll be gone soon enough. Why? Did you think I was planning on coming home for good, is that it?"

"Listen, Ashley," Evie explained, "we have a lot to talk about. Just let us deal with it together. Please? I promise you, there will be no trouble."

"I understand, Evie, I really do. Andrew's passing, and how it happened, has upset us all. Your father was well loved and respected." Then she turned to face Ethan. "But I'm warning you, Ethan. While you're here, keep out of everyone's way. Do you understand? You're going to upset people if you waltz around here like nothing ever happened. I'm telling you that in your own best interest, you understand?"

Evie didn't give him the chance to respond. "That's okay, Ashley. I'll make sure he keeps a low profile." Then she gestured to the door and led Ashley away, while Ethan smiled and took the groceries out of his plastic bag.

"I'll see you around then, Ash," he called out to her as she left.

When Evie closed the door behind her, she kept her voice steady, breathing in a few times to take away the nerves that jittered through her.

"Don't…" she said.

Ethan looked at her and cocked his head to the side, apparently amused by the whole incident. "Don't what?"

"Don't laugh at her, Ethan. Don't annoy her. You know how she can be, and believe it or not she still has a lot of influence around here. She's a Cardew, or have you forgotten? And for God's sake, don't call her Ash. You lost the right to call her that a long time ago."

"Relax. I just don't like her waltzing in like that and telling you what to do in your own home. She's as bad as her brother."

"She's just looking out for me is all, and Mason's an asshole, and always has been, you know that."

Then she saw the shock on his face. *She's just looking out for me.* As if the idea that she needed protection from him was a terrible notion.

"Evie," he said. "You don't need her looking out for you. Seriously? Is that what you think?"

"I'm more worried that you don't think that."

"Sorry, what?"

"Come on, Ethan, think about it. You know this town, you know how long people's memories are here. They haven't forgotten Michael. And they've every right to be scared. And yes, before you ask, I *do* feel nervous. And don't tell me I don't have every right to feel that way. Twenty years is a long time. I need to get used to having you around the same as everyone else does."

He stood still and looked at her for a moment, and she could see he was disappointed. His expectations of her had been higher. He thought she was different from everyone else here. That she was more open, more forgiving.

"Whoa, okay then," he said. "This was a mistake. I see that now. If you want me to leave, then just say so and I'll get going."

He started to walk out of the kitchen and for a second, she thought of letting him go. It would be easier that way. Just have him walk back out of her life again and allow things to carry on as normal.

"No, Ethan, wait," she said.

He stopped in the doorway and turned to face her. "What?" he asked.

She pulled up a chair and sat back down at the table and waited for him to come and sit beside her. When he did, she asked him. "The truth this time. Okay?"

He said nothing. Just waited for her to continue.

"You didn't come back here because of Dad. I know you didn't."

"I never denied that. I told you, there are things I need to clear up."

"I know. But what I still don't know is what you mean by that. *Clearing things up.*"

He nodded and looked at her. His face serious, the doubt right there. She could see he wasn't sure how she was going to react.

"I need to talk to you about what happened that day, Evie. The day Michael died. I wanted to talk to Dad about it, but…"

"You want to drag up the past, you mean."

"Really, Evie? Can you look me in the eye and tell me you think that's it? I know you aren't entirely sure what happened that day. It wasn't just Mom who had her doubts, I know…"

She was too angry with him now to even look at him, and she got up and walked over to the kitchen cabinet, pulled open a drawer and took out a key. The key to Andrew's house. When she placed it on the table in front of her brother, she didn't look at him, just explained. "It's the key to Dad's place. The house just after Chris Maxwell's. You know the one?"

He picked up the key and nodded, started to say something, but she interrupted.

"I need to think things through, Ethan. You can come here whenever you want to, but for a few days at least I need to be alone. If you want Mom to move over there with you then I can ask her."

"Please, Evie—"

"No, Ethan. Just take your things and go."

She waited in the kitchen while he went upstairs and packed his few things and she wondered how she was going to explain this to Carole. Her mom would be angry with her, but she had a right to some space, surely? A right to sit in her own house and quietly think things through?

On the way out, she handed him his bag with the groceries. She'd added a few extra essentials, so he didn't need to go back to the store. She wanted him out of the way. The less he was seen about town, the better.

"It's just some basic stuff," she explained. "Just so you can last a few days."

"Thanks," he said.

When he leaned over and kissed her cheek, she didn't pull away, though she wanted to. There was something in his voice, in the way he turned away from her, the way he avoided her gaze sometimes, that made her even more wary of him now than the day he arrived. But she tried not to show it as she led him to the door.

"See you tomorrow," was all she said, then she closed the door and waited until she heard the click of the gate and the sound of his footsteps on the road, before locking it and pulling across the chain.

In the kitchen, she did the same. Slid shut the locks, top and bottom and pulled the curtains closed. She was sealed in tight, but it did little to take away the anxiety or answer the question.

Just who is it you're trying to keep out, Evie?

CHAPTER ELEVEN

March 2015

She sat in the living room in the gathering darkness and tried to order her thoughts.

What the hell did Ethan mean when he said, *Help me find out what really happened that day*?

She should tell him it was impossible. Her memory was vague and composed of moments that seemed to have no connection. She could remember her father finding her in the forest. She could remember the smell of the cabin as it burned. She could remember that deer lying on the forest floor and the limpness in her limbs when she saw the blood. She could remember Ethan's face when the police took him away. How ashamed he looked, guilty even. The strange expression in his eyes. Not quite a plea for help, more a plea for forgiveness. *I'm sorry*, that was what it suggested.

And now he was asking her to question everything. To give him a chance. To remember things she'd learned to forget, things she had needed to forget. He was asking her to listen to him. There was something deluded about it, because it was almost as if he was trying to convince her he was innocent. That he hadn't committed the most terrible crime imaginable. If her father had been here still, she would have gone to him and asked, *What do you think? What would you do?*

He was resolute when it came to his son. Ethan was never to be forgiven and he would have said that the things he wanted to "clear up" didn't matter. He had lost his right to be heard years ago as far as Andrew was concerned.

*

The doorbell startled her, and she had to think for a moment who it could be, ringing the bell so insistently. Then she remembered she had locked the door, the chain pulled tight, sealing her in and keeping everyone else out.

"Evie," she heard her mom calling, "open the door, dammit."

When she opened it, Carole was standing on the front step glaring at her, before she pushed past her and headed to the kitchen with her bags.

"Why did you bolt the door like that? How was I supposed to get in?" she complained.

"Sorry," Evie replied. "Force of habit."

"Yes, well, try and remember I'm here, will you?"

Her mom busied herself taking the groceries out and putting things in the cupboards and the fridge.

"I had to go all over town to get some decent stuff, but I managed to get some fresh vegetables and a chicken for tonight," she said. "We need some proper food."

Then she clicked on the coffee machine and took three cups from the cupboard.

"Where's Ethan?" she asked as she sat down and kicked off her shoes.

Evie pulled out a chair and sat opposite her mother. It was Ethan's chair, she realized, and she found herself mimicking her brother's actions of a few days ago – tracing the scratches in the wood of the table, circling the stain left from a water glass. Avoiding eye contact and giving herself a couple of seconds to gather her thoughts.

"What is it, Evie?" her mom asked.

"I asked him to spend a few days over at Dad's," she finally admitted.

"What?" her mom gasped.

"No, please let me explain…" Evie protested.

But Carole wasn't listening. "How could you do that, Evie? How could you chase him away again?"

"I didn't *chase him away*. I just asked him to stay at Dad's for a while."

"What difference does it make? You basically let him know he isn't welcome here. How do you think that must make him feel, Evie?"

But it was true. He wasn't welcome. She wanted to explain how she felt to her mother, and show that it wasn't so unreasonable under the circumstances. But she knew her mom wouldn't listen. As usual, she was focused on Ethan's feelings, as if no one else mattered as much, as if no one else was suffering.

"I just need a bit of space," Evie said eventually, too tired argue. "That's not so much to ask, is it?"

"And your brother needs to know that his family is here for him after all he's been through. That's you and me, Evie. We're all he has. He needs to know he can rely on us."

And now an argument was unavoidable. Her mom was clearly not going to back down.

"And what about me? Why does that never matter to you? Why is it always Ethan you think of first?"

"Oh, Evie! That's not true."

"Isn't it? Then let me have some space. Listen to me when I tell you this is all too much. I need to adjust to it. Dad just died in a horrible accident and my brother, whom I haven't seen in over twenty years, is back home telling me he's innocent and asking me to help him in ways I don't think I can."

"He needs your help… he really does." She spoke softly and slowly, trying to defuse the situation. Trying to persuade her, Evie realized, the softness in her voice the same tone she had used with her when she was a child.

But today, she wasn't in the mood to be persuaded or appeased or shushed.

"Why should I help him, Mom? Why should I believe him? I just… I…"

"Why the doubt?" Carole replied, her voice a little stringent now, a little colder. "He's your brother, Evie. Your flesh and blood. And, in case you've forgotten, he's been through hell; he's endured things he should never have suffered."

"You say it like he's the only one."

"You know I don't mean it that way."

"No, I don't. I really don't. He's not the only one to have suffered. Do you think it was easy for me? Have you forgotten what it did to me? To lose Michael that way? To see my brother go to jail, to have my life turned upside down like that while I was still just a kid."

"You were sixteen, Evie," her tone scornful and impatient.

"What difference does it make? Did you suffer any less because you were an adult? Did Dad? Or Ethan for that matter?"

"No, we were all dragged through hell because of what happened. But please, think about it. Your brother has had to deal with it alone."

"He had you."

"He did, thank God."

And she waited for a few seconds in the hope that her mother would understand. *I needed you too, Mom*, she thought. *I needed you too.* But her mom simply looked at her and waited for her to say something.

"He wants me to remember things I've spent my whole life trying to forget. And I needed to forget them. You, more than anyone, should know that."

"Yes, I know, but…"

"No, let me finish. He set that cabin on fire. And he knew Michael was in there—"

"That's why I've never believed your brother did it. Do you really think he was capable of something that horrific?"

She'd thought her mom's insistence that Ethan could never have done it would have diminished and been replaced by an acceptance of reality and the harsh, honest truth. It disappointed her to think that Carole could still hold such an impossible hope in her heart.

"I don't know why you keep on saying that. There was no one else it could have been. He admitted it. And the evidence—"

"The evidence! What evidence? An argument? Some stupid fuss over a few teenage parties? A photograph? That's not evidence, that's gossip."

"But it was still a reason, though, wasn't it? More reason than anyone else had."

"And what about what you saw, Evie? You were so sure you saw Michael in the forest. You told me over and over again that you saw him. You kept talking about his eyes. You saw him staring at something."

"The doctors explained that. I was confused. That deer I came across in the forest. When I saw the blood I panicked, the shock made me jumble everything up, because I was scared." Her voice wavered as she spoke about it, and she felt her legs begin to tremble and her heart to race. "Dammit, Mom, you made me attend therapy for a whole year so I could talk about all this shit. You know what happened to me."

"Listen, Evie, we're not going to see eye to eye on this, not tonight at least. But please, sleep on it. Think about it. Try, if you can, to forgive him. Your father never did, but you still have the chance."

She couldn't even listen to what her mother had to say anymore. It was too much and she could feel herself shivering with impotence and rage.

"Okay, okay…"

"Right, well, I'm going to go over to Ethan and check that he's okay. Let him know he's welcome to stay here if he wants to. I know you think I have no right to take such a decision, but this was Ethan's home too once, and that still counts for something."

Evie could only nod. The conversation had exhausted her. She just wanted to relax and think of nothing.

*

Carole had stayed over there for hours, and Evie was already in bed when she heard her come home and shuffle upstairs to bed without calling out goodnight to her. And she turned over on her side and tried to sleep. But sleep didn't come. She could only lie there and replay the conversation with her mother and try and keep at bay the images of Michael.

Why did they want her to remember? Why did they insist she go back to that day and re-live that horror? It was unforgivable. They were asking for too much.

And forgiveness? That was something you earned, that was what her father always said. It was something you deserved. Or not. And Andrew never thought Ethan deserved it and he never offered it.

Forgiveness? No, that did not come easy. And now, she wished more than ever that her dad was there to help her.

CHAPTER TWELVE

March 2015

She went looking for his help in the graveyard. There was no headstone yet, and the flowers which had been laid on the mound of earth had withered and faded. Seeing them filled her with an unbearable sadness. *This is how long he's been gone*, she thought. *Long enough for flowers to wilt and turn brown.* She gathered them from the ground and took them over to the trash can by the cemetery gate. When she returned to the grave, she wasn't sure if it made her happier or more forlorn to see it so bare and unadorned, and she made a mental note to go to the florists in the afternoon and buy some potted plants she could set there, until the headstone was ready.

"Hey, Dad," she said as she crouched down on the ground. "It's me, Evie."

Then she waited, hoping for a reply. Imagining his voice as he said hello to her. But the silence only made the truth of it all feel worse. She would never hear his voice again.

Without him she felt helpless, as if a limb had been severed from her body so that she needed to learn how to move again, how to negotiate life from this new position.

"Ethan wants me to forgive him," she continued. Then she paused, because she didn't know what to say, what advice it was she was looking for. She picked up a handful of soil from the grave and rubbed it between her thumb and forefinger and watched as the dirt settled deep into the grooves of her skin.

"What I can't figure out is why," she said. "I don't owe him that, do I? But he seems to think I do. He thinks he deserves my forgiveness. And I'm supposed to be able to do that, right? As his sister? If anyone should forgive him, then it should be me, shouldn't it?"

The voice from behind her startled her and caused her to topple and fall back onto the grass next to the grave.

"I'd say you forgive someone if you believe they've repented. If you know they're truly sorry and are willing to change."

Ashley. She walked over to the grave and held out her hand to help Evie get back on her feet.

"Dammit, Ashley," Evie said as she stood up. "You scared the hell out of me."

"Why, who did you think it was? Your father?"

"That's not funny."

"Sorry. You're right, that was pretty crass."

"What do you want?"

"I just saw you sitting here, and you looked so sad and like you could do with a friend, so I came over. Is that so bad?"

It wasn't. It was kind and Evie nodded and said, "No it's not. Thanks."

She didn't want Ashley there, but now that she was, she wondered if she maybe should ask her the question she had wanted to ask her father.

"Can I ask you something?" she asked Ashley.

"About forgiveness you mean?"

"Yeah."

"He paid his dues," Evie said. "Twenty years in jail. That's repentance, isn't it?"

And Ashley looked at her and frowned, as if the question confounded her and she couldn't quite believe she was going to have to explain the difference.

"Evie, you know it's not. Has he ever said sorry for what he did?"

"He admitted it, though, in court. That means something, doesn't it?"

"It does. But that's just the first step, isn't it? You acknowledge what you did wrong, you accept your punishment and then you go away and you think about what you did, and how it makes you feel, and how you're going to change. It's a process."

"Sounds like you don't think Ethan's been through that process."

"Do you believe he has? Has he shown any sign that he has?"

"No," she agreed. "But that doesn't mean he isn't willing to…"

"The way I see it," Ashley said, "is that you don't ask for forgiveness. It's not his to ask for, it's his to receive. But the only way we can give it to him is if he shows us he's sorry. But if you ask for it, if you come back after twenty years and start demanding it, well, then you still have a lot of thinking to do. I'd say you still haven't truly come to terms with what you did. I'd say you're a long, long way from forgiveness."

Ashley was right. Put like that, it sounded so clear and so true. Ethan had no right to demand they forgive him. He would have to show them.

"So what am I supposed to do then? I mean, how do I get him to do that? If twenty years in prison hasn't shown him what to do, then what can he hope to achieve after just a few days back home?"

"I don't know… maybe it just needs time. But look what he's done to you already. I mean, you're sitting at your father's grave asking him for advice, because you don't know what it is Ethan wants or why he came back here. And I'm worried that Ethan hasn't thought about what all this might do to you. So tell him to go home and think things through and take the time to get this right. We'll all still be here for him when he's figured it out."

"And you'll listen to him then, if he does that?"

"Evie, you know we will."

They had left it at that, and Evie had walked home shaken by the truth of the things Ashley had said.

But that last part was not quite the truth, she thought.

They would never listen to him and Ashley knew it. They had stopped listening twenty years ago. All they'd ever heard here was the whisper of gossip and the screech of scandal.

CHAPTER THIRTEEN

April 1995

"Look at this! When is it going to stop?"

Andrew had stormed into the kitchen and thrown the newspaper on the table then slumped in his chair, as if defeated by his outburst, the despair exhausting him.

Evie looked at the paper. Some scandal-hungry tabloid with the big, bold headline: *Guilty!*

When she scanned the opening lines, she caught flashes of shrill exaggerations, each word a punch to the gut, and she blinked, hoping to stop them penetrating deep enough to hurt her.

Brutal. Gruesome. Violent. Jealous rage. Community torn apart. Secrets. Shame.

She knew the story by heart, but every time she read it, she failed to recognize her family in the words on the page. Especially Ethan. She could never accept the way the world now saw him. The picture the newspaper painted was of a coldblooded murderer. Carole's conviction that her son was innocent was portrayed as some sort of sad delusion, while Andrew's quiet rage became a source of gleeful fascination, as if they were waiting for him to explode.

How could anyone read all this and believe it?

But she knew they did. She knew people in this very town devoured those headlines and believed every word. Years of knowing them, years of friendship were not enough to make them question the supposed truth printed there on the front pages for all the world to see.

"Why did you buy it?" Evie asked him.

"I didn't. I found it in the mailbox. Do you think I'd allow this filth into my own house?"

"Oh…" was all she could say.

"What is it they want from us, Evie?" he asked her.

"I don't know," she replied. "Maybe they just hate us. Or they're just doing it for money. Tragedy sells and they know it."

Andrew picked up the paper and flicked through it. Page after page of the story, photos of Michael, the town, her brother, illustrating each fresh headline.

She reached over to take it from him, but he pulled away.

"I mean," he said as he flipped through the pages, "this is what they all think of us too now, isn't it? This is who our friends and neighbors think we are."

Her mom walked in and saw them sitting there, saw the paper in Andrew's hands. "Where did that come from?" she asked. And she walked over and plucked the paper from his hands, tearing it and crumpling it as she threw it in the trashcan. "I won't have this trash in my house, Andrew. Do you understand that? I refuse to have this dirt in my house."

"Someone posted it in the mailbox," Evie explained.

And it was her mom's turn then to slump on the chair and fold herself into a knot of despair. "Oh… I see…"

"I can't take the shame much longer," Andrew said, his voice small and low and uncertain. "Knowing this is what they think of us. That they'll never forgive us—"

"It will settle," Carole said. "People here know us. They know who we really are. They know this is all lies."

"Do they?" Andrew asked. "They say we're standing by him. They say we think he's innocent. They say—"

"And we are standing by him," Carole replied. "And when we visit him in Cañon City—"

"Oh, come on, you can't be serious, Carole. If you think I'm setting one foot in that prison, you're crazy. People will think—"

"I don't care what they think, Andrew. I know my son. And so do you."

"No, Carole, that's where you're wrong. I have no idea who Ethan is and if you were honest with yourself, then you'd admit it: neither do you."

"How can you say that? Your own son—"

"He's not my son. Ethan McCallister is no longer my son. He's what they say he is. A murderer. Goddammit, he admitted it. He confessed. So stop deluding yourself."

"Please…" but the tears clogged her throat and silenced her.

Evie was surprised it had taken so long for things to come to a head. The tension had been building for weeks, all through the trial and up to Ethan's conviction. A simmering silence that was always going to erupt, and now, this morning, the valve had burst.

"I'll never forgive you for this, Andrew. Never! You can't abandon him in that prison."

"He can rot there for all I care," he shouted in reply.

And there were more words thrown.

Her father's voice growing louder with every insult he threw in her mother's face: *Shame. Disgrace. Justice. Michael.*

And Carole begging him to understand: *Mistake. Lies. Love. Believe.* That was all Evie heard.

But there was no space in between these words where they could meet. The distance was too great.

And then a flash of something. A flame almost. That was what it looked like, as if something had exploded and the force of it, the shock wave, hit Carole and sent her reeling. Evie saw her fall to the floor, as her father's rage made its presence known at last, with a smack, and a cry, then a moan.

She looked down and saw her mother lying on the floor. Saw her eyes welling with tears and her mouth contorted in pain as she cried out to her.

"Evie… Evie…"

Then the sound of her father's feet as he shuffled by, and a door slamming someplace.

But he didn't keep his word. He did visit. Just the once. But he did go.

*

On the drive over to Cañon City, she had been nervous. The idea of seeing Ethan left her nauseous. Ethan, her brother, who now had another name: *murderer*. She had thought about that as they moved through the valleys and crossed the open plains, the landscape slowly giving way to open vistas, then towns, then an ugly sprawl of concrete, as if the view beyond the window was indicative of some other change. Ethan moving from the tranquility of lakes, mountains and forests to this harsher place where the air already seemed grayer and thicker, and where the buildings sprouted inelegantly from the ground. Ethan, who had transformed from a shy, gentle brother into something unfathomable and monstrous. Someone who deserved to be shut away in a city like this.

She had wanted to tell her parents that she still couldn't believe it, because when she tried to think of Ethan as someone capable of causing harm, she felt betrayed. Not by her brother, but by the people who had accused him. The people who had pointed to him and declared him evil. That wasn't who he was, surely?

That Andrew had been among the most vocal of the accusers shocked her to her core, and for the length of the journey she had watched him in the hope that there would be some indication in his face as to why he had agreed to join them on the visit. Perhaps now that things had had time to settle down, he was ready to forgive his son at last, or at least to accept that they would all have to find a way to come to terms with what happened.

When the sentence had come through, Andrew had sat stony faced in the courtroom, staring at Ethan as he was taken away, and when Ethan had turned to look up at them, his voice had echoed out across the room.

"You're not my son!" The spit and venom of his tone caused Evie to flinch and lean away from him as he stood up and began to make his way out of the court, repeating those words with a conviction and anger that was terrifying. "You are not my son!"

She had wanted to run to him and say, *You're right. This is not who he is. A murderer? No, he can't be. He's your son. And he's my brother. He's Ethan.*

But she didn't dare. The energy that radiated from her father at that moment was too great, too frightening. And in the three weeks following Ethan's incarceration, she had seen nothing to convince her that her father's rage had diminished.

"Don't ever mention his name to me, do you understand? Don't talk to me about him, ever again," was the reply she received whenever she tried to talk to Andrew about what had happened. It had been Mom who had intervened and led her away with a whispered, "Just leave him be for now, Evie. He'll come round when he's ready."

"Will he?" she replied. "I can't ever see him forgiving Ethan."

And she could see her mom straining to say something, trying to come to Andrew's defense. But she couldn't, because a piece of her knew Evie was right. And again, those words screamed in the courtroom seemed to rebound and reverberate. A terrible memory that would haunt them forever.

You're not my son.

As they drew closer to their destination, Evie looked at her father. His shoulders tense, his gaze fixed to the road, the line of his jaw

firm and determined, and she knew she would need to brace herself
for what was to come. He was here for a reason, and Evie knew
he would not be kind or forgiving.

An intuition which was to prove correct.

When the gray bulk of the prison loomed into view, Evie gasped
and reached out for her mom's hand, squeezing it tight. She could
feel her heart racing, the threatening mass of the penitentiary elicit-
ing a panicked response within her. Her instinct was to demand he
turn the car around and take them away from this place. Because
to be confronted with the fact that this was where Ethan would
spend the next twenty years was horrifying.

Andrew parked the car in the parking lot adjacent to the
building, and they walked to the gate and announced their arrival
to the guard. When they told him the name of the inmate they
had come to visit, Evie thought she saw a flicker of disgust on
the guard's face and it struck her then that they were tainted by
association, that, even here, so far from home, the crimes of the
son, and the brother, were also theirs.

They shared Ethan's culpability, that was how it felt as they
made their way through the security check. Bags emptied, papers
checked, jackets and shoes taken off. They were being inspected,
checked, judged. All over again.

And she had wanted to turn around and leave—and could see
from her mom's expression that she felt the same way—because
the whole process felt like a violation. It was meant to feel that
way, she understood that. It was a way to make them understand
that Ethan was theirs now. Their responsibility, their charge. He
belonged to them. To the prison walls, and the uniformed guards
and the voice which barked instructions through the loudspeaker.

Only Andrew remained impassive in the face of it all. And
Evie could see the way his own words had immunized him; he

didn't feel the terror of this institution, of what it would do to his son, because an unbridgeable distance now existed between them. Because Ethan was not his son. He had handed him over and washed his hands of him.

They were taken to a separate room, because it was their first visit.

"The next time we'll ask that only one of you come," they were told. And they nodded, as if there would be other times. Not knowing that this was the only visit the three of them would make here together. Andrew would see to that.

For ten minutes they sat in the small room, waiting for Ethan to arrive, partitioned behind a Perspex screen that separated them from the room on the other side. Evie wondered what she was going to say to him, but the screen separating them consumed her attention and numbed her to the point that she couldn't think. Sitting there within those intimidating walls, it felt as if the whole place was designed to stop you from thinking. You were supposed to let the time pass. Close your mind to it all. Though there was only one question, really. The one she had not been able to ask until now, because she still wanted to hold onto the lie that Ethan could never have killed Michael. But this place, these prison walls left her with no place to hide and the question could no longer be ignored. Why did you do such a terrible thing? That was all she wanted to know. The one thing which was still so shocking and unfathomable.

Ethan was brought into the room. A guard explained they had an hour, then walked over to the door, where he stood watching them. His presence at once oppressive and unobtrusive. There and not there. Observing. Waiting. Staying silent. Ready to intervene at any moment.

Immediately, Evie noticed that Ethan seemed to pay the guard no attention. A few weeks inside had apparently been enough for him to become accustomed to this ever-present shadow. And it surprised her that he seemed to be so steady, so controlled. That the setting, the circumstances, hadn't affected him as much as she'd imagined they would have. As if he had chosen this. She had expected to see someone broken and frightened. Instead, her brother sat there, upright and confident, almost defiant, as if his incarceration had confirmed to him everything he knew about himself.

She thought about what such a defiant look could mean, and what mental reserves he had needed to call upon in order to maintain his dignity. She hadn't expected his resolve to survive it all—the trial, the plea change, the conviction, the whole official declaration that, in the eyes of the law, he was guilty. He was a murderer. How could he not collapse under the weight of such a terrible label?

During the long formal process, as Ethan had moved from innocence to guilt, from arrest, to confession, then conviction, Evie had managed to maintain a small level of doubt, a tiny hope that it was all a mistake somehow. But now, there he was, sitting in front of her, and it was like seeing the brother she knew, the brother she loved, the brother who could never have done any of the things they said he had done slowly become the thing they said he was. This monster. This murderer. And it shocked her a little when she realized she was scared of him now. That the impact of the label, that awful word—murderer—was unavoidable.

Now that he was in front of her, she wanted to look him in the eye and ask him, "How did you become this man?" But Andrew got in the way. He was the first to speak and the power of his words ensured both she and her mom were shocked into silence.

Even before Ethan had the chance to say much more beyond the introductory pleasantries, Andrew held up his hand and told him to stop.

"We haven't come here to listen to you," he said.

Ethan shrank back in disbelief, before his expression reverted to one of quiet resignation, as if whatever Andrew had to say was something he had already learned to tune out.

And she wished she could do the same. Find some way to block her father, and not hear the cruel things he had to say. Not to have to face them, to have to believe them.

"You've shamed us, Ethan. I hope you know that?"

And again, when Ethan tried to reply, Andrew raised his hand to stop him from speaking.

"No. Listen. You killed that poor boy and I'll never understand why."

Carole had tried to intervene. "Andrew, please, it isn't right to be going over it all…"

Andrew had turned to her with a fierce look in his eyes and Evie saw his hands clench as if he needed to control himself, to keep down something violent.

The guard saw it too and walked over and told Andrew, in a quiet but strangely forceful tone, that "disruption of any sort was not tolerated."

"I'm just here to say what I need to say, and then we'll be gone," Andrew replied. "I won't be disruptive, don't worry."

The guard nodded and walked back to his place by the door, but his interference had worked. Andrew took a deep breath, closed his eyes and composed himself, then carried on, Ethan looking at him all the while with that same, impassive look on his face, as if Andrew meant very little to him. As if he knew that whatever his dad had to say was wrong.

"Okay, so here it is. We will never be coming here again. No visits, no letters, no telephone calls. As far as we are concerned you do not exist—"

"Andrew, stop, that's not true," Carole protested.

But he didn't even acknowledge she had spoken.

"Your mom will understand in due course. As will Evie. When they think about what you did to that boy, they'll feel as I do, I'm sure of it. They'll feel all the shame and disgust and contempt that I have had to endure. And if you think I'm being harsh then let me tell you, I've restrained myself, because I must. But trust me, there are no words to describe how I feel about you."

He stood up then and nodded to the guard.

"We're all done here," he said.

"No, wait," Carole said. "I'm not done. I'm not—"

"Yes, you are, Carole. Now come on."

"No, I don't agree with a word of it, Ethan. Not one word."

The guard intervened again then, walked over to Ethan and ushered him out of the door, while behind them, some other official appeared and led them away, back down the corridor and to the exit, where they collected their things before walking outside.

The whole visit had taken just over half an hour and Evie had felt as if she had barely had time to breathe or even say hello. While her father had made his little speech, she had sat there squeezing her mom's hand and biting her lip, trying her best to hold back the tears that had stung her eyes and tightened her throat. And she wished she had had the chance to let Ethan know that she still thought of him as her brother. That he would always be her brother. That whatever the reasons for Andrew's anger, she could not imagine disowning him. But when she looked at her father, she understood that this was stupid, wishful thinking, and she would need to be careful from now on not to hope for such things.

But I will visit him again, she thought. *This can't be the last time.* It would be too cruel to leave him there, rotting, alone.

And she whispered to her mom as they walked back to the parking lot, "We'll see him again, won't we?"

Her mom looked at her and shook her head. "No, not for a while yet, I don't think."

"But—"

Her question cut short as Andrew shouted out to them.

"Are you two coming?"

Later, Evie had realized that this was the start of it all. The strange, heartbreaking transformation that came over her father as he collapsed under the weight of his own shame and guilt. That was the day he began his own slow, quiet retreat from the world. The day he started punishing himself for the sins of his son.

CHAPTER FOURTEEN

March 2015

The mornings were always the most difficult and again she woke too early, her head fuzzy from a night of disrupted sleep. This morning there was also an echo of a long-forgotten voice. Dr. Newton trying to move her forward toward some sort of clarity: *Why do you think you can't remember what you saw?*

She had always thought it was as much an accusation as a question. As if the blackness which had overwhelmed her and stripped her of her ability to remember was a choice she had made and something she could control. She remembered the way it made her feel, every time Dr. Newton asked her that, the overwhelming need she had to escape. She always tried to avoid giving an answer, and steer the conversation in another direction, but Dr. Newton was too persuasive, too persistent. Week after week, she sat in that stark room and was forced to confront it.

Why do you think you can't remember what you saw?

And Evie had stared at the photographs on the wall and tried to find an escape route there among the idealized scenes. But it hadn't felt like a lie not being able to remember. The emptiness in her head, that blackness, it was real, and she had admitted as much.

"Do you want to know what I see when I try and remember that day?" she had asked the doctor.

"Tell me."

"Black. That's all. Black. It's like being underwater. Deep under water. There's no light. Just blackness."

"And before the black?"

Before the black. *Did such a time exist?* She had woken with the steady weight of that blackness as if it was something that had never left her. When she lifted her arm, she could feel it in the muscles of her biceps and in her shoulder, the strain constricting her neck and making it difficult to breathe. She was underwater again, so deep that the light from the surface was unable to penetrate. There was only dark and cold and an increasing paralysis.

Dr. Newton had tried so hard to explain that the weight she felt, that suffocation, was a symptom. A physical sign that her body was rebelling, fighting her wish to keep it all inside.

"Do you think there is something there, Evie?" she had asked. "Something that needs to come to the surface if you are ever going to heal?"

Yes, she had felt it in every fiber of her body. She hadn't been completely unaware. *But that wasn't the issue,* she thought. *The choice, in the end, was hers: let it rise to the surface or push it down. That was also a form of healing. Amnesia as analgesic.*

The more time she had spent with Dr. Newton, the more she had believed it was possible to analyze a thing to the point of destruction. It was as true now as it was then, she realized. Ethan's return was more than just a physical intrusion. He was also an unwanted presence in her mind. A source of memories and pain and things best left alone.

Now, her own body was telling her not to do it, not to go back into the past, and her muscles insisting she stay in bed and wait until it was all over. "Have no part of it," they seemed to be saying. And she pulled the covers up around her and buried herself deep in their folds and tried to keep the world at bay for just a little longer.

But the day crashed in on her in the end, the cellphone at her bedside ringing and ringing and ringing until she could no longer ignore it. The trouble and upheaval had already arrived.

"Evie, you need to get over here."

She could tell he was struggling to remain calm and trying to control the slight waver in his voice.

"What is it, Ethan?" she asked. "Is everything okay?"

"No, it's not, but I can't explain it over the phone. Can you just come over and see for yourself? Oh, and don't wake Mom. I don't want to worry her."

He was standing on the roadside looking out for her as she walked down the road, and she wondered for a second why he was out there in the cold morning, his hair already matted to his head, his face covered in a light sheen of rain.

Then she saw the reason.

A splash of glossy red paint was spattered across the front windows and the door, like the gash a knife would make. On the small paved path that led from the road to the house, someone had painted the word "Murderer!" in quick, messy brushstrokes.

Evie looked at it and tried to figure out what it meant. Not the text so much as the fact that someone felt compelled to do such a thing. The fact that someone must have been watching the house closely and had seen that Ethan had spent the night alone there unsettled her and made her nervous. She had been expecting people to talk, but nothing like this.

"Perhaps you shouldn't have paraded around town so confidently yesterday," she said as she moved past him and headed inside.

It was only when she went to open the door that she noticed one of the front windows had also been smashed in.

"Shit," she said. "As if I don't have enough to worry about."

Behind her she heard Ethan cough. He was expecting her to turn around so he could say something, but she didn't want to talk to him just then. She just wanted in from the rain and the cold.

She wanted a hot cup of coffee and maybe even a bite of breakfast. Because only when she was calm and warm and fed would she be able to think about who had done it.

Whoever it was, she was going to have to talk to them. Whatever they thought about her brother, he had paid his dues and would be gone soon. There was no need to go hounding him.

In the kitchen, she set about making some coffee and a sandwich, the layout of the room as familiar to her as her own kitchen.

Ethan watched her in silence, sensing that he needed to let her get on with things and that he could only start the conversation once she was ready.

At the sink, she stood and looked out at the small patch of garden, listening to the coffee machine drip. The vegetables her father had planted in tidy rows were there, under the ground, waiting to push through. Beetroot, carrots and potatoes, her dad's staple crop. Good and reliable and easy to grow.

Now it would be up to her, she realized, to tend to this meager harvest. And for some reason, the thought of that, of carrying on with the things he had set in motion and could now no longer finish, was enough to make her cry. It was only the sputtering of the coffee machine that brought her back.

"How about you pour us both a cup?" Ethan asked her.

"Sure," she said.

He noticed her tears as she walked toward him.

"Evie, I'm so sorry," he said. "I never thought me being here would cause so much trouble. I'm really sorry."

"No, it's not that," she explained as she set the cups on the table. "I was just remembering Dad. It hits me like that sometimes, and I'm not always prepared for it. It'll pass, I'm sure."

She walked over to the fridge and gathered together some things for breakfast. Cheese and butter and milk, a small jar of strawberry jelly, then set it on a tray and took it all to the table.

"It's not much of a breakfast," she said, "but it'll get us started for the day."

But the shock of those red blazoned words left them with little appetite.

"Listen," she said. "We should try and get that mess cleaned up before everyone sees it and the whole town starts talking about it."

"You don't want to call the police about it? I mean, it's a lot of damage."

"I don't want it there when Mom wakes up. I don't want her to see it."

"Why?" he said.

"It'll only upset her, and I don't think I can handle her fussing and worrying to be honest."

"If you say so… Listen, I'm really sorry, about—"

"Forget it, okay? Let's just finish up here and make a start on cleaning the door."

He nodded and drank down his coffee. "Do you know if Dad had a brush or something?" he asked.

"If he did it will be out in the garage. The key's hanging up on the hook by the door."

He took the key, then went to get his jacket and shoes while she sat at the table and thought about the paint, the words daubed there on the garden path.

Mason, she thought. *Only Mason would be stupid enough to do something like this. But would he have the guts?* she wondered.

In the garage, Ethan found the things he needed and a wooden board he could fix around the broken windowpane.

"Just until we can get a glazier out."

She watched as he busied himself with mending the window, and then realized she was happier with him being inside the house. She could tend to the mess in the garden and deal with any passers-by who stopped to ask questions.

She had just made a start on the door when she heard footsteps on the gravel path behind her. When she turned around, Ashley was there.

"Morning, Ashley," she said, before turning back to the door and dipping a scrubbing brush in the bucket of soapy water Ethan had given her.

"What happened here?" Ashley asked.

"Ethan had a visitor. And not a very friendly one."

"So I see. You should tell the police about this. Just in case."

She put the brush down and turned to face Ashley.

"In case what?"

"Oh, come on, Evie, you know there are plenty of people around who aren't happy about Ethan being here. And staying in Andrew's house too, so soon after we all said goodbye to him, well…"

"I already told you, he's just here to sort a few things out. Just for a few days. Surely you can all let him have a few days here at home after all this time?"

"Look at the door, Evie. I think that answers your question."

"Was it you?"

"Sorry, what?"

"Was it? Did you do this? Or maybe it was your brother?"

"You know what, I'm going to pretend you didn't ask me that. You're under a lot of strain, and you don't know what you're saying. But when you're ready to apologize, you know where to find me." Then she turned and walked away.

Evie watched her for a while then turned back to see Ethan standing there.

"So you think Ashley did this?" he asked her.

"No. More likely Mason. But listen, if he did, then let me handle it, okay?"

He shook his head and took the brush out of the bucket.

"The window's boarded up. Why don't you let me do this?"

"I mean it. Ashley. Hell, everyone. Just let me deal with them."

"Hey, you know me. I'd never cross Ashley Cardew."

She thought she saw him smile just a little and wondered if there were other reasons he had come back here. Not just Andrew and Michael. But all the other unfinished things too. She watched him kneel by the door and swipe his index finger through the paint, his finger sticky and red as he turned it toward him and frowned then shook his head.

"Gloss paint," he said. "We're going to need turpentine or something if this is going to come off."

She didn't reply. All she saw was the red there, coating his hands. A thick globule of it trickling down his finger into his palm. She watched as he looked at it, then grabbed an old cloth and tried to smear it away.

But the red wouldn't wash away. He could wipe it and wipe it, but it would never be gone. That stain, that terrible stain. She could already feel it, fuzzing up her head and weakening her legs.

Her mother's voice, like an echo from another time, made her jump and want to flee. "My God, what the hell happened here?"

CHAPTER FIFTEEN
Journal Entry, March 1995

Here's something I'll never understand. How easy it is for some people to crush happiness with gossip and laughter and shame.

You keep telling me it's important I remember the good things, the happy moments. You want me to take that positive energy and use it to balance out everything that came afterward, all the horror and the pain. You promise me it will help.

Those good things? They were ruined before Michael died. All that happiness? They took it from us long before Michael was trapped in that burning cabin.

But okay then, Dr. Newton, let me try and remember the good things, the happy times. Because it's true, we were happy last summer. We had endless sun-filled days ahead of us and the freedom to do whatever we wanted.

As I write, I can almost hear you asking me, *So tell me about it, Evie. Describe the summer to me.*

Last summer meant one thing to me and one thing only. I fell in love for the very first time. I understood for the first time how it felt to be completely consumed by another person.

I don't know if I can explain it. I just felt relaxed when I was with him. I could be myself and not have to worry about saying the right thing or doing the right thing or looking the right way. I could just be me. I could just be Evie McCallister.

Just writing about him is so hard. I caught a flash of him just then. That's what happens whenever I think of him. I remember these small tender moments. This time, it was Michael tracing his finger over my arm and counting the freckles on my pale skin and brushing away a stray strand of hair from my eyes, so he could look at me properly and say, *I love those flecks of copper in your eyes, the way they flash when you smile. I can always tell when you're happy.*

I don't think I will ever be this close to someone else again. It's impossible. Who could ever replace Michael? That's why I don't want to remember any of it, even the happy things because it hurts too much to remember him. It hurts too much to feel the loss. But I have to remember, don't I? That's what you keep telling me, so, here goes…

We didn't wait long to get together. From that first moment at the lake we knew the energy between us was impossible to resist. I remember Ashley linking her arm around mine as we walked home and asking me, "Whoa, what's with you guys?" And it made me feel so good inside to know that someone else had noticed the connection between us. I wasn't imagining it. It was real and other people could see it.

When I asked her what she meant she laughed and told me her skin had tingled as she watched us together. She thought we had collided. That was the word she used. As if we were planets or something that had come together and then, *boom!*

She was right. That was exactly how it felt, but I couldn't admit it to her. Because it felt too disorienting and it frightened me as much as it excited me. I had been hit by something so powerful it had left me unable to speak. And putting words to it would diminish it too in some way. I didn't want to describe it or talk about it, I just wanted to feel it.

Remember the happiness. Well, that was the happiness. And if you want to know how it started to fade then I can tell you in one word: Mason.

All summer he had been a lurking presence. I remember walking home from the lake with Ashley the day she introduced us all to Michael. Mason had walked a few steps behind us and listened in on our conversation. And I had known instinctively that I had to be careful.

He had been watching me all afternoon. I would look over and see him staring at me, not even trying to avert his gaze. I knew how he felt about me. I knew too he couldn't accept that I didn't feel the same way. Sometimes I even felt sorry for him, because I could imagine how hurt he must have been. But seeing him that day, it suddenly struck me that he didn't feel anything toward me, he simply wanted to possess me.

And for the first time I was wary of him and I had inched closer to Michael so he could shield me from Mason's gaze. I could feel Mason's anger. I could see the darkness expanding in his eyes as he watched us. A hint of what was to come.

When we arrived home from the lake that afternoon Michael whispered to me as he headed back to the hotel with Ashley and Mason, "Meet me later at the lake? By the boathouse at eight?" and I had nodded and felt his arm brush against me, the goosebumps on my skin emerging in response to his touch.

When I met him at the lake that night, we didn't say a word. He took my hand and smiled at me and together we walked into the forest, the shadows offering us the privacy we needed to finally explore one another away from those prying eyes and penetrating stares.

But it was more than his touch, I want you to know that. It was more than this physical attraction. That night, I understood it immediately, as we talked and talked and talked. Here was someone who paid attention. Here was someone who understood me. Here was someone who cared.

He had noticed Ethan had teased me down by the lake. Had seen the way it embarrassed and upset me. And he wasn't scared to ask me about it.

"Why did he have to tease you like that? Can he not see how uncomfortable it made you?"

I wasn't used to being asked questions like that or to having someone pay me such close attention. I'd accepted long ago that you were expected to hide any fears you had, to accept any laughter, or teasing or criticism as the legitimate response to your weakness. And now, here was Michael questioning all of that and letting me see that a different response was possible, that a kinder response was better and was something I deserved. I'd never met someone like that before. I hadn't realized until then that I needed someone like that. Someone who listened. Someone who cared.

So I told him everything about the lake. About that day, when I was six years old and had nearly drowned. How Ethan had pulled me from the water.

"It's so strange that he would tease you about it," he said. "I mean, he must know how it feels. He must know why it scares you still."

And I had wanted to say something in my brother's defense, but he put his fingers to my lips and said. "No, you don't need to make excuses for him."

I thought then, *I would go into the water for you. If you asked me to, I would do it for you.* And I told him so.

"Really?" he said. "Just like that?"

And he smiled and caressed me as I asked him, "If you held my hand, I would. Would you hold my hand?"

"I'd never let it go," he said.

And my heart beat faster in a confusing rhythm of panic and joy. *He would never let me go*, I thought. *All I had to do was take his hand, if I dared to.*

And I did dare. All summer I gave myself over to that heady mix of panic and joy.

You keep asking me if we were happy that summer. But the more I think about that word—happy—the less sure I am, because more than anything we just wanted to have fun. More than anything, we just wanted to let everything go, and just be. When you first asked me to describe that summer, I couldn't tell you. I couldn't find the right word. You suggested happy and I agreed. But now I think I have a better word. Joyous. That's what it was. It was joyous. Something beyond happiness.

Because that kind of joy comes from being with people you love. Because that's all you need to be happy really, isn't it? I think it is anyway. You just need people who accept you as you are. And that's all we did. We were together and that was enough. That was all we needed. Every day we hung out and listened to music, drank a few beers, smoked a little. Danced, sometimes. And had sex. But it wasn't everything.

That summer. That perfect, joyous summer. Me and Michael, Ethan and Ashley, together in our own little world. A space where we could hide away, where adults couldn't find us and tell us what to do. Where we were free to simply be.

You keep telling me to remember the happier times. But you never ask me what that feels like. You never seem to consider what it does to me to realize Michael is gone forever. And I can't fill that loss with happy memories. The gap he left behind is too big.

And dammit, how can any of this be therapeutic? How can it help? Sitting here writing all this down, what good does it do? If I was brave enough, I would ask you. But I'm not brave. So I sit there and listen while you tell me to give it time. To take it step by step. But when I try to piece it together, when I think back to that summer, it doesn't fill me with joy. It fills me with sadness.

Because the joy was turned to shame, our laughter drowned out by mockery, our fun turned into scandal. We stepped out of line and we paid the price.

I feel sick thinking about it. About Mason and his vindictive little campaign. He didn't know what he had started, and I'm not even sure he meant it to go that far, but it doesn't matter. When you act out of jealousy and hate, nothing good can ever come from it. All that ever comes from it is pain.

CHAPTER SIXTEEN

July 1994

Ashley had decorated the cabin with Christmas lights and the effect was deliriously disorienting. Every time Evie opened the door and walked inside, she had the feeling she was entering a different world. Some fairytale place that was kept hidden and secret from the world.

She had added her own touches too. Strewn pots of incense around the place, which she lit as soon as she arrived. The smoky haze, the thick spice-laden scent, the dim glittering lights, all created something illusory and the more time they spent there, the less they wanted to leave.

It was magical. That was what she thought.

Michael had set up the music and he was an expert when it came to creating the right atmosphere. Thumping beats that pounded through your body and made you want to dance and sing and sweat. Ambient and trance tracks, for when you preferred to relax, to just sit and talk and smoke a little and hang with one another.

She knew, even when she was right there living it, right there in the middle of it, that this was a special summer. The sort of moment that could never be experienced again. You were never this young again, tasting life for the first time like this. Nothing would ever come close to this. But being aware of it made it more special and she wanted to pay attention to every tiny moment, to be aware of every sensory overload. To commit it to memory with every cell in her body so that a piece of it would stay with her forever.

It was during one of those pounding dance moments that Mason showed up unexpectedly.

Michael had turned up the volume and the lights were twinkling, red and blue and green and gold, the air thick with patchouli oil and incense. She was turning and turning in time to the music, her head rolling back on her shoulders, the weight of it pulling her round and round. The beat of the music was a slow repetitive rhythm, primal and easy to move to, and she was half-aware of the bodies around her as they moved as one sweat drenched mass.

When she felt an arm touch her, then wrap around her waist, she didn't think to look. She just moved together with his body and they swayed with the beat. When one tune blended into the next, she let her head fall back on his shoulder and turned and looked up at him, waiting for a kiss.

When his lips touched hers, his tongue brushing her teeth she had felt immediately that something wasn't right and stepped back to see Mason there, holding her and pushing against her again, searching for her lips.

"Mason!" she screamed. "What the actual fuck?"

And he smiled at her, then laughed, his laughter echoing around the room as the music was turned off and the lights went on.

"What the hell do you think you're doing, Mason?" she yelled at him.

And he stared at her, his mouth pursed in a sneer, his eyes greedy and fierce.

"Just thought I'd join in with the party," he said. And then he sauntered around the room appraising it. "Quite a set up you've got going on here."

"Listen, Mason," Ashley said. "You can't crash in here and start grabbing people like that. What the fuck do you think you're doing?"

"What am *I* doing? I can ask you guys the same thing. What the hell do you think you're doing? Does Dad know about this? That you've squatted one of his cabins? That you've turned it into party central? I bet he doesn't, does he?"

"Is that a threat? Are you fucking threatening us?" Ashley said.

"He has a right to know, Ash. This is his property. You can't go vandalizing it."

"We're not," Evie said. "We made it look nice. Look! It's just a few lights dammit. What's wrong with that?"

"Nothing, I guess," he said. "I mean, I can live with it, I suppose."

"What do you mean?" Ethan asked him.

"I mean it's not my choice of decoration, but it doesn't annoy me. I'll get used to it."

"Huh?" Ethan said. "So what's this then? You're inviting yourself to come join the party, is that it?"

"Why not? Is it invitation only then? Is this some sort of exclusive members club? A dilapidated shack in the woods? You think the Christmas lights add a touch of sophistication or something?"

"No one invited you, Mason," Ethan said. "And if you don't like the décor, well you don't need to hang around. It's personality that's the membership criteria."

And they had all laughed at that, Michael spurting out a flume of beer that he'd been sipping from a bottle when Ethan made his cutting remark.

Then Michael turned the music back on and the lights were dimmed and Evie felt the atmosphere change, the beat of the music oppressive and almost threatening, the way it thumped like a heartbeat and synchronized with their laughter.

She looked at Mason and saw him step back, saw him swallow and blink away the humiliation. And for a split second she wanted to walk toward him and touch him and say sorry, tell him it would be okay, but when she moved toward him, he looked at her and she realized that instead of sympathy in his eyes she saw venom, instead of friendship she saw cruelty.

"You guys are going to pay for this, I swear. You guys are in so much trouble."

Then he turned and stormed out of the cabin while the music played, and the smoke swirled, and the lights twinkled as if he had never been there.

As the following days then weeks passed without incident, and their secret hangout remained hidden, they thought he had let it go. They forgot about him. They partied harder. Let the pleasure take over.

They should have known. Mason never let go. That wasn't his style.

CHAPTER SEVENTEEN

March 2015

They had just finished eating when the doorbell rang. The sound harsh enough to make them all jump. When Evie opened the door and saw it was Ryan, she breathed a sigh of relief.

"Is everything okay?" Ryan asked her.

"Sure," she replied. "Why?"

"I heard about that incident over at your father's house," he said.

"Incident. I wouldn't go so far as to call it that."

Ryan came inside and followed her into the kitchen. "Why didn't you call me? You promised you'd call me if there was any trouble."

"It was no big deal, Ryan. We're fine," Carole replied when she saw him enter.

"Oh, Mrs. McCallister," Ryan said. "I didn't know you were still here."

"So am I," Ethan said.

"Ethan," was all Ryan could say when he saw Ethan standing there. And for a second everyone in the room stood still, unsure what to say or do, until Ethan set things in motion once again.

"Listen," Ethan said. "I don't know what that was all about. I'm not here looking for trouble."

"That's okay," Ryan replied. "I just wanted to see that you were all okay was all. That incident with the paint. It might seem like a small thing, but things like that can escalate quickly even in a quiet place like Georgetown. We're not so used to trouble here, despite everything."

"Despite me, you mean?" Ethan replied.

Carole was quick to try and pacify him and she walked over to Ethan and put a hand on his shoulder.

"Listen," she said. "Why don't you sit down, and I'll make us all some coffee. Ryan's just doing his job and I, for one, am happy about that. It's nice to know there are people looking out for us, don't you think?"

"It's just a shame it's necessary," Ethan replied.

"Yes, well, that's just the way it is."

Evie noticed the way her mother placed herself between Ethan and Ryan. The way she made sure she could hold Ethan's gaze and look him straight in the eye. It seemed like such a practiced move. As if, in all these years, her mother had needed to do this often—calm her son, placate him, hold his attention for a few moments until he calmed down.

And it worked, it seemed to release the tension in Ethan's shoulders, and he went to the table and pulled out a chair and sat down.

"Sorry," he said. "I guess I'm more on edge about it all than I realized."

"That's okay," Ryan replied. "I can understand that."

"Here," Evie said as she pulled out a chair. "Sit down and have a cup of coffee. I suppose you're here about more than a splash of paint."

Ryan sat down and took off his coat. He was trying to look casual, Evie noticed, but he fumbled with the coat as he tried to drape it over the back of the chair and when it fell to the floor, Evie picked it up and hung it for him, then pulled up a chair beside him to make sure she was sitting between Ryan and her brother.

"How was the course?" Evie asked him, trying to calm things a little.

"The course?"

"In Denver?"

"Oh, right. Exhausting. I only got back a couple of hours ago."

She saw the tiredness in him then. The shadows on his face, the little pinch of a frown around his eyes as he struggled to concentrate and keep the tiredness at bay. If they had been alone, she would have put an arm around him, looked after him in some way. But instead, they sat at the table, the three of them, and waited for Carole to bring the coffee over, but she fussed around with cups and plates and then went looking for something.

"What do you need?" Evie asked.

"Do you not have any cookies?"

"In the tin by the coffee canister."

And Carole laughed in response. "Right under my nose, as usual!" But her attempt to sound lighthearted couldn't disguise the shakiness of her voice. Ryan's presence made her nervous. And it took Evie a second before she understood that it was because of Ethan; her mom wasn't entirely sure how he would react when confronted with a police officer, even if it was only Ryan.

When she finally stopped fussing and sat down beside Ethan, she heard Ryan cough. It was the same small, official sort of cough she had heard years ago, when the whole investigation into Michael's death was still ongoing. The officers who investigated the case had also coughed, she remembered, just before they started a serious conversation. It was a way of readying themselves. A way of letting everyone in the room know that what they were about to say required your full attention. She'd always wondered if it was something they were taught during their police training.

She looked across at Ethan and watched as he took a spoon of sugar from the bowl and slowly stirred it into his coffee, focusing on the small act with an unusual level of concentration. Anything to avoid looking at Ryan. He was bracing himself, Evie realized. Bracing himself for some sort of admonition.

"I don't suppose you have any idea as to who could have vandalized your property?" Ryan asked.

It wasn't entirely clear who he was addressing. Like Ethan, he focused on stirring his teaspoon in his cup of coffee and Evie had to smile at his awkwardness, at the stilted official tone of his voice and his strange choice of words. He wasn't cut out for confrontation. Why he had ever decided to join the police at all was a mystery to Evie and she often thought it was a mystery to Ryan too.

"Does it really matter?" Evie replied. "I mean, what's the point in wasting time trying to find out who did it. No one wants any trouble, Ryan. Ethan's not here to pick fights with people who'd prefer he was still stuck in jail."

"I know," Ryan replied. And then he seemed to gain his composure and remember why he was there. The slight shift in his tone of voice, taking Evie by surprise, because it contained more authority than she had imagined possible. "I do need to ask, though, why it is you're still here."

"Ryan," Carole replied before Ethan had a chance to utter a word of explanation. "Has it ever occurred to you, or anyone in this Godforsaken town, that Ethan might want to be with his family at a time like this? We just buried Andrew. Does no one here have an ounce of compassion or understanding anymore?"

Ryan flushed red and swallowed and stuttered a reply. "Oh, of course, I didn't mean—"

"It's okay, Ryan," Ethan interrupted. "I know you've got a job to do and like I said, I'm not here to cause any trouble."

"And if other people want to go making a fuss, then I don't really know what you think we can do about it," Carole added.

"Mom," Ethan said, "just forget about it, okay? Something like this was bound to happen and, all things considered, it's not that big a deal really, is it? A splash of paint?"

Carole turned to face him and shook her head.

"It tells you everything you need to know about how little anyone here has moved on. I'd say that's a big deal. You might have come here looking for forgiveness, but no one here is going to offer it."

"Forgiveness?" Ryan asked. And Evie saw his face drain of color, saw him blink in disbelief.

She wanted to say something, to offer some sort of explanation, but she couldn't explain something she didn't understand herself.

"Is that really what you're looking for, Ethan?" Ryan asked. "Is that honestly why you're here?"

"He has every right to ask for it," Carole said.

And now it was Ryan's turn to be shocked into silence.

But something about the honesty of Carole's unwitting revelation seemed to strengthen Ethan's resolve. "I went to jail for twenty years," he began. "I've paid my dues."

Evie saw Ryan's hand tighten around his cup and his knuckles turn white. He was holding back from speaking but it was taking him all the self-control he possessed to sit there and remain silent.

"You say that as if you think the punishment was unwarranted," Ryan said.

"It was, but not for the reasons—"

"Ethan, please," Carole interrupted. "You don't need to say anything."

"No, I do," Ethan replied. And he looked at Carole as if he was asking for permission. And with a small nod of her head, and a defeated droop of her shoulders, she let him know that he could continue.

"I served my time and I deserved it. For what I did, I deserved it. But anyone who knew how I felt about Michael would know I could never have harmed him. And for twenty years, I've had time to think about what happened, and all the mistakes I've made, and I've realized that if I could go back, I'd do it differently."

"Ethan," Ryan said. "None of that makes any sense."

"Please just let me finish," Ethan replied. And Ryan nodded his head and gestured for him to go on. "I'm not here to ask for forgiveness for the things I have done. But I am here to ask that I be forgiven for the things I didn't do."

Ryan let go of his cup and leaned back in his chair and let out a heavy sigh, then closed his eyes and let his chin fall on his chest. He was giving himself time, Evie could see. Letting whatever thoughts were in his head settle because he knew that if he were to speak his mind, if he were to say what he thought about Ethan's proclamation, he would say something there was no coming back from.

And again, Evie found herself appreciating his calmness. That quiet reserve he had perhaps made him more suited to the job than Evie had given him credit for.

"Okay," he finally said as he raised his head and opened his eyes. "That was a lot to take in, Ethan, and I can't say I really understand much of it. So all I will say is that you need to take care. You keep saying you're not here to cause any trouble, and I believe you. But please think about what you just said, and what you think it will do to people here if you tell them what you just told me. There will be more than just a splash of paint if you push things too far is all I'm saying, Ethan. And I know you don't want to put your mother or your sister in the line of fire, but if you set out to do what you just said you want to do, then that's what's going to happen, and, in all honesty, I can't let you do that."

"I'm not here to cause trouble," Ethan protested.

"But that's what's going to happen," Ryan replied. "I need to know you understand that. I need you to tell me you'll leave well alone."

"Well alone?" Ethan replied. "Well alone? Ryan, did you hear a word I said? Did you understand any of it?"

"I understand that twenty years ago you confessed. You served twenty years for that crime and that, in all those years, you never denied or proclaimed your innocence. I understand that what you're asking is impossible. And I'm going to be straight with you. I don't understand what you're out to prove. But I know this town, Ethan. I know the people who live here, and you'd do well to listen to me. Do not leave this house and tell them what you just told me."

"It's okay, Ryan," Carole said. "I promise we'll cause no trouble." Ethan was about to say something but again she reached out to him and placed a hand on his shoulder with the practiced calm and authority that still surprised Evie. She saw her brother lean back in his chair and purse his lips.

He would stay quiet, for now, Evie realized. He would bite his tongue and nod to Ryan and agree to whatever it was Carole was saying. He would see Ryan to the door and tell him "thanks for coming" and he would be calm and quiet and respectful.

And Ryan would leave the house and think that he had taken control of the situation. He would walk back home thinking he had defused a bomb which could have shattered the town into small pieces once again.

But when the door closed, and Ryan walked away, he didn't hear Ethan say: "This fucking place. To hell with this stupid town and everyone in it." He didn't hear the cup as it shattered to the floor and splintered into a thousand irreparable pieces while Ethan wailed a howl of rage and impotence. "They don't know me! They don't know who I am!"

And Evie looked at him and shuddered. *It's true*, she thought. *We don't know you, Ethan. We don't know you at all.*

CHAPTER EIGHTEEN

March 2015

After Ethan's outburst, even Carole had slumped on the sofa in the living room and when Evie went in to check on her, she shook her head and said, "What happened to us, Evie? Our family. We used to be so close, we used to be so happy, or something close to it. I didn't imagine that, did I?"

But Evie couldn't answer. It was too big a question in that instant. They sat there in silence, overwhelmed by their thoughts.

"Listen," Carole said. "I need to be alone, just so I can collect my thoughts."

Evie needed to do the same, so she pulled on her walking shoes and put on her jacket then shouted out to Ethan to let him know she was going for a walk.

He was still sitting at the kitchen table, his head in his hands, and she wasn't sure he heard her or even noticed her presence. When she said, "see you," he didn't look up or utter a reply.

Perhaps that should have been a warning, but she decided to leave him alone and headed out. It was a crisp night, the moon just a sliver of silver in the ink-blue sky, and a smattering of gauzy stars, but she knew every detail of the path around the lake, every rock and stone as familiar to her as her own voice. So she headed through town and down to the water.

When she passed the bar, she almost went inside. She could hear music as she walked by. Singing and a band playing guitars.

On any other night she would have gone inside, the good cheer of the music something she could not ignore. It was always the perfect antidote to loneliness.

But Ethan's words were still ringing in her ears and they had unsettled her.

I am here to ask that I be forgiven for the things I didn't do.

He was heading for disappointment, and that scared her. Because she wasn't sure if he would be able to bear the weight of it, despite his resolve. Those years away, they had changed him, of course they had, but they hadn't hardened him. She had seen it in his eyes, the vulnerability he tried to disguise with bravado. In that way, he was the same. Uncertain, and unsure. Easily harmed.

At a bend in the path, she could just make out the outline of a bench in the dark and she sat down and listened to the water lap the shore for a moment. The hypnotic rhythm of it, soothing her and helping to clear her head.

Her thoughts were all messed up again and contorted by the emotions of the last few days. First her father's funeral, and now all this with Ethan. She needed to step back and breathe. Give herself the chance to think things through. She needed to absorb the little bruise of pain she could feel swelling in her chest when she thought of her mother's question: *What happened to us, Evie?* The sadness and longing those words contained, to get back to a place which could never exist now, was too immense. Evie had carried that question within her too all those years, without ever acknowledging it. That sadness and longing were a part of her too.

Somewhere over the lake, Mount Saxon loomed. She could feel its presence. The mountain, a living, breathing thing. Her father, now forever a part of its story. That was what she believed. The mountain had claimed him, and he belonged to it. His body may be buried in the churchyard, but the rest of him was still there, inside that impermeable rock. Looking down on them, watching over them.

In the darkness, Evie thought she could hear her father's voice. Low and calm and clear. Guiding her still.

Start with yourself, Evie, he said. *Ask yourself the question: can I forgive him?*

There would be consequences to any forgiveness. A re-writing of the past would bring as many questions as it answered, would offer up new problems for old. It could destroy as much as it could heal.

And that strange statement of his, she kept returning to it.

…to be forgiven for the things I didn't do.

What did you not do? she thought. But as she sat there and thought it through, there was only one conclusion she could draw. *I didn't kill Michael Deacon.* That was what Ethan was saying. That was why he had come home.

"I'm not sure I have the stamina or the strength to face this," she whispered to her father in the dark.

Then tell him that, she heard Andrew say. *Tell him he has to go. Protect yourself, Evie.*

But as the water lapped against the pebbles on the shore and the moon rose higher over the mountainside, her mother's question returned, a counterpoint to her father's.

What happened to us, Evie?

If she was to ask herself that—if she was to say, *What happened to you, Evie?*—what would her answer be? Her honest answer?

Because she had been one of them, hadn't she? She had allowed herself to believe the brother she loved was capable of a monstrous, terrible thing. She had allowed herself to forget the brother she knew and had replaced him with this other man. The man with the blood-stained hands. The convicted murderer. But these were labels others had given him. Labels she had accepted without question.

Deep down, something told her he wasn't who they claimed him to be. A monster? No, she couldn't use that word to describe her brother. And if it was instinct rather than proof which made her think this, if it was simply blind faith, well, who was to say she was wrong? Sometimes you had to trust your gut because your gut spoke the truth.

She turned and faced the mountainside.

"I'm sorry," she said to her father. "If Ethan genuinely believes he is innocent then I have to listen to what he has to say, because he wouldn't make a claim like that without having a reason. Not after all this time. If he's really suffered for twenty years for something he didn't do, then we all have to listen to him. We owe it to him."

She got up from the bench and made for home. She wasn't sure how she was going to explain it, this sudden change of heart, to Ethan or to anyone else for that matter. Maybe that wasn't quite what it was. The deep sadness she had felt for so long every time she thought of her brother, the pain of his incarceration. It was doubt that caused the pain, she realized. The small but unshakable doubt she had always had. Could Ethan really have done something so terrible?

Maybe if she tried to explain it this way, to Ashley and to everyone else, they would understand and maybe even listen to her. She could ask for that understanding, even if Ethan couldn't. She could make people listen.

For the first time, she started to believe in the possibility of it and that she might be able to do it. But Ethan never gave her a chance.

*

The music had stopped. No singing. No guitars. Only raised voices and a commotion of some sort. She stood outside the bar and listened, but above the noise she couldn't make out what was being said or recognize any of the voices.

She would have walked on if she hadn't seen her mom rush down the road toward her. "Is he in there?" she asked.

"Who?"

"Ethan. Is he in there?"

Her mom didn't give her a chance to reply. When she got to the door, she pushed past and entered the bar, leaving Evie outside, bewildered and trembling. It took her a couple of seconds before she could pull herself together and figure out that she needed to get inside and help her out. If Ethan was in there, and all this commotion was because of him, then Carole couldn't be left to sort it out by herself.

When Evie pushed open the door and stepped inside, the atmosphere overwhelmed her. The bar was hot and smelled of sweat and heated argument and something masculine. Someone had turned on all the overhead lights so that the room was a harsh, fluorescent white and her eyes needed to adjust to the brightness. It took her a moment before she spotted Ethan.

She saw her mom pushing through a group of men toward him. She was calling his name, but Ethan didn't hear her and no one else seemed to notice her as she struggled to make her way to her son.

Instead, a group were crowded around her brother as he sat on a stool at the bar. His jaw was clenched, and Evie could see the muscles in his neck and shoulders were stiff, as if he was readying himself for what was coming. The punches, the kicks, the blows. But for now, it was only words which were being thrown. And Evie saw who it was throwing them.

Mason.

His face was close to Ethan's and Evie saw a hand on Mason's shoulder, someone holding him back, making sure he didn't get any closer. Because Evie could see that if he did, the violence would burst out of him and there would be no holding him back.

"No one wants you here," Mason was shouting at Ethan. "Don't you understand that? Just get out of this town."

"I don't want any trouble, Mason," Ethan replied.

And through the sweat and the breath of a room full of men all chanting their agreement, "We don't want you here, you don't belong here anymore," Evie heard her mom desperately trying to make herself heard above the noise.

"It's okay," she was saying as she maneuvered toward the bar. "I'll take him home with me. He's not looking for trouble, he's just here to say goodbye to his father."

But either no one heard her, or they chose to ignore her. They moved closer to Ethan and tightened the crush of bodies around him and Evie could feel their heat, their energy and the musky smell of male aggression.

"We know what you're all about, Ethan," Mason said. "You don't think we've forgotten, do you? What you did to Michael?"

"I did nothing to him," Ethan replied.

The room fell silent, as if everyone needed to absorb what Ethan had just said. No one quite believing they had heard him correctly.

Evie counted the seconds. One, two, three. Expecting a rush of energy any moment.

"Nothing?" Mason sneered. "Well, a court declared otherwise. And I know everyone here would disagree with you, Ethan. We all saw that cabin burn to the ground. We all know you set the place on fire. Hell, you admitted as much. No, Ethan McCallister, you have blood on your hands, and everyone here knows it."

And then Mason turned away from him and looked around the room, first to Carole, then to Evie.

"And if you know what's good for you, and what's good for your mom and Evie, then you'll get out of here."

In the quiet, Carole had managed to push her way to the front at last and she placed herself between Mason and Ethan. She looked small, standing there between them, as if the crowd around her could crush her in an instant.

And perhaps it was her smallness that moved them. Her vulnerability, enough to calm things, to let people shake themselves awake from the fevered violence which was about to overwhelm them, as Evie saw them all take a small step back.

"Come on," Carole said as she took Ethan's elbow. "Let's go." She turned and looked at Evie.

"Open that door, will you?" she asked her.

It was only then that Evie realized she had been standing there frozen and motionless the whole while. Fear had once again rendered her incapable of action. If Carole hadn't been there, who knows what would have happened. Something bloodier, for sure. Evie would not have been able to stop it.

Ethan stood up from the barstool, and once again she saw the defiance there, in the slowness of his movements. The way he took his time lifting his jacket from the stool and then putting it back on. The indolence of his stare as he leaned over the bar and lifted a glass to his lips then drained it of its contents. The beer disappearing down his throat in long, slow gulps. And all the while, he held Mason's gaze, daring him to say something.

But Mason was not used to such defiance and, unprepared for it, he had no response, save to look away. Evie saw the small smile that crept across Ethan's lips as Mason backed down. The small triumph of the moment emboldened him even more.

As he walked away from the bar, Carole pushed people aside as she led him to the door. Evie felt her stomach tense, knowing there was something coming.

"Tell Ashley I said hi, will you Mason?" Ethan said as they left.

*

"What the hell did you think you were doing?" Evie screamed at Ethan once they were safely home. "*Tell Ashley I said hi?* Are you crazy or something?"

"Okay, I'm sorry," Ethan conceded. "That was uncalled for. But the arrogant son of a bitch. He deserved it."

"No, he didn't," Carole interjected. "It was a stupid thing to say and you know it. And mind your language. There's no need for it."

"Dammit, to hell with my language," Ethan said. "I should never have come back here. I mean, who am I kidding? Thinking anyone here was going to listen. They all made up their minds about me years ago. There's blood on my hands. That's all they need to know, right? Who cares about the truth?"

"I do," Evie whispered.

"What?" Ethan replied.

Those words seemed to pull him out of himself. He looked at her and seemed to blink himself back into the moment.

"I care about the truth," Evie said. "I was thinking about it when I was out walking. What you said earlier about wanting to be forgiven for the things you didn't do. I have no idea what you mean by that, and you've had twenty years to set the record straight. Twenty years in which you were silent. Not once in all that time did you challenge the decision of the court, and it's going to take a lot to convince people that your silence was anything other than an admission of guilt."

He looked at her but didn't reply, as if he didn't agree with what she said but didn't see the point in explaining why. All she could do was continue.

"I can't help thinking, though, that you would never come back here after all this time and say something like that if it wasn't true. So maybe you need to start with me. If you can convince me, then maybe there's a chance you can convince the rest of them."

He looked at her, but she couldn't read the expression on his face. What she had said was an admission. She doubted him still. The certainty she had developed over the years was the same as everyone else's. She believed he had gone to jail for good reason. Because Michael's blood was on his hands. And the pain she felt whenever she thought of that had not diminished.

"I see," Ethan said. "I see…" All he could do was look at her and shake his head. An expression close to disgust on his face which he didn't try to hide.

"I'm off to bed," he said as he brushed past her.

Then, she felt it coming again. The old familiarity of the blood as it rushed to her head. The dizziness, the nausea as she panicked.

The fear squeezing her belly tight. If the truth was different to the one they had believed all these years, if Ethan was not responsible, then they owed it to Michael to find out what really happened.

Michael. There is no stopping her memories now. He's there again, in her heart, in her mind and this time, there is no silencing him.

CHAPTER NINETEEN

Journal Entry, April 1995

We had hopes and dreams. I know every teenage kid does. I know it wasn't just us. But that was how it felt, as if we were the only ones dreaming. And I wanted to believe in it so much. All those plans we made. I don't know if Michael meant it when he talked to me, when we lay out on the porch of the cabin at night, smoking cigarettes. Perhaps he was just passing the time, musing on things because there was nothing better to do. But I like to think that he felt the same as me. A little fizz of excitement at the possibilities.

You want to know how I felt about him. What he was like. But it's so hard to describe. You just felt him, was all. He was so present. So there. And I know what you'd say to that. You'd tell me to give you an example. *Show me what he was like, Evie.* That's what you'd say, isn't it?

God, and I don't want to remember any of this, because it hurts to know that this is all it will ever be. That those dreams and hopes and silly plans can never be any more than that. He's gone, and all of this went with him.

But okay, let me think.

Okay, there was this one night. We were lying in a hammock, out on the porch at the cabin. It was one of those hot, sticky sorts of night with too many insects in the air and not enough of a breeze to cool things down. Through the trees it was possible to see stars. I had laughed because it felt too much, but Michael just stroked my arm and gazed at the sky and kept on talking, his voice sweet and low, soothing and coaxing. When he spoke, I felt myself slide into a strange sort of space. This calm, empty sort of place where nothing much mattered. It was as if the universe had shrunk down to just the two of us.

Little by little, I knew I was revealing myself in ways I never thought possible. When I say that Michael was exciting, I think, what I'm really talking about is this. It was exciting to feel so close to someone else. It was amazing to be able to trust someone this way. And it's this I miss most of all.

For the others, he was just someone different. Someone new in a small town. But to me, he was the boy who gave me that first real look at myself. With him, I was more than little lost Evie, the girl who needed watching over, the girl who needed protecting. And I was feeling my way toward her, finally unafraid to discover who she was. Who she *really* was.

"Did you love him?"

You asked me that once, and I didn't answer. I didn't think it was any of your business. I still don't. But the answer is yes, of course. I loved him.

That night, we talked about the future for the first time. We dreamed about a life beyond Georgetown. A life after the summer.

"We could go on a road trip, the two of us," Michael had joked. "Bum around California like we're a couple of Beats in a Kerouac novel."

I'd laughed, but I remember holding my breath and thinking, *Careful, Evie. Don't aim too high. Don't dream too much.* Though it was already too late. As soon as he said it, I had wanted it so badly.

I think we both knew it was just a dream. We both knew it would never happen. Though I would have done it. I would have gone to California with him. I would have done whatever he asked me to. Anything to be with him just one minute longer, one day more.

He'd smiled when I told him that and turned it into a game.

"Would you kiss me for three whole minutes on Main Street?"

"Yes."

"Would you share your last stick of gum with me?"

"Yes."

"Would you nurse me if I got sick?"

"Of course."

"Would you jump in the lake with me and swim out to the deepest point?"

"I…"

"No?"

"Yes," I laughed. "Yes, yes, yes, yes, yes."

Why did I lie about that? I guess because it would have spoiled the moment to say no. A piece of me wanted to say yes to everything. Who knows, maybe even a piece of me wanted to do it. To slip under the glassy black surface of the water with him and dive until we touched the bottom. *He would pull me to the surface*, I thought. *I could trust him.*

"Would you take me on a road trip round California?" I asked him. "Would you show me the sights? The Golden Gate Bridge, Yosemite, Big Sur…"

And he kissed me, on my neck, on my ear, on my lips and said, "Yes. Yes, yes, yes, yes, yes, yes, yes."

You're right to tell me that I should remember him this way. I know I can't have that image of that burning cabin haunting me for the rest of my life. These are good memories. But what good does it do to remember what I've lost? What good does it do to have only a bunch of nice memories? I want him to be here still. I want those dreams to still be a possibility. I want our plans to become reality. I want him to be here with me still. Alive.

These are tiny seeds you're planting, aren't they? These questions, these conversations? You want me to understand what it is that happened to him. You want me to feel that loss. Because you think I need to. Because you think that's the only way I'll open up those hidden memories and finally face the truth about what happened. If I want to get better then I need to feel the loss, feel the pain. I need to remember. But right now, all I want to do is dream again. Imagine a different outcome. Right now, I want to keep my dreams alive. I want to turn back time and have none of it happen.

All of this is impossible, and no amount of talking can ever change what happened. But forgetting it can help—it can make it seem, at least, that the past was somehow different.

And that's all I can do. I know it's not what you want but I have to. I have to forget, I need a past I can control, a past I can be at ease with. And if that past is a lie and a pretense, well, then so be it.

CHAPTER TWENTY
March 2015

She blinked into the sunlight and lifted her head, expecting to see the room. But instead, she was lying on the forest floor, wet moss and pine needles sticking to her cheek. *No*, she thought. *I can't be here. I can't be.*

She closed her eyes and counted her breath as she inhaled, then exhaled, waiting until she felt the pinch of stress behind her temples release, then opened her eyes and looked up, trying to get her bearings. The trees towered above her and tapered to thin, peaked tops. She watched them sway in the breeze, saw that the sky above was patchy with cloud and that the light was a dusty orange. The color of late afternoon.

How the hell did I get here?

She tried to think back. Remembered waking that night and checking the clock at 2 a.m. Before that, there had been trouble of some sort. Faces in a crowd, angry and dangerous. Then an old familiar panic. She could touch it almost. See it, smell it. It was unforgettable after all, that fiery red, and it was rushing toward her. Unstoppable now. Her sleep had been restless and troubled by dreams she could not recall, but the feel of them remained. A dull ache in her head and in her limbs. And she had a vague recollection now of running uphill in the watery gray morning light.

No, she thought. *This can't be happening to me again.*

She exhaled and focused on the sky. Listened to the shiver of the pines and waited for it to come back to her. But there was nothing. The in-between, the stretch of day from morning to this moment, had disappeared. Her memory had been swallowed by some inexplicable and fast descending darkness, just as it had been in those months after Michael's death. Back then, the same panic, the same fear would overwhelm her, and her brain would shut itself down. She would feel it coming sometimes, some trigger catching her unawares, followed by the rush to her head, a fiery assault of red, and then the blackness as she fell.

She had lost so many days to it, she thought she would never recover. It had taken years of work with Dr. Newton to make it stop. And now, after just a few days, Ethan had flicked a switch and here she was again, frightened and confused and fighting memories she thought would never trouble her again.

Is this what you want, Ethan? She thought. *Do you really want me to suffer like this?*

She looked at her hands, some strange instinct taking over, and saw mud there, and small pieces of grit stuck in the folds of skin in her palms and under her nails. And something else, something red. Bright and shocking. A sob caught in her throat, and she felt her mouth open into a wail as she stared at her fingers and shook her head.

"No," she said. "No."

A voice behind her.

"Dad?"

She thought she would faint at the sound of her name as it echoed through the trees. Someone shouting out to her. "Evie! Evie!"

But she couldn't answer. She simply lay there in the damp, muddy clearing and waited as the voice drew closer and closer.

When a hand touched her shoulder, she flinched and didn't dare look.

Her father was dead, she knew that. That was not a thing she would forget. When the figure crouched down beside her and called out her name again, softly this time, she turned to look, expecting to see some apparition, but instead there they were, those blue eyes again. The color the same as always. The creases of age around the lids a recent addition. But recognizably him, all the same.

"Ethan?" she said.

He wrapped his arms around her and drew her close, and she gave herself over to it, even as she squeezed away a scream and felt her teeth clench in something close to terror, when she remembered they had been here before.

*

He took her back to Andrew's house and laid her down on the sofa and folded a blanket around her, then went into the kitchen and set about making coffee.

She listened as he fumbled around, opening and closing cupboard doors, not knowing where anything was, and she thought to call out to him and tell him the spoons were in the second drawer next to the sink, the coffee in a jar labeled sugar, the cups draining in the rack—the only two Andrew possessed—but she couldn't find her voice.

Two's all I need. No one comes here for coffee, just you, had been her father's explanation when she had suggested he buy some more.

Eventually she heard the coffee machine click into action and the spoons rattle in the cups, and the small click of a tut as Ethan stumbled back into the room, balancing a serving tray. She had no idea where he had found it or why her father even possessed it. It was probably some remnant left over from the days they lived together as a family. Only her mom would have thought to buy a thing like that. Something as optimistic and hospitable as a serving tray.

Ethan set it down on the low table next to the sofa, then took a seat beside her in the shabby armchair her father had always used. It smelled vaguely of him still. Traces of linseed oil and cigarettes, and she wondered if her brother realized this was what he was breathing in as he sat there—the last traces of their father. Soon the smell of him would disappear. A few days of open windows and he'd be gone.

She lifted the cup from the tray and swallowed down a hot mouthful of sugary coffee. The only way to keep the tears at bay.

"Are you okay?" Ethan began. "What happened?"

She didn't know why he thought she would be able to answer that and she wondered if he had forgotten the terror which had threatened to consume her twenty years ago.

"The same thing that happened before, I guess," she eventually told him. "I blacked out."

"But I thought they'd helped you with that." There was concern in his eyes, and she knew it was genuine. After all this time, after all that had happened, he still worried about her, he still cared about her. She was still his kid sister.

"They did. That psychologist, Doctor Newton, she helped me a bit."

"With what?"

But it was impossible to explain all those conversations with Dr. Newton. All the things she had learned about the complicated ways shock and trauma can affect memory, how triggers can overwhelm the system. It was too long ago and she didn't have the energy to talk about it.

"She just taught me how to cope with things when I felt they were overwhelming me."

"Is it because of what happened? Did you feel overwhelmed?"

"When?"

"The door? All that nonsense in the bar?"

"Right, I guess so, I mean—"

"A bit of broken glass and a daub of graffiti. That was enough to make you black out, to make you run to the forest in the middle of the night?"

"It made me think of Michael," she said. "And I remembered something else too. That deer. The wound in its stomach. The blood round its mouth. I remembered it lying there on the forest floor. I dreamed about it . And Michael, I—"

"Stop it, Evie. Stop it!"

"Sorry, I didn't mean to... It was just, waking up there, of all places…"

Evie eased herself up into a sitting position and placed the cup back on the table beside her and noticed the bare patch of the carpet around Andrew's chair where his work boots had worn it down to the thread. She focused on it, made it the only thing in the room. No Michael, no Ethan, no gasping for air, just this: a threadbare carpet and the memory of her father.

"He would never take off his shoes," she said. "Wore the carpet clean away in the end."

"Sorry?"

She pointed at the carpet and Ethan looked down.

"Right," he said. But she could tell he didn't understand. Her grief was different to his and she supposed it always would be.

"I'm allowed to miss him, Ethan," she said. "He's only been dead a couple of weeks."

"I know, I'm sorry. I just… well, maybe we don't miss him in the same way, I guess."

"You can't force people to believe you didn't do it, Ethan," she told him. "It's too much to expect that of people." The words spilled out before she had time to think, and her voice was more agitated than she intended. Which was for the best. A second longer and she would have kept the thought to herself, even though she knew it needed saying.

"Something happened that day, Evie, and I can't simply *forget it*," he replied. "You must understand that, surely?"

She was about to tell him that she didn't understand it, when footsteps crunched on the gravel path to the house and a key fumbled in the lock. The door creaked open then slammed shut. Carole.

"That'll be Mom," Ethan said. "I texted her to tell her we were over here." Then he got up from the chair and headed to the hallway.

Evie tried to get up, because she didn't want her mother to see her like this. It would only worry her. But the fog in her head seemed to inhibit her and push her deeper back into the sofa.

From the living room she heard them talking in the hallway, their voices low.

"No, don't get up," her mom said as she walked into the living room.

Evie ignored her. It seemed important for some reason that she stood up and walked over to her, and she said, "I'm okay, honestly, I'm okay."

"Look at the state of you, Evie, you are *not* okay."

She watched as Carole took off her coat while Ethan stood there, arms hanging at his side, not knowing what to say or do.

"I'm fine. I swear it."

Carole walked over to her and took her by the elbow and led her back to the sofa. "That'll be why your brother found you in the forest in your pajamas, I suppose?"

They both sat down, and Evie felt it again—the creeping drowsiness, the blurring of things. The after-effects of her blackout had not quite faded and for a second she thought it was going to wash over her again. She could feel the room begin to swirl around her, her mom's face moving in and out of focus.

"Evie," she could hear her say. "Evie are you okay?"

Then, "Ethan, go and fetch her a glass of water, will you?"

When she finally managed to speak and say she was okay, her lips felt thick and swollen, as if she had been punched. All she wanted to do was fall into a deep sleep.

"Did you black out?" Carole asked her.

"Yes," she replied. "Ethan found me, brought back me here. But I have no idea how I got there. I remember being in bed, at home… I was in my own bed, in my own house, asleep… I mean… How, Mom? How…?"

Carole pulled her close, the way she used to do when Evie was a child. "Oh, Evie," she said.

Ethan set down the glass of water on the small table beside the sofa and stood over them, waiting. His awkwardness caused Carole to peel away from Evie and lean back into the sofa.

"I didn't know about any of this," he said. "If I thought being here would hurt you, I'd have thought twice about coming back. I'm sorry, Evie, I've rushed into things when I had no right to."

Evie took a sip of water and beckoned to Ethan to sit down. Her gesture surprised him, and she sensed his nervousness as he sat on the chair opposite her and waited for her to say something.

"Are you sure you're okay?" Mom asked her. "You look so tired."

"I'm fine," Evie nodded. "I just need you to be honest with me," she said.

And she caught the furtive glance Ethan threw in Carole's direction.

"We have been honest with you, Evie," she said. "I don't know what you mean."

She turned to face her mom and was glad she had enough energy to keep her voice steady. "What I mean is that it's obvious you still think Ethan is innocent, and it's obvious too that Ethan thinks the same—"

"I never said that, Evie—" Ethan interrupted.

"Maybe not straight out, but it's why you're here, though, isn't it? I mean, that's what you meant when you said you wanted to clear things up, isn't it?"

"Listen, Evie," Carole said. "You know I never thought your brother killed Michael. And you must remember that Ethan denied it too—"

"What?" Evie said. "He admitted it. In court. He pleaded guilty. Mom, you can't—"

"What she means," Ethan interrupted, "is there were reasons why I did that. It was complicated and I was young and scared and I made a mistake, but I... Dammit, I don't know how to explain any of this."

For a few seconds they sat there in silence, no one knowing what to say. Evie wasn't even sure if she was capable of listening. She could feel the exhaustion seeping into her. The strain of her blackout fogging up her head and weakening her body. But she had to try and concentrate. If they were going to tell her the truth now, then she had to listen.

"I just don't know how you can expect me to believe that," she said.

"Believe what?" her mother asked.

"Mom, did you hear what Ethan just said? He's suggesting he was forced to make that plea. That he was forced to lie and go to jail for something he didn't do. For twenty years! I mean, you can't expect me to accept that without question. You must understand how absurd it sounds. He can't have... I mean... I..."

She couldn't find the words to explain how hopeless it made her feel. What they were suggesting made no sense whatsoever. Because there was no reason why anyone would do something so inexplicable, something so irrational and so damaging.

"Do you remember," Ethan asked her, "that day you all came to visit me in jail, just after I'd been incarcerated?"

She wasn't sure why he brought that up or what it had to do with anything, and she struggled to remember.

"More or less," she said. "But it's such a long time ago. Why? Is it important?"

"Do you remember Dad that day?" he asked her.

And Evie saw Carole shift in her seat and tuck her hands beneath her thighs as if she was struggling to contain something. But she stayed quiet and let Ethan speak.

"All I remember was how angry he was. The way he shouted at you and didn't let you speak," Evie replied.

Ethan leaned forward in his chair and waited until she looked at him. He held her gaze to be sure that she was listening carefully and that he had her full attention. It made her nervous and she felt the palms of her hands become clammy with sweat.

"He was so nervous," Ethan said. "Do you remember?"

"Was he?" She turned to face her mom, hoping for some confirmation, but Carole didn't look at her and stayed seated with her hands beneath her thighs and her gaze on Ethan.

"He was," Ethan said. "He was frightened I would say something stupid. He didn't want me to speak. So he made that little speech, remember?"

She did remember. Not her dad's words exactly, but his energy. It was true there had been something odd about it. His was too jittery. It wasn't just the prison atmosphere that had set him on edge. They had all been intimidated by that. But she knew that she had not felt especially nervous and neither had her mom.

"He was just stressed about it, that was all," she said.

"But the way he spoke to me. His tone was so strange, you must remember that?"

She nodded. Some of it was coming back to her. Andrew's tone had been weird, it was true, but she couldn't think what it was about it that made her feel so uncomfortable.

"It was as if he had prepared what he had to say," Ethan continued. "Like he'd memorized it."

Evie looked at him and frowned again, confused why he needed to mention it and what the point was.

"What your brother is trying to say, Evie," Carole said, "is that your father came with us that day to make sure Ethan stayed quiet. He was there, basically, to intimidate him—"

"Mom," Ethan interrupted. "Come on, that's not quite how it was."

Her mom leaned away from him a little, surprised he would contradict her about this. "All I mean, Ethan, is that—"

But now it was Evie's turn to intervene. She'd had enough. If they were suggesting, even for one second, that her father had implicated his own son in a crime he didn't commit then there was no way she was going to sit there and listen to them. She had been prepared to give them a chance, had been prepared to hear what they had to say, but if this was the story they were going to push, then she was not going to listen to it. They'd pushed it too far. And it was too much for her. There were too many pieces that needed to be slotted into place, and her brain was incapable of processing it all and making sense of anything. A couple of hours earlier, she had been lying curled up on the forest floor, the cold of the ground seeping through her, and now here she was, sitting in her dead father's living room, her mother and brother fussing over her when all she wanted was some breathing space.

"Listen," Evie said as she stood up, the wobble in her legs forcing Ethan to jump up and catch her by the arm to steady her. "I still need to sleep this off. I can't take any of this in. It's too much. I want to go home."

"Here, let me help you," Ethan said.

"No, I'm okay. Please, just leave me alone for a bit."

She took a long, deep breath, then headed out into the hallway and picked up her dad's old coat from the peg by the door.

"I'll see you later," she called back to them.

If they replied, she didn't hear them, their voices drowned out by that other voice: *You watch out for yourself, Evie. Don't let them push you to remember things you'd do better to forget.*

She walked home, her legs trembling and weak, and she thought she would need to crawl the last stretch up the hill as she rounded the bend in the road. Then she saw her home, the lights on, welcoming her.

Forget? she thought. She'd spent a whole lifetime forgetting, but what good did it do her?

Forget, no, not this time. Maybe Ethan was right. Maybe it was time to remember.

CHAPTER TWENTY-ONE

September 1994

"What do you remember, Evie? Take your time." The police officer was patient, but she had nothing to say. How do you explain what you can't remember? "Okay, why don't we start with the forest? Tell us about the forest. Your father found you there. Do you know why you went there, Evie?"

But the room was windowless and claustrophobic, and the air so warm and stuffy, it made her woozy and unable to focus. The officer questioning her had a low drone of a voice she didn't like, and his eyes were black as shiny buttons; his gaze was impassive, yet it felt like a threat for some reason. Every time she looked at him, she imagined he understood things about her that others didn't. That he could see right inside her head to the memories and secrets she wanted to keep hidden.

She didn't like him. Didn't trust him. All she wanted to do was run from that room and never look back. But he kept on asking her that question. "Tell us about the forest, Evie. Your father found you there. Why there? Why did you go there?"

It was Mason who told them he had seen her running from the lake toward the forest. But she didn't remember seeing him that day. Yet it seemed impossible she could forget such a thing. So surely Mason had made a mistake?

"Mason Cardew claims he saw you running away from the lake and up the hill toward the forest," the officer told her. "Can you remember why you were running?"

She had stared at him in silence. She couldn't speak, couldn't even nod her head to acknowledge the question. All she could do was look away and try to avoid the unfathomable black of his eyes.

"He says he called out to you as you ran past him," the officer persisted. "But that you didn't stop, you didn't even acknowledge he was there. He ran after you because he was worried about you. He said you looked as though you were in a trance. That you looked frightened."

Evie frowned and shook her head and tried so hard to recall it. But nothing he told her made sense. She had not seen Mason that day, she was sure of it. The lake, though, there was something she couldn't quite grasp. The memory was just out of reach. The water, and the lake. Yes, something about that seemed familiar. Maybe Mason remembered it correctly after all.

"He thought you were running away from someone," the officer continued. "You kept looking over your shoulder as if to check if someone was coming after you. He said that when he tried to help you, you wouldn't let him. Can you confirm any of this?"

And again, she knew she should say something, she understood she should react in some way and she tried to think. She tried to remember running from the lake. Mason coming after her. But there was nothing. And so she sat and stared at the wall behind the police officer's head and tried to think of something to say. What could she tell him about something that didn't exist? There was a void, that's all there was. A black hole where her memory should have been. And what good was that to him? It wouldn't help him figure things out.

"Mason," she said. "He always worries about me. Even when there's no need to. Sometimes I think he just wants to run after me for the fun of it. He likes to think he can protect me, but there's nothing I need protection from. Not from him at least. But he's strange that way. He always has been."

The officer had looked at her and blinked and she could see he didn't understand why she was telling him this. But she didn't know how to explain Mason to him. The way he had always hovered about her like a buzzing fly. The way he had set out to destroy the happiness she had found with Michael. It wasn't something she understood herself yet and she had no way of explaining it.

"So you weren't running from someone then?" the officer continued.

"I don't know. Mason seems to think I was. But I don't remember. I really don't remember. If he says I was there, then I guess I'll have to take his word for it."

"He said he called your name at least three times," the officer said. "Did you not hear him? He says when he grabbed your arm and asked you what was wrong, you couldn't speak. He said you had stared at him as though you didn't recognize him. That you seemed terrified. Were you terrified, Evie?"

And she thought she caught a flash of something. Thought she heard Mason calling to her.

Evie, what's wrong?

Was it Mason who asked her that?

The officer noticed the way she had blinked away the memory, and so he pushed on. "Mason said he had to shake you to try and get you to speak." Then he looked down at some papers on the table in front of him and scanned them, his voice a monotonous drone that seemed to stupefy her. "According to Mason Cardew, you were incoherent and the only thing he understood was *Michael.* He said you kept muttering that name over and over until you pulled free from him and ran to the forest. Do you remember that? Were you running from Michael, Evie?"

But again, all she could do was stare at him and shake her head. No, she remembered none of this. If it was there in those statements, then it must have happened, but she had no recollection of it.

"I don't know. Maybe I was running from Mason. That's also possible, don't you think?"

The officer nodded, and she watched as he made a note on a pad that lay on the table in front of him. "It's possible," he conceded. "Do you remember that then? Do you remember running from Mason Cardew?"

"No. All I remember is that my father brought me home," she said.

"He found you in the forest, didn't he? Close to the cabins where Michael died?"

"Yes, he found me and brought me home."

"Okay, can you tell me a little bit more about that? What happened before your father found you? You were in the forest and the cabins were on fire. Did you smell the smoke? Did you see the fire?"

But he had lost her already. Her memory following its meandering path.

"There was blood on Ethan's hands," she said.

"I'm sorry?" the officer said. "We were talking about the forest. About the fire."

But she ignored him and carried on.

"He was at home, in the kitchen, and there was blood on his hands. I think, maybe it was from that deer. There was a deer, you see, in the forest. I think a cougar had gotten to it."

"Evie, wait a minute, we need to go back a bit."

And she looked at him and stared at his black, empty eyes and frowned in confusion.

"I thought you wanted to know what happened?" she asked him.

"Yes, we do, and there's a lot we need to clarify, but—"

"It was dead," she said.

And he waited for her to continue but she looked at him, forcing herself to focus on those black eyes. *Let me talk*, she thought. *Just let me talk.* And she saw him exhale as he relented at last.

"Do you mean the deer?" he asked her. "The deer was dead?"

"Yes. Was it a cougar, do you think? My father thought so."

"Are you sure it was a deer?" the officer asked her.

And she wondered why he would ask her that. Yes, she was sure.

But again, he asked her, "Are you sure it was a deer?"

"It was dead. There was a gash in its stomach. There was blood. Yes, it was a deer. I'm sure of it. Why would I... Oh, but its eyes…"

And he had waited for her to explain it. Why she felt it was important to tell him about this. About the blood she had seen that day and the way the pupils of the deer's eyes had been filled with black. The death visible in that dark, empty expanse. The terrible finality of it.

But the memory mutated. Those large brown eyes transforming as she tried to fix on them, and she watched as they turned from brown to blue. A blue that slowly filled with black. She remembered watching as the pupils widened and filled the eye, until the blue was mostly gone, diminished to a bright rim of light around this pool of dark matter. She had watched him die.

And she had seen red too. The unmistakable red of blood. A trickle of it on pale skin. But this vision was no deer. Those eyes. Those beautiful blue eyes. She had watched him die. And she could no longer contain it then.

"Michael," she sobbed. "Michael."

"What do you mean?" the officer had asked her. "What about Michael?"

"There was blood. A trickle of blood. And his eyes…"

"Are you talking about the deer, Evie?"

"What?"

"Was it Michael's blood? Michael's eyes?" All she had to do was choose. Yes or no. And he pushed her again. "Evie? Evie? Did you see Michael? Was Michael with you in the forest? Was he bleeding?"

Yes or no. Yes or no. The question swirled before her eyes and she tried to answer, she tried to make a decision, she opened her mouth to speak, but all that came was a sob followed swiftly by that all familiar blackness.

*

The police took Ethan in for questioning in the morning. They all assumed he would be home by mid-afternoon at the latest. But when five o'clock became six, and then seven, her mom began to worry. When Andrew called from the police station to update them with the news, Evie watched in disbelief as she heard her mom gasp then drop the phone and slump to the floor in tears.

"What it is?" she asked. "What's wrong?" But her mom could only sob and shake her head. Evie picked up the phone and was relieved her dad had stayed on the line.

"Is she okay?" he asked her.

"No, she's not. What's going on, Dad?"

And that was when he told her, and she felt her whole world collapse again.

"It's Ethan," Andrew said. "They've charged him with Michael's murder."

And she heard her mother crying and whispering, "That can't be right. It just can't be."

*

When Andrew came home later that evening, he had little to tell them. In his shock and confusion, the process they had explained to him at the station was too complicated to understand. All he knew was that Ethan was to be moved to a detention center in Cañon City and that they would need to find an attorney.

"I mean, how do you go about such a thing?" he said.

And Carole had cried, "We shouldn't have to. There is no way Ethan did this. They've made a huge mistake."

Evie had looked at her dad and had been surprised. She had expected him to be filled with energy and resolve. Determined to help Ethan in any way he could. But he seemed strangely quiet and resigned and Evie wondered just how firmly he believed in Ethan's innocence.

"He'll be okay, won't he?" she asked him.

But he had shrugged and shaken his head. "I don't know," he said. "We'll have to wait and see what the attorney says."

She had slept badly that night, visions of the forest and Ethan washing his hands tormenting her. She felt she was missing something. That somewhere among those visions was a clue of some sort. A vital piece of information that she wasn't seeing but that could help her brother get out of the terrible situation he found himself in.

When she woke the next morning and went down for breakfast, her parents were preparing to drive to the detention center and had somehow already arranged legal counsel.

"Are you okay to stay home alone?" Carole asked her. "There's a lot to do and I don't think it will do you any good to get involved in all of this. It's too awful."

Evie had wanted to say that she didn't want to be alone, that she was still suffering the effects of everything that had happened—she could feel it in her muscles, in the constriction in her belly and the squeeze of stress in her skull.

"Would it be okay if I asked Ashley to come over and keep me company?" she asked. "I think I need someone to talk to."

Her mom hesitated. Of all the people Evie could have wanted to console her, it was clear she thought Ashley was not the right choice. "Are you sure about that?" she asked.

"Why? Is there anyone else I can call?"

"Listen," Andrew interrupted, "we need to get going. Just make a decision, will you?"

So she watched them leave and then called Ashley and explained what had happened and asked her to come over. A mistake, as it turned out. Her mom's instincts had been correct.

"Oh my God!" she had wailed down the line. "Poor, Ethan. Shit, Evie, what are we going to do? How can this be happening?"

Evie had to lean away from the receiver, had to try and block it all out, Ashley's reaction too overwhelming for her. She just wanted someone to talk to, someone to wrap an arm around her and comfort her. She wished she had gone with her parents. Calling Ashley had been a mistake, but now it was too late. She was on her way over and Evie wondered if the shakiness of her voice was due to panic or exhilaration.

Evie didn't know if she could handle having Ashley around when she was in such a state of agitation. She desperately wanted to tell her about Michael. She wanted to tell her about the pain she felt every time she thought about him, every time the realization hit her that he was gone. It was indescribable. The empty feeling inside her, unbearable. She had forced herself not to think about him because it was the only way she could make it through each day. But hiding from the truth, pushing down the pain wasn't something she could sustain. She needed someone to talk to. Someone who understood how special Michael was and how much she had loved him.

When Ashley arrived, Evie heard the doorbell ring and she called out to her to come on in.

Evie was sitting in the living room, still dressed in her pajamas, her hair tied back in a disheveled ponytail and the specks of sleep encrusted in her eyes.

"Oh, you look like shit," Ashley said when she saw her. "Can I get you anything? Some coffee or something?"

"That'd be good, thanks," she said. She followed Ashley into the kitchen and caught sight of her reflection in the hallway mirror. She looked like a wraith or some figure from a B-movie, and she almost laughed when she saw herself.

"Here," Ashley said as she set two cups of coffee on the table then went to fetch some cookies from the jar. "I want you to tell me everything that happened. How the hell did they pin this on Ethan? Ethan, of all people!"

"Ashley, quit it will you? It's not some TV show. This is real."

"I'm just shocked is all. Everyone is. Ethan means a lot to us, you know he does. When I told my parents what had happened they could barely believe it. And Mason turned so white when he heard the news."

Evie couldn't bare to think of it, the way the news would now be spreading like wildfire through the town. Everyone talking and whispering and coming up with their own crazy theories as to what had happened. And Mason, there was no way that his reaction could have stemmed from sympathy. He was most likely just shocked to discover that his actions had consequences. That his spiteful little campaign had in some way contributed to the spotlight falling on Ethan. She vowed to confront him about it. She would let him know that she would never forgive him for what he had done.

"Can I ask you something?" she asked Ashley.

"Sure, you know you can."

"Do you think Ethan could have done it?"

Ashley looked at her and Evie spotted it immediately, the tiniest of twitches in the corner of her eye. An indication that she was thinking about it, that she needed to think about it. She wasn't able to say without hesitation that Ethan was innocent. The possibility existed, however small, that he could have done it.

"No," Ashley said. "There's just no way he could have done it."

"Then why did they charge him?" Evie asked her. "And so quickly too. I mean, it's only been a few days, what evidence can they have?"

"I don't know. I guess they must have something, though. I mean they need evidence, right? They can't just charge someone without evidence."

"I wish I could remember what happened. Why can't I remember what happened? What the hell is wrong with me, Ashley?"

"Nothing," Ashley said, and pulled her chair closer and wrapped an arm around her. "Shit, Evie, I'm so sorry. I'm really sorry."

"Me too," Evie replied. "I mean this affects you too, doesn't it? You and Ethan, I mean…"

"God," Ashley said, "I never thought of that."

Evie looked at her, surprised that Ashley had apparently not given it any consideration. If Ethan was going to be convicted then she would never see him again. The future plans they had would be shattered; surely she had thought of that?

"Oh," was all Evie could utter in response.

"Shit," Ashley continued, "people are going to say I was the girlfriend of a murderer. Fuck."

"What?" Evie said.

"I mean, they're going to ask me to take sides now, aren't they? They're going to ask me the same question you did—if I think he was capable of doing it. Shit, Evie. What the hell am I supposed to do? What the hell am I supposed to say?"

Evie wanted to tell her: *you're supposed to support him. You're supposed to ignore that little twitch of doubt and stand by him. You're supposed to know him well enough to be able to say without hesitation and without a shadow of doubt, that he could never have done this.*

This was how it was going to be from now on, Evie realized. People you knew your whole life, people you trusted, would be filled with doubt and hesitation. People you would seek out when you needed comfort and consolation would no longer be there when you needed them. There would be no more shoulders to cry on.

"I'd say you have to decide," she told Ashley. "Do you believe him, or don't you? Will you choose to stand by him, or will you choose to walk away."

Ashley blinked, as if having the choices laid out before her like that was perplexing.

"Yeah, you're right," she answered. "You're right."

But Evie didn't need to ask her what the decision would be. It was obvious. They were on their own.

*

When her parents arrived home, they looked hopeless. Evie watched them as they walked from the car to the front door. Their shoulders slightly stooped, their heads bowed. Neither of them spoke and when Evie asked them how it had gone, they said nothing and just walked to the living room and slumped down onto the sofa.

When Evie asked again what had happened, she saw them look at one another before he nodded and said to Carole, "Why don't you tell her? I'm too tired now, and I don't think I have the energy to go through it all again."

Then he stood up and walked out of the room, squeezing her shoulder as he walked past her and headed to the stairs. "Sorry," he said. "I just need some sleep. Maybe I can tell you more tomorrow, but for now…"

Evie nodded then walked over to the sofa and sat down beside her mom and took hold of her hand.

"Are you okay?" she asked her.

"Not really. It's been exhausting."

"Just tell me what's going on."

Her mom had squeezed Evie's hand and composed herself, then told her what they had learned from the attorney and during their visit to the detention center.

It wasn't entirely clear to Evie how they had come to such a conclusion and she struggled to understand how the police had been able to look at such circumstantial evidence and use it to charge her brother. But she was in no shape to take it in. All she could do was accept what her mom was telling her.

Ethan had been seen arguing with Michael a couple of days before his death. It was related to all that mess which had been stirred up by the photographs Mason had distributed around town. Those stupid photographs.

Just thinking about them made her skin tingle with shame. She would never forgive Mason for what he did. He had made her feel so embarrassed and anxious. Even now, remembering how people had laughed at her, and gossiped about her, made her feel sick. The way her happiness had been turned into something sordid, it was cruel. She couldn't understand why Ethan would have fought with Michael about it. They had all been victims of Mason's cruelty. Why take it out on Michael? It made no sense and she wondered who it was that had reported seeing Ethan and Michael arguing. Michael had never mentioned it to her, and it was the sort of thing he would have talked to her about. He would never have kept something like that from her.

"Are you sure?" she asked her mom. "Michael never mentioned an argument to me…"

"I'm only telling you what they told me, Evie."

If that had been the only statement made against Ethan, then perhaps it wouldn't have mattered. But there was more. Some of the firefighters had spotted him running from the forest as they were heading up to the cabins. They thought he was simply fleeing the blaze and it was only when Michael's remains were discovered that they had informed the police that they had seen him fleeing the scene.

"But how can they be sure it was Ethan?" she asked.

"I don't know, Evie, we didn't go into the detail. I just heard that this was what had happened."

"Well, okay, but it still doesn't mean anything. People run from fires."

"I know, but there's other evidence too. I don't know how they gathered it. Traces of gasoline, blood. I didn't get the whole story, and the attorney was still trying to evaluate things and check everything was being processed correctly. There was an issue with parts of Ethan's statement apparently."

Evie sat there and tried to think. She would have seen him running, surely? And her dad would have too. The fire had not been burning for long when they had fled, she was sure of that. *Dammit,* she thought. *Why can't I just get a clear picture in my head?* She remembered Ethan taking off his clothes and trying to wash away the dirt and the smoke and the blood. *Or trying to wash away the evidence,* she suddenly thought. But no, that couldn't be right. She refused to believe it.

"Anyway," she heard her mom say. "It all seems to add up to enough evidence to charge him. And I don't know what we're supposed to do to help him. But please, Evie, if you can just think back to what happened, if you can just try and remember what you saw. For Ethan. Please, do it for Ethan."

CHAPTER TWENTY-TWO

April 1995

They had gone over it a thousand times, or so it felt. What she would say. What she would not say. They had tried to anticipate the questions she would be asked and the statements she should make in response. They had explained the process repeatedly and so thoroughly, she thought she would collapse under the weight of expectation they were placing upon her.

She was supposed to clear Ethan somehow, that was how it felt. But no matter how many times she went over that day with them, she could never figure out how anything she said could be of any use in her brother's defense. A "witness" who could remember so little, whose memories were incoherent and jumbled up, what use was she to anyone?

But they had insisted she testify.

Right up until the day of the trial she hoped some reason would be found to prevent it. Her state of mind, those blackouts, the apparent delusions, she thought any one of those things could qualify her as unreliable, and she had begged her mom to try and convince someone, anyone, that she should not be made to undergo such an ordeal.

A psychologist was eventually appointed to talk to her, and he had declared that under the right conditions she would be able to undergo questioning. As a witness, her testimony was too important to be withheld. She had wondered about that, why both the defense and the prosecution should see the benefit of her taking the stand. It felt dangerous, as if one wrong word could be enough to undermine her brother.

The night before the trial, she had sat with her mom in the darkness of the living room, both of them too agitated to sleep, and she had curled up with her head on her mom's lap and allowed herself to be soothed as her mom caressed her head.

"I wish I didn't have to do this," she said.

"I know, sweetie, I know. But tomorrow evening, we'll sit here together again, and it will be over."

Sweetie. Her mom hadn't called her that in years. And she knew then how bad it was going to be.

*

The opening statements were precise and succinct, but no matter how hard Evie tried to stay focused, she found herself slipping into a sort of half-sleep, her eyes open, but her brain barely aware of what was happening. After a while, she realized she had been counting her breath all along, measuring the pause between inhalation and exhalation. It was a coping mechanism she had learned from Dr. Newton, her brain automatically shutting down, in order to help her cope. She was trying to remove herself from the room.

She didn't hear when her name was called and it was only when she felt a squeeze on her elbow that she became aware of what was happening.

"It's time," she heard someone say.

She was led to the stand and asked to confirm her name. When she looked across to her parents, their faces were ashen, the lines of worry traced on their foreheads and around their eyes, making them look older than they seemed just a few days before. She had to stifle a sob and try to remember what the attorney had told her when he had coached her.

"If you start to feel nervous, just look at the clock on the back wall and count the hands for a few seconds. It helps."

And she nodded but was unable to focus on it for more than a few seconds at a time, because when she did so she didn't hear the questions which were being put to her.

The whole thing was a blur and she wasn't sure in the end if she had answered the questions correctly. If she had remembered the answers she had practiced. If she had been any help at all.

"Did you see Michael Deacon in the forest the day he died?"

"Yes."

"Was he alive when you saw him?"

"I think so, yes."

"You think so, can you explain that?"

"He was there... he was..."

That had been a mistake. It was the other way around. She thought she had seen him in the forest. He had been alive. He was lying on the ground. He was alive, and then... But she had no time to correct the mistake and wasn't entirely sure if she had answered incorrectly. When she failed to explain for the third time, the prosecutor moved on.

"Did you see your brother, Ethan McCallister, go to the cabin?"

"No."

"Did you see Ethan in the forest?"

"I think so, yes."

And the prosecutor refined his question.

"Did you see Ethan McCallister in the forest the day Michael Deacon died?"

"No, I don't think so. But the days are all messed up."

"Okay, let's talk about a different day. Did you know that Ethan had argued with Michael a few days before his death?"

"No."

And the next question followed but she was still stuck on the previous one.

"Michael would have told me if he had had an argument with Ethan. He told me everything. And Ethan too, he would have wanted to talk to me about something like that. We're close. We talk."

She heard the defense attorney make some sort of request that the records note she had been confused. She thought perhaps they would pause, but the prosecutor was allowed to continue.

"Can you tell me why you ran from the lake?"

"I don't know. I can't remember anything about that," she said. "I just know I was running from something."

"Something?"

"Yes."

"So not from someone?"

"I don't know. Maybe. I just ran."

And she thought about it again, remembered her labored breath, the heavy thud of her footsteps on the forest floor, and how her heart had raced; and she remembered she had not dared to look around. *Run*, was all she had thought. *Run as fast as you can. Just get away from it.*

"Evie?" the prosecutor was asking her. But she didn't acknowledge him. She didn't want to listen to his questions anymore. She didn't want to answer. Whatever she had been told to say, she had forgotten. She just wanted to take her seat beside her parents again and forget it all. She just wanted to go home. To be somewhere safe.

She felt herself slip into that dark place again, heard the blood rush in her ears, saw the clock on the walk tick-tick-ticking away the seconds. And then she slumped and fell. The last thing she heard was her father's voice yelling across the court room.

"Look what you've done, Ethan. Look what you've done."

Later she would wonder about that. What did her fainting have to do with Ethan? Why did her father blame him for it? It was the prosecutor and his damn questions that had caused it. Ethan wasn't to blame.

By the time she came round, she was in a backroom of the courthouse and there was some discussion going on as to whether she should be allowed to continue to testify.

"You can't put her through that," she heard her mom say. "She's not stable enough yet to be put through this. She's been traumatized by all of this for God's sake! Get a doctor to look at her, they'll confirm it."

Though in the end, it didn't matter. In the end she didn't need to face further examination. None of them did. Ethan made sure of that.

*

No one saw it coming. Her mom more than anyone had been convinced that the trial would prove inconclusive.

"There's no real evidence," Carole explained. "No one seems to know what happened exactly."

And Evie had started to think it was true. What did they know, after all? Only that there had been an argument. And she allowed herself a brief moment of hope that everything might work out okay.

"As if that's enough of a reason to kill somebody," her mom continued.

"But the gasoline and the blood. They found traces on his clothes. That can't be dismissed so easily," Andrew reminded her.

"Okay, so they had a bust up earlier in the week and maybe some of Michael's blood came onto Ethan's T-shirt. It still doesn't put him there at the crime."

"And the gasoline?" Evie asked her. "What about the gasoline? Ethan can't explain that."

"Of course he can. He tanked gas. How often has he done that? And who the hell remembers something like that? He must have filled the tank a thousand times. You wouldn't be able to say when you did it. So maybe he filled the car the day Michael died? I don't know."

"Listen," Andrew said. "Let's leave it to the lawyers to prove it one way or another. We can talk about this all day, but it won't make any difference."

"It does make a difference, Andrew. It makes all the difference. If there's any doubt, any doubt whatsoever then they can't convict him of this. And there is doubt, you know there is, so we need to believe him. We need to support him. He's your son, Andrew. Why can't you stand up for him?"

And who knows, perhaps the evidence against him would not have been enough. But, in the end, the arguments for and against had been unnecessary. A call early morning changed everything. She had listened to her dad as he nodded and sighed and said, "I see, I see."

Then he walked into the living room and told them to sit down.

"What is it, Andrew?" Carole had pleaded. "Is everything okay?"

"He's changed his plea," he explained. "The trial's been stopped. Ethan's pleaded guilty."

CHAPTER TWENTY-THREE

March 2015

Her mom shook her very gently.

"Evie," she whispered. "Evie, wake up."

It took her a few minutes to come round. The sight of her mother leaning over her was disorienting and she had to focus carefully on her face, take in the fine lines around her eyes, the gray at her temples, the short neat haircut, before she understood that she was not remembering some other day, from years ago.

When she looked out the window, she saw it was dark outside, but she couldn't tell if it was morning or night.

"What time is it?" Evie asked.

"A little before seven," Carole replied.

"In the morning?"

"Yes."

"I slept away a whole day?"

"Yes. I guess you needed to."

Evie sat up in the bed and rubbed her eyes and tried to think why her mother was whispering.

"You don't need to whisper," she said. "I told you I'm okay."

"I don't want to wake your brother," Carole replied, her voice still low.

"Ethan? Isn't he over at Dad's?"

"No, he didn't want to stay there after all that business with the paint and the bar, so I told him to come home. It's safer for him here."

She wanted to explain that this was her home now, the place she had made safe for herself, a refuge which had now been invaded by Ethan, by her mother and by the past—and they were all uninvited guests. But she was too tired and too groggy.

She flopped back onto the bed, felt her head sink into the pillow, and was struck by a fleeting déjà vu. The sound of her mom's whispering voice pulling her back to a day, years ago, Ashley sitting beside her on the bed, the two of them whispering secrets now long forgotten, and she felt a pang of loss as the memory filtered through. Ashley, the close friendship she had lost. Another bit of damage Ethan had caused.

"You okay?" her mother asked, whispering still and reaching out to stroke her hair, just as she did when she was a small child.

"I'm just tired. I forgot the way these blackouts wipe me out. What did you want to talk to me about?"

"There's something you need to know, about Ethan."

And there's something I need to talk to you about too, Evie thought. Though she wondered if her mom was ready to listen to her. That blind spot Carole had when it came to criticism of Ethan was still there, and there was no shifting it.

If Evie had the strength, she might have tried one more time to explain how it felt to know she would always take Ethan's side. She would tell her: *When you left, it felt like an accusation, like a finger pointed at me and at Dad, saying, "Look how easily they abandoned their own brother, their own son."*

Did she not understand how it felt to be looked upon with such a critical eye by someone you loved? Did she not understand that this was the answer to her question, *What happened to us, Evie?* She had left them, that was what had happened.

But Evie didn't have the energy to talk about any of this, not yet, and besides, it would only lead to an argument. "I'm not sure I can talk right now," Evie said. "My head's still swimming and to be honest, there's only one thing I want to know."

"And what's that?"

"I just want to know what he thinks he can achieve with all this. Does he really think people will listen to him or believe him? He must know that's impossible. No one confesses to a murder they didn't commit. No one."

Her mom tilted her head and let her chin fall onto her chest. She was taking a moment to compose herself, and Evie felt the muscles in her throat contract and her arms tense.

"Let me ask you something," Carole said. "If it were you, if you were the one who had sat in jail all those years knowing you were innocent, how would you feel? What would you do? Would twenty years make a difference? Would you give up? Or would you keep on believing in yourself? Because that's what happened to your brother over twenty years. That's what he came to understand."

It wasn't a fair question, Evie thought. She had gone over it a thousand times. And for what? What could she say or do to change the facts? Facts which suggested only one possible truth—whether they liked it or not, whether they wanted to believe it or not. Ethan was guilty.

"Have you forgotten?" she asked her.

"Forgotten what?"

"How many times I was asked. Over and over until I collapsed under the weight of it. *What did you see, Evie? What did you see?* They asked me that question until I couldn't think straight. And I told them what I saw. I told them the truth, and you told them yourself. You confirmed it to the police, to the court. Ethan came home that day and there was blood on his hands and on his T-shirt and he wouldn't tell you what had happened, he wouldn't tell you how all that blood got there. You saw Andrew carry me home, you saw how paralyzed I was by it. And now Ethan's back here and he's asking me to remember all that, and—"

"Listen, Evie. That blood was from a deer. The way you talk about it, it sounds as if you believe it was Michael's blood. But it wasn't, Evie, and you need to stop believing you saw things that weren't there."

She closed her eyes and winced as a flash of something blue flickered beyond her eyes. She saw the blue fill with black again. It was there, she could feel it. It was not something she'd imagined. She didn't need to believe it or deny it. It was simply there. It was simply the truth.

"Evie," she heard her mom say. "Evie, are you okay?"

"Listen, Mom," she said. "I woke up on the forest floor yesterday, half-frozen and with no idea how I got there. And now you're sitting here asking me how I would feel if I had been in Ethan's position. Well, let me ask you the same thing. If you woke up in the forest, with no idea how you got there, how would you feel? It's been years since that happened to me, and now Ethan's back and it's as if I've been thrown back twenty years, and I can't go back to that, Mom. I can't. You must know that."

"Okay," Carole said. "Okay. But there was no way we could have anticipated you would collapse."

"Then you have forgotten. Then you don't know me at all. Ethan wasn't the only one to suffer through all of this, and I'll never understand why you can't accept that. I lost Michael and I never really thought you understood how that felt. It wasn't just some teenage romance. I was young, but I loved him, Mom. I really did. And I just wish you would acknowledge what happened to me. It's not just Ethan who suffered. It never was."

"That's not fair, Evie, I do. I know exactly how much we suffered. *All* of us. You, me, your father. And if you think that we didn't understand what Michael meant to you, then I'm so sorry. I know he meant a lot to you."

"Then *show* it sometimes."

Carole hesitated, on the brink of saying something, then holding back. Evie propped herself up on her pillow and tried to focus. The conversation, so early in the morning, had already left her feeling light-headed and in need of more sleep. Her head felt fuzzy and dense, as if she had been kept awake the whole night.

"Why is he back here?" Evie asked. "Honestly, what did he tell you?"

"Do you trust him, Evie?"

"Should I?"

"I trust him," Carole replied. "If that's any help? I always did."

"He needs to earn it, though, don't you think?"

"He does, but I'd like to think you at least give him a chance to do so. I feel like you're shutting him out before he's even had the chance to explain himself. Do you think at least you can find it in your heart to listen to what he has to say?"

Evie closed her eyes and exhaled slowly and felt some of the tension release as she concentrated on each breath.

Yesterday, for a moment, she had imagined she could forgive him. But now? Could she forgive him today? No, was the honest answer. She couldn't. But Carole wouldn't want to hear that.

When she opened her eyes, she pulled back the covers and got out of bed, without looking at her mom, without answering the question. She wanted coffee and breakfast and a normal start to the day. She wanted to be away from her mom, just long enough to catch her breath and think.

She wasn't sure if she wanted to spend the next days or weeks watching Ethan antagonize people who were her friends and neighbors. People she had come to rely on over the years and who meant a lot to her. These neighbors and friends meant more to her now than her mom or Ethan, she realized—they were the only truly steadfast things in her life. She didn't want to jeopardize that. Once things had calmed down again, once Carole and Ethan were back in Boulder, she'd be left here on her own again to pick up the pieces.

And yet… he was her brother, and family was supposed to mean something, wasn't it? But that meant she was going to have to trust him and she wasn't sure she could yet, because he had destroyed their lives already once, had brought her dad to the brink of his sanity, why should she let him destroy them again?

CHAPTER TWENTY-FOUR

August 1995

Almost a year had passed since Michael's death. A year of pain and confusion. After Ethan's conviction, there was an empty space in their lives and the happiness they had known had shattered irreparably into a million tiny pieces. With it, her mom and dad's relationship crumbled, and the days were filled only with arguments and slamming doors.

Though there were some moments of calm. A brief respite from the chaos that lulled Evie into thinking they would somehow get through it all. That whatever happened, they would be able to withstand the pain that Ethan's conviction had caused. But the calm was just a settling of things. They were just absorbing the shock. Once the reality of what had happened hit, there would be no more peace.

In the last year, none of them had spoken about the way their lives were going to change. Andrew especially refused to discuss it, and Evie wondered sometimes if his silence was more a hope that he could pretend none of it had ever happened. But it turned out her dad's reticence was more than simply a denial of their sad new reality. His need for solitude increased with every passing week. Days could go by without them seeing him at all. He would hole up in his studio and scream at anyone who ventured over there to talk to him.

"Get out!" the cry whenever someone knocked on the door.

When she asked her mom if they should do something to help him, she had told her, "Leave him be, Evie. He just needs time to absorb all this. We all do."

And Evie agreed, at first. They had needed to keep their emotions in check during the trial, because that was the only way to get through it. You needed to get through each day in a sort of emotional neutral gear, because, if you dared let anything through—anger, confusion, hurt or disbelief—then it would eat away at you.

But as the anniversary of Michael's death approached, it seemed the time had come for release. And her father's release was strange and frightening.

She was walking home from school when she saw him lock the door to the studio. She was about to call out to him and tell him to wait for her to catch up so they could walk home together, when he took a right turn and followed the road down toward the iron bridge.

She would have left it at that, just let him head off on one of his solitary walks, if she hadn't seen him swing a bag over his shoulder.

It was one of her old school bags. A small, leather backpack she hadn't used for years because it was no longer big enough to carry all the books she needed.

What's he doing with my bag? she thought.

And something about the way he walked troubled her too.

He was a slow sort of walker, usually. One of those people who tended to amble along and gave themselves time to take in all the details. All the things most people failed to see, but which he paid attention to because the details of the world were where he found his inspiration.

But as he headed to the bridge, Evie noticed he was almost running. And he was nervous too. Twice he had looked over his shoulder, as if he needed to be sure no one was following him.

It wasn't curiosity that caused her to go after him. It was concern. When she saw he was headed up the hill and into the forest, taking the path that led to the cabins where Michael had died, she thought to call out to him.

In a panic, she started to make her way over the bridge, hoping to catch him. But his pace was too fast. His legs stronger than hers and more used to pulling up the steeper stretches. She had needed to stop a few times and catch her breath. The weight of her backpack was slowing her down and it took her a while before she thought to ditch it. Just set it down among the ferns and pick it up later. Once she'd done so, she felt her pace quicken immediately.

But her frequent stops and dithering had meant she'd lost him. Up ahead, the path forked, one leading up out of the trees and toward the summit and open views of the lake, the other winding its way deeper into the pines.

Somewhere in those trees lay the clearing, and the granite stone she often sought out, and, beyond that, deeper still, the dark, sad place where Michael had died.

She didn't need to think about where her father was headed. This was no sight-seeing mission. He wasn't up here for the views. So she followed the path, deeper into the trees and tried not to think of Michael.

When she saw him come to a stop, she hid behind the trees and watched him, fear and instinct warning her she should not get close.

Through the branches, she saw him kneeling on the ground, bent over a hole. He was scraping away at the earth, and digging with his bare hands, and there was an agitation to his movements, as if he had been overcome by an urge he couldn't control, his hands scratching at the ground, directed by some unseen force.

He was murmuring too. Fast, whispered words she could not hear, but the rhythm felt like a prayer of sorts, some sort of incantation that made her fearful. She did not dare get any closer for fear he would realize she was there.

When the hole was complete, he leaned across it and opened the backpack and Evie watched as he undid the buckles and straps and reached inside and pulled something out, but in the shadowed light, she couldn't see what it was exactly. It appeared to be a metal box, but she wasn't sure.

She watched as he placed it in the hole and began to cover it over with dirt, then patted the earth down with the palms of his hands, before covering it with leaves and pine needles. She concentrated on the spot to memorize it. To one side she saw there was a moss-covered rock, about the size of her fist and, on the other side a small pile of twigs lay on the ground, one of them covered in green needles, as if it had only just been snapped off the tree. It was enough to provide a way-marker. She would be able to find the hole once he left. But she kept her eye on the spot just the same, taking care to observe him as he pulled the backpack over his shoulder and dusted himself off.

She held her breath as he stood up and hoped that he would not turn around and head back the way he came. Prayed that he would head down the track into the woods and then loop back up onto the path that went around the hill on the other side and back down to the road. It was the shortest route from here. The sensible path to take as the light began to fade and evening to fall.

But he stood over the hole for a few minutes, and Evie wondered if he was ever going to leave. It looked as though he was standing guard there, too scared to leave, as if the contents needed protection.

What did you just bury there? she thought.

When he lowered his head, she saw his lips move as he quietly uttered what she could only assume was some sort of prayer. He had that solemnness about him. Suddenly, she heard her heart pound, and felt her curiosity dwindle as she was overwhelmed by something closer to fear. Because the way he stood there, head bowed over the mysterious hole, sent a shiver through her. She had seen this solemnity the year before at Michael's memorial service. And when he finally raised his head and made the sign of the cross, it was like déjà vu.

For almost half an hour after she had watched him walk away, she had sat there listening out for his footsteps, making sure he wasn't about to return, the image of her father at Michael's memorial service haunting her. Michael's death seemed so vivid again, and the weight of sadness pulling at her was something her body had not forgotten.

Whatever her dad had buried there, it had something to do with Michael. The two moments were linked in some strange way. The only way to understand the connection was to overcome her fear and scratch at the ground to unearth whatever it was down there.

The light was fading by the time she dared to walk out from behind her hiding place and toward the small clearing where he had been digging. Every crack of a twig, every swish of leaves in the breeze made her jump with fright, and she looked around to check her dad wasn't there.

It took her a moment to find the right spot. The rock and twigs which had seemed so clear to her as she sat crouched behind the trees were more difficult to find up close, and it was only when she saw the disturbed ground, the loose way Andrew had scattered the leaves over the soil, that she knew for sure she had found the right spot.

She got to her knees and started to dig, the soil getting under her nails and filling the cracks in her skin. He had not dug down deep and after only a few minutes of scraping she saw the tin box appear under the soil. She tugged at it and eased it from the ground. Once she had seen what was inside, it would go back into the hole and be covered up just as he had left it. She didn't want him to come back to retrieve it and notice that his hiding place had been disturbed. Because she knew he would realize it was her. She was the only one who came to these woods with any frequency.

She looked at her hands and dirty nails and made a mental note to wash them in the small creek at the bottom of the woods. If her father saw the dirt there, he might quickly understand what she had done.

Her fingers trembled as she brushed the soil from the box. When she opened it, she saw there was an envelope inside, blank and new, with no name or address, and the seal folded in rather than licked shut.

She lifted the flap and felt inside for the contents. A letter, she assumed. But when she eased it out and turned it over, she got a shock.

Not a letter at all, but photographs of them all partying in the cabin. It was shocking to see them again. Michael and Ethan dancing drunken and half-naked. Her and Ashley smoking and laughing and watching the boys as they cavorted round the room. Their hair a mess, their mascara smudged. The photos were so sharp, so focused. Whoever took them had known what they were doing. Had known too that they were there, partying in the disused cabin. They'd been spied on for weeks, was what she always thought. But why? It was just a bit of teenage fun. Some vodka, some music, some weed, sex. The usual rebellion. But to look at those photos was to see something else. Something sinister almost. Bacchanalian and wild. Something to be discouraged and punished.

And that was definitely what the photographer had in mind when they stood there in the shadows, clicking away. When they printed out those images and then spread them about town. It was a punishment. Though what they had really done wrong, she never knew. They were having fun, that was all it was. None of them had deserved to be punished for it. To be humiliated for being young and free. And Michael, poor, beautiful Michael. He'd paid the ultimate price for being spirited and wild.

She slipped the photograph back in the envelope and put it back in the box, then laid it in the hole and covered it up, thinking of her father as she did so. Because it troubled her to think about why he had gone to all this trouble to bury a box in the forest. To bury that photograph. That particular memory. It was as if he wanted to bury the past and ensure those memories never returned.

It hurt her to think that those happy moments had been so tarnished by scandal and tragedy that her father thought they should be eliminated like this. Despite it all, she would do anything to go back to those days with Michael. To re-live them. To have him beside her again.

CHAPTER TWENTY-FIVE

July 1994

None of them would have thought to claim one of the abandoned cabins for the summer. But Michael was bolder than them and saw opportunities they never imagined. It was easier for him, Evie sometimes thought. He was the outsider. If it all went wrong, he could just walk away, and never have to deal with the consequences.

Though they didn't put up much resistance. That rebelliousness or disobedience or whatever it was that showed itself that summer, had always been there. Michael just knew how to bring it out of them.

But it never felt like they were doing anything wrong. Rebelliousness, disobedience, Evie never really thought there was much wrong with that and she could never figure out why everyone got so upset when they discovered they'd been having parties there all summer. It was what teenagers were supposed to do, after all—push the boundaries.

It should have been that way. A happy, carefree time. A long, lazy summer filled with laughter and fun and pleasure. If they'd been left alone, that's how it would have been. But some people don't want others to be happy. Some people don't want others to have fun. Some people prefer to destroy such things.

It took a special kind of vindictiveness to do what was done to them. To stand outside the cabin and spy on them. To sit there, night after night, click-click-clicking a camera and documenting the whole thing. Gathering evidence and passing judgment. It takes a cruel mind to do a thing like that, is what she always thought. To look at a bunch of kids having fun and decide they had to be punished for it. You had to be a special sort of creep to turn happiness into pain and pain into tragedy.

*

Those damn photographs. They started appearing around town one morning without warning. Scattered around the grocery store. Attached to lampposts. Slipped through letterboxes. Each with their own little caption. Every word an exquisite little piece of meanness and petty revenge.

Her father came down to breakfast and saw one lying face down on the doormat. When he turned it over and looked at it, he had turned pale and walked into the kitchen holding it between his thumb and forefinger as if it was something filthy.

They were all seated at the table in the kitchen eating breakfast and when he threw it toward Ethan it fluttered down and landed in his bowl of cereal.

"Hey, what are you doing?" Ethan protested as he fished out the photograph, which was dripping with milk.

Then he turned it over and spread it out on the table. It was weird. For a few suspended seconds they sat there staring at it. Then she heard her mom cry out a tiny "Oh!" as Ethan picked it up and crumpled it in his hands.

But they had all seen it. A grainy shot, taken at night, from a distance, but it was clear enough to see what was going on. The four of them looking debauched and deranged, slumped in the living room of the cabin in various states of undress and disarray, the caption succinct and neatly typed: *Wasted #1*. As if it was a work of art. The first in a series.

For a moment the room was still, everyone waiting for her dad to say something. Because they could feel the quiet rage that was building within him.

When he pulled out his chair and sat at the table, she was almost relieved. Perhaps he'd be reasonable about it. That was what she hoped. She remembered relaxing a little and exhaling.

Then he glowered at them. "Are you going to explain this?"

But she couldn't say anything, and Ethan just sat there, stiff with anxiety.

"Answer me!" he screamed. And he stood up quickly and grabbed Ethan by the shoulders, spinning him round and pulling him up so they were face to face, eye to eye.

"Answer me, God damn it!"

Her mom screamed at him, begging him to calm down, pleading with him until he snapped out of his rage. Evie could see it in his eyes, the way his pupils contracted, as if he was regaining his focus and coming back into the room. He let Ethan go and threw him back against the table with such force the bowl of cereal toppled and spilled over the surface.

And while Mom fussed and rushed about trying to mop up the mess, while Dad paced the room and tried to steady his breath, and while Ethan sat there with his head in his hands, she picked up the crumpled photo and smoothed it down and looked at it again.

And in the noise and chaos of the kitchen she tried to make it good.

"It's not as bad as it looks," she said.

They had all turned to look at her as if they couldn't believe what she had just said.

"What?" Andrew cried. Then he grabbed the photo and pressed it up against her face. "Look at it," he seethed. "Look at the state of you. What is it? Drugs? Drink? And Michael, is that Michael your lying next to?"

She tried to explain it. She tried to tell him that it was just a party, that what he thought he saw there was nothing really. It was just a party. They had done nothing wrong. But he shot her down.

"No, Evie, you be quiet. I want to hear what your brother has to say about this. What the hell were you doing dragging your sister, your *sister*, into this…" he threw the photo on the table in disgust. "How, Ethan? I mean…"

And she'd never forget Ethan's voice, how frail it sounded, how panicked as he pleaded with his father to listen.

"Whoever did this just wanted to cause trouble. Please, just think about it, will you? Someone was out there, watching us, taking photos of us. What kind of person would do something like that?"

And it was then she understood the full horror of that photograph. It hit her like a punch to the gut, so hard and with such force that she got up from the table and vomited on the kitchen floor, causing her dad to shout at Ethan as if it was his fault.

"Look what you've done to her. My God, Ethan, you're supposed to take care of her. How many times do I have to tell you?"

She'd wanted to protest, to explain to him that she could look after herself now. That it was unfair to keep up this pressure on Ethan. He wasn't responsible for her anymore. He hadn't been for years. But she couldn't speak, she was still retching and weakened from vomiting.

Then Andrew had turned to Carole, and she would never forget what he said.

"I want him out of this house," he said. "Do you understand? Out."

Carole begged him, trying to get him to see that he was over-reacting. Trying to tell him that he needed to listen to what we had to say.

But Andrew didn't care. Something irrational had taken hold of him and he wasn't making any sense. "I won't have him behaving like that under my roof. What he does in his own home is his own business, but here, in my house. What are people going to think of us?"

"It's *our* home, Andrew," Carole had tried to explain. "You are not the only person who gets to decide what happens here."

But Andrew had refused to listen. Whatever it was that possessed him had taken over. And looking back, she thought it was because he knew. He could feel it coming. Could hear the whispering tongues, could see the disapproving gazes, could feel the shame rising.

"I expected better of you, Evie," he told her. "And Ashley too. I thought you were both decent girls."

She'd wanted to defend herself, to ask him what he thought they'd done wrong. *Decent girls.* What did that mean? What sort of expectation was that? What sort of judgment was that? But the pain in his eyes was so visible, his disappointment something she could feel as it oozed from his every pore.

Then, somehow, she found the words. Somehow, she managed to look him in the eye and ask, "Have you forgotten what it's like to be young? To make mistakes?"

It seemed to stop him in his tracks, the fact that she had challenged him catching him off guard. She saw the change come over him, a softening of his eyes, a calm as he thought about what she had said, and she wanted to tell him she was sorry. Sorry about the photograph, sorry if it had embarrassed him.

But Ethan chose that moment to interrupt. He was staring at the photo and shaking his head. "Who would do this?" he said. "Who the hell would do this?"

Then his eyes seemed to sharpen into focus as if he had suddenly understood something. He stood up quickly and ran into the hall, grabbing his coat as he left the house.

She knew immediately where he was headed and who he planned to confront. Mason was behind it, he had to be. It would make sense. Anyone could see it.

"Let me go after him," she said to her mom. "I think I can stop him." And Carole had nodded, while her dad stood there, emptied of energy after his angry outburst and seemingly incapable of knowing what to do.

*

She ran over to the hotel, hoping to catch Ethan before he got there, but she was too late. When she arrived, she saw him out on the front lawn with Ashley, their conversation animated and loud.

"Did Mason do this?" he asked Ashley as he thrust the photo at her.

Ashley calmly took the photo from him and looked at it, and then frowned.

"I was just about to call you. They're all over town apparently. Everyone's talking about it. My dad is so mad at us."

"Listen, I don't give a damn about any of that. Did Mason do this?" Ethan repeated.

"Sorry, what? Come on, Ethan, why would he do a thing like that?"

"You know damn well why. Because he's a petty, vindictive, spoiled little brat who can't stand not to get what he wants. The idea that we shut him out, he couldn't handle it."

Ashley stared at Ethan aghast, unable to speak for a moment.

"Is that what you think of him, Ethan? Really?"

And he had nodded.

"Well then fuck you. Seriously, how can you think such a thing? Mason can be annoying, but he's not some weirdo vindictive voyeur. You've gone too far, Ethan."

"Oh come on, Ashley. How many times has he hurt you then? None? Really? Admit it, it must be him. He's got a camera, one of those good ones with a long lens, hasn't he?"

"So?"

"Ashley, please. Think about it. You know I wouldn't say this if I didn't think there was a good reason. You know how angry he was with us because we shut him out."

"He was angry because we laughed at him, Ethan. And the way Michael sneered at him too."

"Yeah, okay, fair enough, that was a shitty thing to do. But it was different this time."

"Maybe, I don't know… But just go, okay? If you want to ask Mason about it, then you can. Just leave me out of it. But if I find out that you've spread lies that Mason is behind this, then I swear to God, Ethan, I'll never speak to you again."

Evie had run over to them then and taken hold of Ethan's arm to let him know she was there and told him that maybe Ashley was right, they should head home and calm down before it all got out of hand.

As she tried to lead Ethan away, she saw Michael standing in the doorway of the hotel, signaling to her. Call me, he was gesturing. She smiled and nodded, and felt her mood lift, just knowing he was there, waiting for her still.

They walked home slowly but Ethan was seething, and she heard him muttering as they walked. He was determined to prove that only Mason could have done such a thing.

"When Dad knows who was behind this, he'll stand by us," Ethan said. "He'll never let that little shit Mason get away with it."

But Evie thought of the rage and the hurt she'd seen in their dad's eyes. Stand by them? She wasn't so sure.

*

When they got home, Andrew had calmed down just enough to accept that he was not the sort of father to throw his son out of the house. He was, however, the sort of father who took refuge in his studio. The sort of father who preferred to simmer in solitude while he figured things out.

"I'm not going to lie," he told them. "I'm disappointed in both of you. And shocked too that you thought it was acceptable to run wild like that."

It was an awkward sort of peace, maintained mostly through Andrew's absence, but they all assumed that, eventually, Andrew would calm down and life would return to normal.

But events took a very different course. Things moving so fast that no one had time to react or understand what was going on.

*

They had all kept a low profile since the photographs appeared. The humiliation was too great. The looks on people's faces, the smiles, the sniggers. Evie had thought she would never live it down and there were days when she wanted to stay at home and never have to face the world again.

Andrew had made it clear that she was to stay away from the hotel and from Michael. As far as he was concerned, it was Michael who had got them into this mess and led them astray. She had protested and said it wasn't fair to blame only Michael. But her dad didn't listen, and she wondered if it was simply easier for him to react this way—to blame the outsider and pretend that without him they would never have "run wild" as he put it.

But every time she thought of Michael alone in the hotel with no one to talk to or support him, it worried her. He would be as upset as she was, she imagined, and it was wrong that he had to suffer the humiliation in isolation with no one around to talk to about it.

But when she'd told Ethan how much she wanted to see Michael, how much she needed to know he was okay, he had looked at her with shock and surprise.

"Why?" he asked her. "This *is* all his fault. His damn parties and his crazy ideas. Dad's right, if it wasn't for him, we wouldn't be in this mess."

She had looked at him aghast and upset that he still crumbled under pressure from their dad. That he still felt incapable of standing up to Andrew and demanding they be treated like the adults they almost were. It made her realize that the freedom she thought they had grasped because of Michael was just an illusion. When it came down to it, they were still as fearful and obedient as they had always been.

"I should never have let Michael persuade me to let you join in," Ethan had told her. "I mean you're only sixteen. It is sordid, isn't it?"

Sordid. One of the photos had been captioned with that little delight. Of all the words that were thrown at them that summer, that was the one that hurt the most. The way it sullied them. The way it labeled their joy, their fun, and their innocence as something dirty and bad and contemptible. She could never get over that word for some reason.

But Ethan seemed to think that it was correct. And that it was all Michael's fault.

"It's true, Evie. Without him, none of this would have happened."

She lost count of the times he said that. It was almost as if he needed to repeat it because, in his heart, he didn't really believe it. It was only through repetition of it that he could get the idea to take hold. As if he was forcing himself to believe something he knew was not true.

It was crazy and unfair. And a way of letting them off the hook, she thought. As if they couldn't take responsibility for their own decisions. But they could. She might have only been sixteen, but no one had dragged her up there to that cabin. She went willingly. She went because she wanted to be with Michael. And she told him so.

"That's not how it works Evie," Ethan told her. "You're just a kid, Michael should have laid off you."

She didn't know what he meant by that. Of course that was how it worked. You made a decision, and sometimes the decision was good and sometimes it was bad. And she'd made a bad decision. Because she was young and stupid. Because it didn't seem so wrong. And she'd probably never do it again. So what was the big deal?

But she could see the worry in Ethan's face. That look he had when he thought he'd let Dad down, when he thought he'd done something stupid. *Why did he always have to feel so responsible for everything,* she wondered? But she knew the answer to that. Dad had always made Ethan responsible for everything. He still blamed Ethan for things he should have long ago forgiven. It was time Ethan confronted him about that. And it was time they both acknowledged that she was not a kid anymore, that she could make decisions for herself, that she should be allowed to make mistakes. Mistakes that were hers and hers alone.

*

A couple of hours later, Mason came over. He knocked on the door and smiled politely when Carole opened.

"Mason," she heard her mom say, her voice quivering because he had taken her by surprise. "What brings you here?"

He smiled, but Evie could see he was nervous, as if he had already decided he had made a mistake by coming over and was on the point of leaving when Ethan came down the stairs and said, "What do you want, Mason?"

"Just a quiet word, that's all. Is that okay?" He put the question to Carole, knowing she would say yes. Mason had always known how to charm her with his manners and that soft-spoken voice he always used to fool people into thinking he was harmless.

They walked into the living room and Evie followed and when her mom tried to pull her away—"Let's leave them to talk, Evie"—Evie had glared back.

"What? I've as much right to talk to Mason as Ethan has."

And her mom had relented and walked away, too tired to get involved it seemed in any more teenage drama.

Evie thought Ethan would remain calm about it. That he wouldn't give Mason the pleasure of seeing how angry he was.

But Mason's smiling face, his insolent smirk was too much for her brother to handle.

"What the fuck were you thinking, Mason? It's sick. You're fucking sick."

"What! I was just taking a few photos. I wasn't the one knee deep in a drugged-up orgy."

If the conversation was going to be nothing more than trading insults then she didn't want to be a part of it.

"Oh for fuck's sake," Ethan shouted. "Are you serious? It was just a party, Mason. I know you don't know much about parties, seeing as how you're never invited to any, but guess what? This is what they're like. People dance and drink and have a laugh."

"Naked?"

"Oh, God, you're not listening to me. Why did you do this? Spy on us? Humiliate us? What's wrong with you? Or is this how you get your kicks then, is that it?"

Mason ignored him. "It's Evie that upset me the most," Mason said, his tone patronizing and insincere. "I thought she was better than this."

"Oh no. You leave her out of this okay? You have no right to judge her or say such a thing. No right at all."

"Why? I mean that's her in the photos, isn't it? Fucking Michael?"

And it was too much then. Ethan lunged and hit Mason with a punch straight above his eye. The cut spurting blood immediately.

"Look what you've done!" Mason cried.

But Ethan was unrepentant. Evie watched as Mason wiped away a smear of blood above his eye and leaned toward Ethan, the veins in his neck bulging with anger.

"You're a piece of shit, Ethan," he cried.

"Just be glad I didn't hit you twice. Stay away from us, you hear? Stay away."

"Oh, don't worry. I never want to set eyes on you again. And I'll tell you another thing. After this, Ashley won't want to see you either."

Ethan screamed, his face contorted with rage. "You're going to pay for this, I swear. Watch your back, Mason. You watch your back."

She had never seen him like this before. The anger. The act of violence. Sometimes he was just like Dad, she thought. When it took hold of him, his temper was the same. And she felt a shiver of fear race through her. Because she didn't recognize him. She didn't recognize her own brother.

CHAPTER TWENTY-SIX

March 2015

Their voices came through in slow drifts, distant at first, then becoming clearer. She had not been listening and felt only half-aware of her surroundings. They were sitting at the kitchen table again, the three of them, and her mom was saying something, and Ethan was staring at her intently.

Evie had no idea how long they had been talking to her as she sat at the kitchen table, and she struggled to focus on what they were saying.

When her mom touched her hand, and patted it to check she was listening, Evie looked at her, then shook her head. A few things they had said had filtered through, but all the words had jumbled in her head and none of them made sense.

Witness. Remember. Innocence. Help us.

She stared at the table and let the words swirl in and out of her head in different orders, hoping with each new configuration that some sense would eventually materialize.

"Evie," her mom said. "There's something you need to know. It might help you understand why Ethan needs to do this."

She waited for her brother to say something, but he sat there in silence. Clearly, he was going to let Carole do all the talking. Looking at them then, it struck her that they wanted her to be the messenger. She was the one who would be sent out into town to make the case on Ethan's behalf. She was the only one people would listen to. But she couldn't do it, she thought. She *wouldn't* do it. If they had something to say to the people in this town, then they should have the courage to say it themselves.

"I know this is difficult for you, Evie, but do you remember the day Michael died?" Carole asked her.

"Just bits and pieces. But you know that. Please don't keep asking me about it."

"I know there was a lot of confusion as to what really happened that day," Carole continued. "But there are missing pieces still."

Was there so much confusion? Evie wondered. She had told them what little she could remember, but it had never seemed that confusing. What was known had always been straightforward, she thought. For years she had managed to keep the story simple.

She had run from the lake but couldn't remember why. In the forest she had stumbled upon a kill, the deer with its belly slashed open, the sight of all that blood shocking her into silence and confusion. When Andrew found her, she wasn't sure what it was she had seen. Blood, the only thing she remembered. Blood and Michael. But she had no idea where he was. And then the alarm as the cabin burst into flames. The smoke and the fire and the terror of it.

There was nothing to add to this story. Nothing to take away. This was as close as she had ever come to making sense of that terrible day. She had never been able to fill in that long, dark gap of time between leaving the lakeshore and then coming round in the forest. Only darkness, where her memory should be. And she had never been able to shine a light into its depths. But one thing she did know and understand. The statement she had pieced together with psychologists and lawyers and the police was as close to the truth as she could get.

"I'm not confused about what happened," she told Carole, then turned to Ethan and said, "I've spent years trying to come to terms with that day, Ethan. You weren't here, you didn't see how long it took for me to put it behind me. Do you think I want to go through it all again?"

"No, of course not," he replied. "But there are things that happened, things you don't remember. But I do, I remember them, and I just want you to help me is all. Please?"

"How?" Evie asked. "How can I help you? You said yourself, I don't remember what happened, and I never have. So why would I suddenly remember anything now?"

"Maybe if you learned the truth. Maybe if I told you, about me, about Dad. It might trigger something."

"Dad? What's he got to do with any of this?"

"That's what he's trying to tell you, Evie," Carole said. "Your dad has never been honest about any of this, and—"

"He's dead," Evie said. "He can't defend himself against anything you have to say. We just buried him and now you want to lay it all on him? Mom, it's over. It was over twenty years ago when the court accepted Ethan's plea. Or have you forgotten that? Huh? Did you forget that Ethan pleaded guilty? In court. He stood there and he said it: *I killed Michael.* What more do you need?"

"I did admit it, Evie," Ethan said. "But not for the reason you think."

"Sorry, what?"

"I don't really think you understood how angry Dad was with us that summer. Remember, after those photos?"

"Of course I remember."

"It was worse for me. You know how he was. He never gave me any peace. It was obsessive, when I think about it, the stress he put on me to always be looking out for you. He thought I'd dragged you into the sort of trouble I should have kept you away from. When he learned about what we'd been doing in the cabin that summer, he never forgave me. And the angrier he got about it, the more I started to agree with him. It was true. I had put you in harm's way. I had allowed you to get into trouble. He knew that all he needed to do was keep the pressure on me, keep telling me I should feel ashamed about it, accept it was all my fault. He knew that was all he needed to do to have me doubting myself.

"He was always so good at laying the blame on me, at getting me to accept responsibility for things, even when it wasn't my fault. I don't know why he did that to me, why he put so much on me, but he did, and you know he did."

It was true. She did know it. But she couldn't listen to him as he tried to implicate her father in all of this. He was dead and they should respect that. She began to shake a little as her anger grew. That they would try to turn this around and say that Andrew was somehow to blame for what happened to Michael. That he was in any way to blame. It was outrageous and unfair.

"Stop, please. I know who Dad was. I know what he was capable of and I also know what he was incapable of. I won't sit here and listen to you pinning the blame on him. After you admitted—in court—that you were responsible. You can't come here and tell these lies. And they are lies. I know they are. A truth like that would have come out years ago. Don't tell me you sat there in jail for twenty years for a crime you are now saying was somehow Dad's fault. How can you even think such a thing, never mind say it? Do you seriously want me to tell people that this is what happened? That you're innocent? That Dad did this? Listen to yourself! It's crazy! I won't do it. You're on your own here."

"Evie, please," Ethan implored.

"No!" she replied. "No! Just get out of here. I want nothing to do with this. Nothing!"

He slid his chair back from the table, and she watched as he put on his coat and headed to the front door. When she heard it click shut behind him, she felt a wave of emotion overwhelm her and the tears began to flow.

"How can he do this to me?" she asked Carole. "How can *you* do this to me?"

"We just want to set things straight. Trust me on this. He's trying to do the right thing."

"No, no, he's not. He's causing pain and hurt and you're helping him."

"Evie—"

"Mom, please. Can you leave too? Just go. I need to be alone."

Carole got up from her chair and got ready to leave.

"Just think about it, Evie. There are things you need to know, about what happened. And you need to know why Ethan did the things he did. You owe him that much. But I can't force you to accept or understand that. All we can do is wait until you are ready. All we're asking is that you listen to us. Just listen."

When her mother left, Evie sat alone in the kitchen and wept. There was something to what her brother had said. A truth there that had filtered through from the shadows. A little flicker of a memory. Her dad with her in the forest, stroking her head, wiping the dirt from her hands. Shushing her and comforting her.

Listen to him, Evie. Go and find him and listen to him, she thought she heard him say.

CHAPTER TWENTY-SEVEN

March 2015

She found Ethan down by the lake, walking along the shoreline path. It was the place he always went to when he needed to think. Some things never changed.

"It'll be getting dark soon," she said as she approached him. And she saw him jump as she startled him.

"You shouldn't go sneaking up on people like that."

"Oh, sorry. I thought you'd heard me."

"You want to take a walk with me for a while?" he asked her.

"Sure," she said.

"We can talk too, maybe?"

"Okay… I'm sorry, for asking you to leave. I just…"

"It's okay, Evie. I should have thought about what this is doing to you. I'm sorry. If I could make it easier, I would. I honestly don't want to hurt you, Evie. I swear to you, I don't."

She nodded and drew alongside him, and they walked for a while in silence, taking in the view. The physical closeness of him was something she still needed to adjust to, though already she could sense just how much she wanted him by her side. It was as if he provided a ballast of some sort now that her father was gone. Ethan was something solid to keep her rooted to the ground and secured. Strange that even after all those years away, her instinct was still to stay close to him. It was as if he had never left her, as if he had always been by her side. And in a way, he had. A piece of him had lodged within her a long time ago, and it lay so deep, it would never be shifted. Even tragedy and doubt had been unable to completely dislodge it.

"I guess you must have missed all this," Evie said.

He took in the view and she saw him exhale, the soothing quiet of the sky at that time of day calming him and slowing him down.

"I used up a lot of energy trying not to think about it if I'm honest. That's the only way to get through it. You need to forget the places and people you knew. You'd go crazy if you didn't."

Evie stopped walking, unlocked their arms, and looked at him. "So for twenty years you forgot about us?"

He kept on walking, didn't even turn to face her when he replied, as if he needed to put some space between them so he could think about what he had just said.

"I had to," he said. "It was too painful to think about you all, about this place. I had to stop thinking if I was going to be able to get through it, because I wasn't sure if I had done the right thing. Once the reality of that place hit me, once I was in there and understood what it meant to plead guilty, I didn't think I was going to make it. So you learn not to think, because that's how you get through it. Once you start thinking, you might as well throw yourself against the cell walls. And anyway, here I am, back home again, so, you know…"

She didn't know. She had always tried not to think about what it must have been like for him to be stuck in that jail. The horror of it was something she never wanted to contemplate. But she had never imagined that after all this time he would still call this place his home.

"Some people would say this isn't your home now. You know that, don't you?" she asked him.

"I know. But where else would home be then? This is where I was born, the place I grew up. If this isn't home, then where is? Cañon City? Boulder?"

He gestured at the lake and the mountains, and looked up at the sky, blushed lavender now as the sun began to set. And again, she saw the effect it had upon him. The way his jaw loosened, and his eyes widened.

"And what about you? Do you think I belong here?"

If someone had asked her that question before Ethan's return, her answer would have been quick and certain.

No, she would have said. *This place can never be his home now.*

And there was a tiny piece of her that still thought that. But the degree of certainty had diminished. When she saw him look out over the lake, when she saw him exhale, she understood what he felt. Because she felt the same way herself.

This place contained him. The mountains and the lake, the granite and the pines, they all held fragments of their lives, caught there in the branches and the water and the soil. Every laugh, every tear, every joy, every pain, every memory and every hope. It was all there. And if you stopped to listen, if you stilled yourself and allowed it to come, you could sense it, that trace of immortality in everything. That was what she felt, when she looked over the lake and up at those hills, when she smelled the pines; she belonged here, forever. And so did he. Because Evie knew he felt it too. This place was as much his home as it was hers, and who was she to keep him from that?

And Andrew was here, in all of these things. If Ethan wanted to, he could stand on the shoreline and look up at Mount Saxon, just as she did sometimes, and he would find pieces of his father in everything. That hope he had for reconciliation, for the chance to talk to Andrew again, it wasn't gone, not completely. All he had to do was stand still and listen and wait, and he would find his dad again, just as she had.

But Michael is here too, she thought. His death contaminating everything forever, his cries, tangled in the pine trees. A shudder rushed through her then, and she had to close her eyes and breathe it away. Why could she never be rid of him? Then a voice pulled her out of her thoughts, and she felt a hand squeeze her arm.

"Hey, are you okay?"

"Oh, sorry. I was just thinking was all. Remembering things."

"Dad?"

"Yeah, and…" She didn't want his name on her lips. But Ethan had no fear of it.

"Michael?"

"I don't know if I can help you, Ethan. I want to, but I'm scared. When I remember him, it all comes back and I can feel it again, as if it was yesterday, as if I had just seen him again. His eyes… and… and… what you're asking me to do, it's too much, it's just too much."

"I wouldn't ask you to do it if I didn't need you to, Evie. I hope you know that."

She didn't answer. She couldn't answer. Because it didn't feel like the truth. Not yet. And he had changed his mind before, hadn't he? He had stood in court and lied before, proclaimed his innocence so convincingly there had been a moment when she thought he would walk free. She had plenty of reasons to doubt him, and he had provided her with every one of them.

"Evie," he continued. "I know I can't just walk in here and expect you to trust me. I know it'll take time."

"It will. People need to know why, Ethan. And that means you need to explain what you want, and why you're here."

"A secret is easy to keep if someone else has been blamed, if someone else is sitting in a jail someplace, and everyone is happy that justice has been served. It's easy because you don't have to look the victim of your lies in the eye every day and feel the shame of what you've done to them. And over time you probably even come to believe it. You forget what happened and just shrug it off. Ethan McCallister. He's your man. He did it. Well, I didn't do it, Evie. But someone here did. And I want them to look me in the eye every day and start to feel it. Start to know what they did to me. I want them to understand that it's their turn now."

"Ethan, that sounds too much like revenge…"

"Revenge? Fuck, Evie. Revenge? How about justice? How about fairness? How about truth? Revenge? Are you kidding me? Is that what you think I'm about?"

"Okay, I'm sorry. I just… do you really think someone could keep a secret like that for twenty years? In a small town like this? Do you really think no one would notice?"

"You don't believe me, do you? That's it, isn't it? You still think I did it."

"We've been over that already."

"Have we? Okay, then. Say it. Look me in the eye and tell me you think I didn't kill Michael."

She had known this was coming. It was inevitable. Ever since he rang the doorbell, she had been waiting for him to ask her.

"I think it's up to you to prove you didn't, Ethan. And I know that's not what you want to hear, but it's the truth. If you want me, or anyone else for that matter, to even listen to what you have to say, then you're going to have to prove it."

"Okay, but then you're going to have to let me do it."

She leaned away from him and in that moment she could tell that he must have noticed her doubt, as he then added, "I'm frightened too, of what might happen if I rush. I could hurt too many people again. People I love. But I have to try."

The way he looked at her, the tilt of his head as if he was gauging her response and weighing up her ability to absorb not only this truth, but whatever was to come, left her in no doubt.

She was one of the people who could get hurt here. That was what he was telling her. And he wanted to know if she could handle it. Because she understood now. Ethan knew who had killed Michael. That's why he was here.

And somewhere in the distance she heard a voice. A voice whispering a name. A voice gently sobbing. "Michael, Michael."

It took her a moment to realize the voice was her own.

She had tried so hard to forget him. She had needed to forget him. And now, there he was again. As if he was the one calling to her. As if he had been waiting for her to remember him all these years. And she felt her body slump like a dead weight against her brother as the dizziness and nausea washed over her.

CHAPTER TWENTY-EIGHT

September 1995

He had always been a constant. He had always been so reliable. It was how fathers were supposed to be, she had always thought. They were meant to stay strong, keep calm, steer everyone safely through rough seas. And with Ethan gone, she had needed her father to be this steady presence more than ever.

But in the face of condemnation from people he considered his friends, he crumbled. People had decided Ethan's crime was somehow theirs too. And no matter how unfair it was, no matter how awful it felt to be betrayed by people you thought you could trust and rely upon, there was little they could do to stop them finding the McCallister's guilty by association. They *were* tainted by association and there was nothing they could do to change that. All they could do was accept it and hope that people would come round eventually.

But Andrew seethed at the injustice of it. "They're making us pay for something we didn't do. I mean, what is it they want us to do? Are we supposed to leave our own home, is that it? Are we supposed to accept that we have to share some of the guilt for what happened to Michael and just slink away like criminals? When they look at us, all they think about is Michael. They've forgotten who we really are."

But how could it be otherwise? Evie wondered. When she looked in the mirror, she sometimes saw the same thing. Her brother's violence stared back at her. It was inside of her too, in some way, she could feel it. Something bad in the blood. Inherited from their father. That temper of his. That surliness. Some people called it an artistic temperament, but she had always understood it was something more malign. She wanted to tell him to just give it time, but he never listened to her.

"Leave him be, Evie," Carole told her. "He needs to figure this out for himself."

He figured it out alone, in his studio. Night after night. Week after week. The weeks turning to months. As if to be at home with them was too much for him. As if their family life was something which belonged in the past now and was something he didn't want to look back on. Too many things had changed, and to remember the past was to see everything you had lost. To look back was to understand that the small happiness you once had was now irretrievable.

Sometimes she would go over to his studio to try and speak to him, and check that he was okay, but every time she opened the door he would look up and blink, as if he needed to recall who she was.

"Oh, Evie, it's you," he would say, before turning back to the work at hand.

One evening she had slipped in quietly and watched him paint, her father so absorbed in his work, he barely noticed she was there. She just wanted to be around him for a while, to have him close and know that he was okay.

He was working on a painting with a concentration and energy that verged more on obsession than craft. The only thing which seemed to exist was the canvas in front of him and the ragged old palette, smothered in thick globules of paint.

She had watched as he smeared red paint onto red paint. Purple onto purple. Black onto black. Layering the paint until it was an inch thick. Each brush stroke, small and carefully executed. Each application had a meaning and a purpose, but there was an energy to his movements too, a vigor and something close to violence, in the way he pressed the palette knife to the canvas or flicked the brush.

It was jittery, nervous. And yet, at times, so quiet and calm. He could control this, Evie realized. This energy, this anger, he could use it as he pleased. Each brushstroke was a precise dosage, a distilled rage that could be seen there in the painting itself.

Let him forget me, she thought.

So she sat there, quiet and still and tried to think about the image which was slowly forming on the canvas. That red, fiery forest. He had never used such colors before. His work was always a natural color scheme. The grays, greens and lilacs of the landscape. Such a muted, subtle palette. But this, this burst of red, was something strange. If she had dared to, she would have asked him: *Is this how you feel?*

But she couldn't speak. She could only watch as the paint was layered on, thicker and thicker, the flames rising higher and higher.

She looked at all that red and, despite herself, a flash of something appeared in her mind. A trickle of blood. That hemoglobin red. Those pale blue eyes again. And she squeezed her eyes shut and counted her breaths, slowing everything down, coming to some sort of equilibrium, before opening her eyes again.

Slowly, she began to make out the forms underneath the paint. A collage, built layer upon layer and made up of all the headlines and clippings he must have collected from the papers, papers Mom would not allow in the house because they all screamed the same accusations. Evie watched as Andrew tried to obliterate them with paint, with blood, with red. This forest fire, her father's anger, transforming and becoming clearer and more defined.

Her father was painting the cabin fire, she could see it now. And she called out his name when she understood what she was looking at.

"Michael."

The sound of her voice broke the spell her father was under. He turned to face her and glared, and she looked at him, then looked at the painting and repeated his name.

"Michael," she said, as she pointed at the canvas.

He shook his head. "He's dead. Dead and gone. Don't mention that name in my presence again." His voice so strange, the words so old-fashioned and authoritarian.

"Then why are you painting him?" she asked. "If you want to forget him, then why do this?"

"You're seeing things that aren't there, Evie. Go home, why don't you? Go home and help your mother and leave me alone."

"Not before you answer the question."

She stood up and walked over to him and was surprised at the lightness in her head, at the tremble in her legs. She was afraid of him, she realized. Afraid of her own dad. Afraid of this man who stood there, covered in paint, shaking his head and repeating, "No, no," as if he could contain it all like that, with a simple proclamation, repeated over and over.

"But don't lie to me, Dad. Don't stand there and tell me I'm imagining things."

He looked at her and his eyes creased into a frown as he shook his head. No words, just silence. But a no was a no, even without saying it. When she reached out to him, and placed her hand on his shoulder in an attempt to comfort him, to let him know it was okay to try and figure things out however he needed to, he shuddered, and the paint brush fell from his hands and spattered red paint across the floor in a violent splash of red.

They looked down at it and she gasped a little "Oh!" in surprise. The splash of red flashing through her, like a partially glimpsed event you catch while seated in a speeding car. She wasn't sure what she was looking at. The red on the floor. The splash of it. The paint dripping from the dropped brush as she stood there. That trickle of blood on pale skin.

Then she felt it. A rush of blood to her head. A tingling in her fingers and toes. A ringing in her ears. And then, nothing.

*

She must have fallen, but she had no memory of it. A moment later, or so it seemed, she came to, back in the house, in her bed, her clothes covered in red paint, her mom leaning over her and smoothing her hair from her face and whispering to her.

"Evie, Evie, are you okay?"

But her mom's soft, hushed words couldn't soothe her. All she could see was red. The red of fire, the red of paint, the red of blood. All of it mixing together and swirling her back down into a pit of vertigo.

"Evie? Evie? Oh, help her Andrew, please. What's happened to her?"

"She'll be fine," her father replied. "All she needs is some rest."

She had wanted to tell them that she wasn't fine, that she felt scared and confused and sick. But the bed swayed, and the ceiling swirled and all she could do was close her eyes and wait for it to stop.

"I don't know, Andrew. I don't know. She's so pale. Look at her."

"She just needs to stay away from the studio while I'm working."

"What? What does that have to do with anything?"

"Just tell her to leave me be, is all."

Then she heard him walk away, closing her bedroom door with a gentle click. She felt her mom touch her head, kiss her on the forehead and whisper, "Shh, shh, it will be alright. Don't listen to him."

But she never went over there again. She didn't want to see that painting. She didn't want to know what her father was thinking. She did as she was told. She stayed away and left him alone.

Left him to brood in his studio. Left him to fester. And that was what it was. The grief, the shock, the anger, the frustration; it was an open wound that was slowly poisoning him.

CHAPTER TWENTY-NINE

October 1995

When the breakdown finally came, they weren't ready for it.

The day had been the same as any other. She had helped her mom with the breakfast chores and then caught the bus to school. On the walk to the school bus she had passed her dad's studio and had seen the light on. He was working still, hadn't even gone to bed. She said "Good morning" to him anyway, because maybe he knew she was there. Maybe he looked up, saw it was eight thirty, and thought of her. Maybe.

On the school bus, she sat next to Ashley. It was a recent thing, their reconciliation. For months, during the trial and afterward, Ashley had made a point of ignoring her, as if she was too tainted to even look at. But at some point, something had softened in Ashley and their friendship had tentatively resumed.

It gave Evie hope that maybe this was how it would all work out in the end. That the whole town, given enough time, would come to its senses, and let them back in. At some point, everyone would simply forget.

Later, on the bus ride home, Ashley had asked her if she wanted to come over in the evening and she'd accepted. Anyone watching them would have had difficulty noticing there was still a tension there between them, that they were still finding their way back to the friendship they once had. To a casual observer, they were just two teenage girls making plans.

For the first time in months Evie felt something close to happiness again. Maybe it was possible, after all, to find a way back home. And she found herself hoping this was the first step toward a new life.

When she walked past her father's studio, the lights were off and she hoped her father would be home. She could tell him about her day. How ordinary it had been. It was something he should know about, she thought. He would understand what it meant, an ordinary day. That was all any of them ever wanted. And now, today, here it was at last.

When she arrived home, she called out to her mom, "Hey!" and with that her ordinary day cracked and splintered.

*

It was her mom who had found him.

"I could feel something was wrong. The lights were on all day," she told Evie. "And they're never on all day. Every morning by eleven, he always turns them off. Every day. I've been watching him. Keeping an eye on him."

At three in the afternoon, she had gone over and found the door locked. She had knocked and knocked but there was no response. She had called his name, but again, there was silence. Then she remembered the spare key in the kitchen drawer and she had rushed home to get it.

It took her four attempts to get the key in the lock, her hands were shaking so much, because she knew, she just knew—something was wrong, something terrible.

When she pushed open the door she almost didn't dare go inside. But she forced herself to look. And there he was, lying crumpled on the floor. On his side, thank God. The vomit pooled around him, but there was enough color in his cheeks for Carole to see that he had not choked.

She had checked his pulse and his breathing, then called an ambulance. In the minutes while she waited, she went looking, but it didn't take her long to find the evidence. A bottle of bourbon. A bottle of pills. Something on prescription, but she had no idea what it was. And there, amid the mess of it all, was the easel and the painting set within it. The apparent reason for this attempt at self-destruction. She had looked at it and not understood at first, had picked out the familiar shape of the landscape, the mountains and valleys, the pine forest rising up the sides of the hills, but all of it disfigured and partly concealed by a barrage of newspaper clippings. All those terrible, scandalous words that had been thrown at them in the press. He had clipped them from the papers and arranged them on the canvas like a collage. And splashed over it all, in thick, wild brushstrokes, the unmistakable color of fire and blood.

She panicked then and feared the damage he might have done to himself.

The ambulance had driven him to hospital, but she had not gone with them.

"My daughter will be home soon," she explained. "I need to wait for her."

And that was how Evie found her, sat in the gloom of the kitchen, waiting.

"It's your father," was all she said when Evie walked in.

Then they had taken the car and started the long drive to the hospital where they had waited and waited until finally a doctor came out to tell them Andrew was stable and that they should come back tomorrow when he would be well enough to see them.

*

When they got home, word had spread already. There was a rumor even that Andrew was dead, and a slow procession of visitors had arrived intent on consoling them.

Evie was too tired and shell-shocked to join in the conversations going on around her.

"He's alive. Oh, that's so good to hear, Carole…"

"If there's anything we can do…"

"So shocking all of this. Poor Andrew…"

"It's been too much for him…"

Her mother had nodded and said nothing in reply. Had accepted their sympathy with a quiet fortitude Evie knew hid her true feelings. She had waited for them all to leave before she allowed the tears to flow.

"We should never have left him alone like that," Carole told her. "God knows what he was thinking all this time, cooped up there alone like that. Why was I so stupid, Evie? Why didn't I just go to him?"

Evie needed to remind her that he had been the one who had pushed them away.

"Have you forgotten?" Evie asked her. "Every time anyone knocked on that studio door, he shooed them away. He was the one who demanded to be left alone."

"I know, but… do you really think he wanted to die? Does he really think we can't get through this?" her mom asked her.

Evie had no answer to that. "I don't know," she said.

When her mom started to cry, Evie had leaned across to touch her, but she shrugged Evie off, stood up and headed upstairs to her bedroom. The click of the door as she closed it sounded like the answer to Evie.

"Yes, he really did want to die."

*

They had driven back to the hospital in silence. A two-hour drive, but neither of them could speak, their thoughts too jumbled up. They needed the time to gather themselves together.

When her mom had asked her if she was sure she wanted to go, Evie had said yes, without hesitation.

"Okay," her mom had said. "But let me see him first. I don't want you to see him if he's a mess."

"But what about you, won't it be hard for you to take it?" Evie asked.

"He didn't give me any choice," Carole replied.

It was such a strange, curt sort of reply that Evie was silenced by it. It was only later she realized she should have asked her: *Why are you so angry with him?*

*

He was groggy, but okay. No tubes, no machines, nothing terrifying.

"Hey, Dad," Evie said when she walked over to him. "You okay?"

And he nodded.

"He's a bit disoriented still," her mom explained. "So he can't say very much."

"Right, I see."

For a while they sat there staring at one another, and Evie could feel it already. The unspoken words which were building up and expanding into the silence, pushing and pushing at it until the tension became too great. Something would have to give.

Once a nurse came in and said she needed to run some checks and they had moved away from the bed and watched as she adjusted a canula in her dad's hand and made some notes.

The sight of that needle in his skin, the thickness of the vein, so blue and sinewy, made her turn away and walk over to the window. There was something vulnerable about him. His physical fragility there for everyone to see. Skin so thin, so pale, you could count the pulse there in his vein if you wanted to. You could see how weak it was, the beat, beat, beat which kept him alive.

The beat he had wanted to stop.

When the nurse left, Evie went back to his bedside and took his hand in hers, the hand with the needle in it.

"Does it hurt?" she asked him.

No," he whispered.

Then: "Did you really want to die?"

And he looked her in the eye. "Yes," he said. And his voice was stronger.

It took her mom a few minutes to react. She had leaned back in her chair. Stared at him. And he had turned to face her and stared back. But before Evie could say anything, before she could intervene and apologize for asking the question, her mom spoke.

"You would do that to us?"

He didn't reply.

"My God," she continued, "you would do that. Pile suffering on suffering. Why?"

"I'm sorry," Evie said. "I should never have asked him that. I don't know why I did. I'm sorry—"

"No," Carole replied, "maybe it's a good thing you did."

His voice was difficult to hear at first. It was faint and dry and cracked. A broken whisper. "I can't face it any longer, Carole. That poor boy. That poor boy…"

It took them a minute to understand he was talking about Michael.

"Your dying can't bring him back."

He had said something in reply, but his voice was so fractured, so small, they could barely hear it.

They were leaning over him and asking, "What did you say?" when the nurse came back and told them it was time to go.

"That poor boy. That poor boy."

Evie struggled to make it out and it was only on the drive home that she had finally deciphered her father's whisper.

That phrase. She had heard it before.

Her father, standing over that hole in the ground, burying a box. Burying his memories of Michael. Hoping he could hide it all away. Hoping if he buried it deep, it would not be able to hurt him.

CHAPTER THIRTY

March 2015

The doorbell rang and shattered the peace which had settled over the house. When Evie opened the door, Ryan didn't smile at her. He was brisk and efficient.

"Hello, Evie. Is Ethan home? I was hoping to have a word with him."

"Ryan, come in. I guess you're here about that business in the bar last night?"

"Among other things."

"Right."

She led him into the living room and told him to make himself at home.

"He's upstairs. I'll just go and get him. Do you want a cup of coffee?"

"No, I'm fine thanks."

"Wait, is this official?"

"It's only official if I think it needs to be. I need to hear Ethan's account first."

She didn't hear him come downstairs and was surprised to find him standing behind her.

"Hey, Ryan," Ethan said. "What do you want to talk to me about?"

"I need to talk to Ethan alone, Evie. You don't mind, do you?" Ryan asked her.

But Ethan didn't give her the opportunity to reply. He took her by the elbow and led her to the kitchen.

"Maybe you can get us some coffee or something?"

"I already offered. He doesn't want any."

"Oh, right."

"He's here on official business apparently."

And it was a warning to him. A quick way of alerting him to the fact that he needed to pay attention and think about what he said. She knew Ryan was here for more than just the stupid argument over at the pub. Nothing had happened that evening to really warrant a complaint. Whatever Ryan was here for, Ethan needed to be prepared for it.

The door clicked shut but she could just make out Ethan ask, "So what's this all about then, Ryan?"

She wanted to stay there and listen in, but her mom came out of the kitchen and saw her standing there.

"Who was that?" she asked.

"Ryan. He wants to talk to Ethan about something."

"That business in the bar last night? Oh, that's just stupid, nothing happened!"

And Carole walked toward her and reached out to open the door, but Evie pulled her hand away.

"No, don't. He wants to talk to Ethan alone. I don't think he's here just because of last night."

Her mom paled and her eyes widened. She was trying to quickly think through all the reasons Ryan could be there.

"Let's just give them a minute, okay? If it's anything serious then Ethan will tell us," Evie reassured.

"If it wasn't something serious then there'd be no need to close the door and keep us outside," her mom replied.

She was about to lead her away, but her mom was too fast for her—the panic gave her an unexpected force and energy. She pushed past Evie and into the room.

"Mom?" she heard Ethan say.

"What's this all about, Ryan?" Carole asked.

"Just a quiet visit is all," Ryan replied. "It won't take long."

"Mom, why don't you go for a walk with Evie and I'll tell you all about it when you get back?" Ethan said.

"That's a good idea," Evie added, "and it's nice out."

"Mrs. McCallister, we won't be long, I promise," Ryan said. "I just need to ask Ethan a few questions, that's all."

"Fine, then I guess I'll have to leave you to it," Carole replied. She left the room and headed upstairs, tutting at Evie as she passed by: "*It's nice out*! Seriously? I'm not a child, Evie." The clunk of her bedroom door as she shut it, emphatic in its irritation.

*

When Ryan left, Ethan was pale, as if the conversation had defeated him in some way. She asked him to talk to her, but instead he just shrugged and asked where Carole was.

"Upstairs," she told him.

He headed straight upstairs and she felt so disappointed. There he was, confiding in Carole again. And she wondered why it was he expected her to trust him, when he seemed to have so little faith in her.

She heard the door open and click shut, and Ethan and Carole talking quietly. It was clear they didn't want her to hear what they were talking about.

But she needed to know. She had a right to know. They couldn't keep shutting her out like this. So she headed upstairs, determined to make them tell her what was going on.

When she heard their whispers at the top of the stairs, and she could just make out what they were saying, she realized she would learn more if she stayed behind the door, listening. If they didn't trust her, then she would have to find out like this. They'd left her with no choice.

"I've been wondering," Ethan said. "Maybe I should just have come home straight away?"

"There's no point in thinking that, Ethan. You needed time to adjust and think things through. We both did."

"I feel as though I wasted the last year, though. And I wish Dad was here to help. This is all his problem as much as it is mine. But now it's too late."

"We needed that time to figure out what to do, you know that. Don't you remember how long it took me to get used to the truth when you told me what had happened to Michael? Something that big, you can't just spring it on people. We were right to take our time and try to figure out how to go about it. If your dad hadn't died, we would have had the time, but his accident left us with no choice."

She wasn't sure she'd heard him correctly. A *year*? He'd only been out for a few months, surely? Wasn't that what her mom had told her? It was all she could do to stop herself from bursting through the door right then and demand Ethan explain himself.

"Maybe we need to trust Evie more," Ethan said. "Just tell her more. All this softly, softly approach, it's getting us nowhere."

"No, Ethan, please wait. She's not ready. You have to trust me on this."

"Are you sure?"

"You've seen what's been happening to her, it's exactly what I was worried would happen. She's vulnerable, and you know the truth could throw her off balance."

What truth?

She gripped the handrail of the staircase and held it tight, closing her eyes in the hope she could focus on their conversation. They had come here with a plan and had kept it from her all this time. And all her hopes they would find their way back to one another, that Andrew's death would somehow bring them a little closer and help them deal with the past, felt hopeless and deluded then, and she didn't know if she could carry on listening.

"I do," she heard Ethan say. "But I just don't know if it's worth it anymore. For Evie, I mean. It's going to cause her too much pain, isn't it?"

"Not if we handle it correctly. Trust me, Ethan. We can do it. If you still want to, we can do it."

"I don't know anymore… I don't know…"

"Ethan, why is it you came back here? What is it you want Evie to know? Remind yourself of that."

He was silent for a while, and then, "I want her to know that I didn't kill Michael. I want her to know the truth."

His voice was so clear and strong. His statement so matter of fact that it left no doubt. He believed what he had said. He believed it completely and with a conviction that she knew he would act upon.

"And are you sure that's still what you want?" Carole asked him.

"Yes, but will she believe me? That's what I want to know. I need to be sure of that, *really* sure of it, because if she's never going to believe me, then there's no point in any of this. I'm not here to hurt people or turn their lives upside down."

"Do you remember the trial? How shocked Evie was when you changed your plea? She always wondered why you did that, because it was clear the evidence was too circumstantial, and the testimonies were too conflicting. She was convinced the court would let you off. And then you changed your plea. Just like that. With no warning and no explanation. And she always said it made no sense. She always thought you would have been acquitted. Until you pleaded guilty, she thought you were innocent. She *believed* you were innocent. Even when she was grieving for Michael, even when she felt so hopeless about everything, she could never believe you killed him. And I think, deep down, she knows the truth."

"You sound so sure of that. Are you?"

Was it true? Evie thought. *Did I think Ethan was innocent until he changed his plea?* A piece of her wasn't sure. A piece of her remembered the doubt she had.

But Carole continued, as if she had to convince Ethan. "She could never quite believe you could do something so violent. And to Michael? No, that never made sense to her. And I'm sure she still thinks that."

"Then why did she never say anything? Why did she block it all out?"

"What could she say? That she had a *feeling* they'd got it wrong? No evidence, just a feeling. What good would that have done? And besides, she was so confused and upset, everything she remembered so incoherent. And you just stood up in court and pleaded guilty, so what was there to say? She had to accept that she had got it wrong, that you were guilty, despite what her intuition told her."

"And now?"

"I can feel her edging closer to us, Ethan. I really can."

She heard Ethan take a breath then and exhale, slowly. If she were in the room, she knew she would see his hands were shaking.

Then he spoke. "But that means we have to make her remember. That means we have to make her understand that she knows more than she thinks."

"We always knew that, Ethan."

"And the risks? We've seen what's happening to her. Do you really still think we should do it? Do you still think we should put her through that? As her mother, can you? Because, as her brother, I'm not sure I can. Not anymore."

"But she's close to the truth already. I remember the way she insisted for so long that she saw Michael in the woods, even though everyone told her it was impossible. But that was what she kept repeating. He was in the woods with her and he was bleeding. She remembers him being there."

Evie sank to her knees and steadied herself on the handrail before sitting on the top step of the staircase. A flash of blue flickered in her mind and she couldn't make it go away. Michael's blue eyes, fresh and bright as the sea one minute, and then black as an onyx the next. She wished they would stop talking just long enough for her to blink it away. Just long enough for her to push him to the back of her mind again. *Michael.* Why did they have to mention him? But they kept on talking, unaware that she was sitting there listening.

"Mom, I've spoken to her and she still doesn't remember what she saw that day. She's as vague about it now as she was then. And you must remember the state she was in when Dad brought her home. She was terrified. She could hardly speak. We might not like it that she can't remember, but she's not lying about it. She's not faking any of this."

"I know. But she understands there was a reason she ran from the lake. She knows she was in that forest with Michael. It will be there, somewhere."

"She spent years talking to therapists, trying to get over what happened to her—and trying to remember. If she'd seen Michael, then a therapist would have uncovered it, don't you think?"

"I don't know… I always thought she should have kept going to therapy. She was so close to figuring it out, then your dad stopped her going. She would have remembered given enough time and support, I'm sure of it." She heard her mother pause and sigh as if she needed to catch her breath before she could continue. "I saw it happen, time and time again. She'd come so close to grasping it, but then just as she was about to remember, some sort of self-preservation would kick in and she'd block it out again. She didn't want to see. She didn't want to know. But she has to see it, Ethan. She has to know."

"Before I came back, I thought the same. But now I've seen what it can do to her… the trauma, it never leaves, does it? The fire. Michael's death. What she saw that day. She never recovered from it. All that therapy was to help her cope. What happened was terrible and she was right to try and forget it. To trigger it, could we really live with that?"

"Ethan, I saw that cottage go up in flames with Michael in it. I was there through all that therapy, all those blackouts. Do you honestly think I don't understand what it did to her? But I'm not wrong about this, Ethan. I know I'm not. I know we can get her to understand what happened."

"I don't want her to be hurt is all. She's been through enough. We should be careful before we start opening up old wounds, that's all I'm saying."

"And we will be, Ethan. We will be."

Evie heard the change in her mother's voice, how softly she spoke, how slowly. As if she wasn't sure at all. She would try to take care, but she had no idea what was going to happen. Evie wondered then what difference it made. If you opened an old wound carefully or carelessly, the effect was always the same, was it not? It still bled.

"Damn it," Ethan said. "Why did Dad have to die? He should be here, helping us with this."

"I don't know if he would have been able to help us, for what it's worth."

"You mean he wouldn't have wanted to help us."

"No, I mean I don't think he was in a good place is all, psychologically. He wouldn't have coped with it."

"Are you defending him?"

"No, Ethan. Not at all. But you should listen to me when I try to explain what he was like, toward the end."

"He knew what he did, Mom. Why deny it?"

"I'm not denying it. He did know what he did. And it destroyed him." Carole sighed and paused for a moment before continuing, "Did you know they always commemorated it?"

"What?"

"Michael's death…"

"What's that got to do with anything?"

"I mean your dad and Evie. They remembered him on their own too, they had their own little private ceremony. I think it was Andrew's way of trying to help Evie get over it."

"What do you mean?"

"They went to the forest every year, just the two of them, up to where the cabins used to stand, and laid some flowers. Andrew thought it would help Evie come to terms with it. To go back there and face it. He also thought if she started to associate that place with something other than Michael's death, it would make it all seem less terrifying. I think it might have been the therapist's idea to give the place a different meaning, something more positive."

"Dad took flowers to the forest for Michael? Seriously?"

"Your father was a good man, Ethan. Things like that, remembering the dead, meant something to him. He was touched by all this too and you have to accept that."

"Okay. It just seems a bit weird."

"Everyone deals with these things in their own way. There's nothing weird about needing a ritual. But it gives you an idea of his state of mind. He didn't ever forget what happened. He suffered because of it."

"He was only doing it because of Evie. He just wanted to make sure she never remembered."

"I know that, Ethan. But he did what he thought was right at the time. He was trying to protect her."

"And what about me? What about protecting his son? While he protected her too much."

"He thought he was taking care of her, that's all he wanted to do."

"I know. But what about everyone else? Why did we have to suffer because of it? Why was it always just Evie with him?"

"I don't know, Ethan. I can't speak for him. But his intentions—"

"They were not good, Mom. He thought they were. Shit, so did I in the beginning. But they weren't good, and people have to understand the suffering he caused."

"So we keep going then?"

"Yes, I guess so. We keep going."

Evie sat on the stair and listened and felt her head begin to swirl and her vision begin to blur. She remembered those visits to the forest with her dad and the way they had made her feel, the apprehension she was never allowed to express because it would have upset him if she had done so. Ethan was right when he said Andrew wanted to help her forget what happened in those woods, and she had wanted her dad to believe that he was succeeding.

Those annual trips were meant to be therapeutic, so she never told him how they made her feel. The way her legs would tremble, and her head would fill with noise and fuzz. The way a hot flush of acid would burn in her gut. The way she'd have to conjure up that image of the sea Dr. Newton had taught her to use. She had to let the waves wash over her and sometimes she thought she would be swept away by the force of her panic and the conviction that she was going to die.

And now there it was again, that terrible familiar feeling. That awful panic. She had to get away from it. Far away. But the azure calm wouldn't come, she couldn't recall it. There was no sea. There was no beach, there was no calm, there was no peace, not this time. And so she ran again. She ran, as she always did. Back to the place she knew would provide some sort of answer. Back to the forest.

*

There, among the twigs and the leaves and the dirt, she scrapped away the soil with frantic fingers. Her fingernails raw and bleeding with the effort of it, but the pain was not enough to make her stop. Because there was something there, under the ground. Something lay buried.

A commemoration.

That word. It had rushed at her. Like a punch to the head, between the eyes.

She had left the house and run into the forest. One moment she was sitting on the stairs listening, the next she was on her knees in the clearing. This was where Michael had died. She was sure of it now. What she had seen that day. It was no traumatic hallucination. Michael had been there in the forest and he was dead before he was burned in the fire.

In the mud, her fingers scraped against something hard and metallic. She pulled at it and dug around it, loosening the soil and slowly working it free.

The metal box her father had buried, untarnished despite the years. The seal of thick black paint protecting it from the elements, from the years underground. The lock snapped shut and the dial waiting for the code to be turned. The contents, safe still, until those four digits could be remembered.

She remembered her father burying that box in the ground, filling it with mementos every year. It became their pilgrimage. On the anniversary of Michael's death, they went there together and thought of him, remembered him.

Every year, he dug down to where it lay. Each year a little dirtier, a little more battered and worn, but a safe place despite the elements. It had always amazed her when he turned the dial on the lock and she heard the grind of it, then the gentle click as it opened without complaint. Just that one year he had needed to replace it. And inside, the contents, wrapped in plastic and sealed in their tin, seemed to have remained untouched. Her father would take them out, one by one and examine them, and only when he seemed pleased that nothing had changed, that no damage had occurred, only then did he place them back and add one new item.

Strange things, always. Things she never questioned him about, though. Nor did she bring any items of her own. Over the years she had watched him add these curios to the box. Trinkets was what she called them, because that was what they were, little meaningless things. Though she never told him this; his reverence was too sincere, his need for the ritual too great. Year by year he gave himself over to a superstition he had always prided himself in not possessing.

She could list each item still, she realized, and list them in the order they had gone in the box. One for each of the years she had gone with him. Ten years in total, until it became too much for her. The ritual too obsessive and morbid and strange. Too sad.

Ten years. Ten items.

A blue ceramic bird. A silver whistle. A polished onyx. A wooden bear. A glass dolphin. A silver dollar. A swatch of tartan. A leather bookmark. A thumb-sized music box that played 'Claire de Lune.' A Saint Christopher medal.

He saw something of Michael in each of these things. But she never had. And if she had dared, she would have asked him why he chose these things, asked him why he needed to open that box each year and check on them, and add a new offering.

Though a part of her knew the answer to that. Because she remembered his face when he lifted each item from the box and examined it. The relief there, the joy even, when he saw it had survived another year, undamaged, unbroken. She didn't need a psychologist to explain to her why he needed to control things this way. To have things unchanged and renewed each year. People preserved the memory of the saints in much the same way. Made the dead immortal, untouchable. This was his shrine to Michael.

It was once she had understood this that she had stopped going with him.

Michael was dead. And that was a fact they all needed to accept and learn to live with. There was no ritual that could bring him back. No magic that could be the undoing of any of it.

His mourning of Michael in this way was almost as a punishment, she thought now. A way of making good the damage which had been done.

Every year, after their visit, he would call Michael's parents and offer his condolences. Tell them they had paid their respects to him again. Never quite asking for forgiveness, though that was what he wanted. To hear them say it. Categorically. With no doubt. But all they ever did was thank him and ask perfunctory questions and wish him well. Too polite to ever let the phone go unanswered, even though they knew it would be him. Too devastated still to understand they had a right to deny him the comfort he demanded from them.

Evie fell back and lay on the ground, the box clutched to her chest.

Above, the sky was gray, the light dim. It was raining, she realized, and dusk was drawing near.

How long have I been here?

But she had no way of knowing. The morning already felt like another day. The overheard conversation something she imagined.

It was only that word, "commemoration," which let her know she was not imagining any of it. The dead weight of the box on her chest, another tangible reminder that what Ethan had said was true.

There was something she needed to remember. Something she'd forgotten. Something she didn't ever want to see again. Only now she had no choice. And she screamed at the sky. A sound as shrill as the screech of an eagle.

A sound that was carried by the breeze and lifted into the air. A sound that echoed out across the mountains and the lake.

CHAPTER THIRTY-ONE

August 1996

When the second anniversary of Michael's death came round, she knew what her father would do. He would head to the forest, back to that box he had buried. She had never told him she had seen him in the forest almost a year ago, but when she asked if she could join him, he had looked at her and understood, then nodded.

"Okay, if you think you need to."

They'd headed up the mountain path after lunch, Evie carrying a small bouquet she had fashioned from some flowers from the garden. Her father took nothing.

"I'll say a few words," was all he said when Evie suggested he should bring something too.

At the top of the path, just before it swung left toward the clearing, her father stopped and turned to face her. He looked somber and gray, and for the first time, Evie saw the doubt there on his face. Now that they were close by, he wasn't sure if it was a good idea. He was nervous.

"I've come up here quite a few times, this past year," Andrew said.

"You have? Why?"

"I don't know exactly. Maybe I still need to convince myself that it all really happened."

Evie didn't know why he would feel the need for that. The pain and confusion were the same wherever you were, surely? Even on those days when she thought she was finally free of it, when she realized there had been moments during the day when she hadn't thought about Michael, even on those good days, the pain would make an unexpected entrance and leave her beaten and cowed.

"But it did happen. We can't pretend otherwise," she said.

"I know. I just… this place. I don't want you to walk in there thinking it won't affect you. Because it will and maybe not in a good way, and… well, I'm no expert when it comes to these things."

"It was Dr. Newton who suggested it, remember? Exposure therapy, she called it."

He smiled at her.

"Yeah, well, she probably meant that she should take control of that, and anyway, you know what I think about all that therapy."

"A waste of time?"

"No, it's just, I'm not sure it's really helping you. Those episodes you have, they're not going away, are they?"

"They're not getting any worse either though."

"True…"

"Talking about it, writing things down makes it feel less frightening sometimes, like it's something I can learn to control. It might not look like it's helping, but it is, even if I can only manage to take small steps forward."

"Well, that's a good thing, isn't it?"

"Yeah, it is."

"But this though, this is something different. It's not just talking. This is actually walking back in there and I just want you to be prepared."

"What did you feel the first time you came back here?"

He exhaled and looked up, as if there was something there among the trees that had captured his attention. This was always the way he was when he was being forced to talk about something he would rather ignore. Talking into space made it easier for him. It was a strange, almost childlike trait, Evie always thought. As if he thought that by not looking at you, by not seeing you, he was talking to himself and revealing nothing.

"You know I'm not the superstitious sort, Evie," he began. "The world is as you find it."

He paused, waiting for her to react, but she couldn't think of anything to say, and she wasn't sure where this was heading.

He shook his head and looked around, still avoiding her gaze, still troubled by his lack of ability to express himself clearly. Downhill, a fallen tree trunk lay flat across the forest floor, the bark covered over with moss and sprouting ferns. Andrew headed toward it and sat down, then looked at her and waited for her to come and sit beside him.

She walked over and sat down and was surprised when he took hold of her hand. His grip was firm, and she felt he needed to hold her hand because he needed her support before he could say it.

"Are you okay?" she asked him.

"Yes, I just need to find a way to explain it. I'm not good at this sort of thing."

"You know," she said. "Some people think there's an energy that's left behind when something bad happens, and that you can feel it."

"Are you telling me you believe in ghosts?"

"I don't know if I would call it that, though I guess some people would."

"It's just their own emotions, that's what I think," he said.

"Huh?"

"What they're feeling. The 'energy' is just their own reaction. But they get mixed up, start thinking the fear they sense is something supernatural."

"I'm not going to walk in there and start believing I can sense a ghostly presence, if that's what you're thinking."

And he laughed and put his arm around her.

"I'm glad to hear it."

"So shall we go then?"

She got ready to stand up, but he held her back and said, "No, wait a second."

"Why?"

"What I wanted to say was, you feel it again."

"What?"

"Everything you felt that day. It floods you. Comes back to you. And it can feel like it's happening again. That's what I wanted to explain, I suppose. You remember it all. And I mean all of it. And I just need to know that you're able to deal with it."

"What makes you think I'll react the same way as you did?"

"Maybe you won't. But I just want you to know what's possible. Because it's different for you, isn't it?"

"Is it? Why?"

He looked at her for the first time then, as if she confused him. As if he didn't quite know who she was.

"I don't know what you did or didn't see that day, Evie. Maybe Michael was here. Maybe he wasn't. You say you saw him lying here, and… well, what if it happens again? What if you see that again?"

It worried her that he would say such a thing. And the tone of his voice, his seriousness, made her nervous too, because it sounded as if he considered it a realistic possibility. She *had* seen Michael that day. She *did* know more than she remembered. And she wanted to say something, but he carried on talking before she had the chance to speak.

"Shit," he said. "Maybe this isn't a good idea. I should never have asked you to come here, what the fuck was I thinking? You've come so far. The attacks aren't as bad, and you've been able to put it out of your mind more often. I shouldn't put all of that at risk."

He rarely swore, and to hear him curse was a shock. His emotions had taken over him and loosened his tongue, and it made her uncomfortable because, more and more often, when she looked at him, she wasn't sure she recognized him.

"Dad," she said. "I've spent a year talking about it, a year learning how to contain it. And that's the first step to learning how to cope with it, that's how you learn to function. Bit by bit, step by step. That's what they make you do, the psychologists. They never give you the chance to forget how it made you feel. I confront this every week, every time I set foot in that room with Dr. Newton."

"So you think you can do it?"

"I won't know until I do it. There's no other way to find out."

"Okay. But can I ask you something first?"

"Sure."

"The doctor, she mentioned something, a while back."

"Yeah?"

"She said you were telling the truth when you said you don't remember anything."

"Yeah, she says it's possible."

"Right… and…"

"Do I agree with her?"

"Do you?"

"I think so. I mean, it's true, isn't it? I don't remember anything. And knowing why I can't remember makes it easier, it makes me feel less of a freak."

"Oh, Evie, you're not a 'freak.' Please tell me you don't think that."

"Okay, maybe not. It's just sometimes I think people are waiting for me to have some sudden awakening or something. They think there must be something wrong with me, that my amnesia—or whatever you want to call it—is just some temporary blip. I know Mom is waiting for me to say something. She still believes I can help Ethan. And I feel so guilty about it. Because I want to remember so badly. I want to help him. But there's a reason why I don't remember anything. I know there is."

"You say that as if there is a possibility you did see something."

"Yeah, well, maybe I did. I mean it's possible, isn't it?"

"Okay, listen, Evie, you don't need to go through all of this. There's no point to it. Ethan admitted what he did."

"I know, but—"

"You don't think he's innocent then, do you?"

"Honestly? I don't know."

"But you think it's possible he didn't do it?"

"It's more that I just never imagined he could do a thing like that. Can you?"

"I can't imagine it, no, but I also have to accept that maybe I just don't know my own son."

"But you know he'd never have hurt Michael, don't you? He meant something to Ethan. I know he did. And he meant something to me too. I know how Ethan felt, Dad. And when I think of that, there's a doubt I can't shake off."

"All I know is that whatever argument they had, it ended in that cabin, and maybe we don't need to know any more than that."

He was right, when you stood aside and looked at the facts, there really was only one explanation for it. She knew then that if she had any doubts, they were born of wishful thinking, from wanting things to be different. She wanted Michael to be alive still and she wanted her brother to be home with them. She wanted their futures to unfold just as they'd imagined they would.

"Sometimes I keep hoping it's still all going to work out," she said. "I don't know why. I mean it's never going to work out is it? The dead can't be brought back to life. Michael's never coming back. Ethan's never going to be released."

"You wish for that?"

"I just wish it had never happened."

"We all wish that, Evie."

"Yeah, but maybe you need to force yourself to accept things sometimes. If I go back there I can hardly pretend it didn't happen, can I?"

"Is that what you've been doing then? Pretending?"

"Or just avoiding the truth because I don't want to believe it."

"He did it, Evie. You know that, don't you? We might not want to believe it, but Ethan did this."

"Yeah, I know. I just don't want to believe it."

She didn't tell him the doubt remained. She didn't tell him she was nowhere near as certain as she seemed. She didn't tell him that the voice in her head was loud and clear, *Did he though, Evie? Did he?*

Instead she took his hand when he held it out to her and nodded when he asked her one last time: "Are you sure?" Then they walked into the forest together.

She could feel her heart racing, her breath quickening, and she squeezed Andrew's hand as they walked deeper into the forest. It was darker there, under the canopy, and she hesitated a little as she walked, waiting for her eyes to adjust to the gloom, scared of tripping over a tree root or a hidden boulder.

When they arrived at the clearing, she stared at the ground. It was soft and moist, the green of the moss too vibrant somehow, as if the ground had been nourished by what had happened here. Overhead, the breeze caught the branches and rustled the trees and she caught the smell of the pines, fresh and clean and again, too invigorating. She shook her head.

"You okay?" her dad asked her. She felt his hand tighten its grip, felt the panic as it flooded through him.

"It looks so calm, is all," she said.

And she looked around and tried to take it all in.

They were just trees, she thought. It was just moss. The stones, the pinecones, the caw of a bird, the brush of the breeze. Everything was as it should be. She had been too wary to admit to him that she had been expecting ghosts. Too embarrassed to admit that she did believe that bad energy could be transferred in some way. That the horror of what had happened here would always be felt in the things which remained. The moss could remember the blood as it soaked into the ground. The trees could recall the screams which had shuddered through their branches. The stones still contained the energy of the fire as it cracked and splintered the wood of the cabins.

She believed all this, and she expected to feel it again.

"I don't feel anything," she told him.

"Well, maybe that's a good thing."

"I should feel something though. I mean, what happened here. How can I not feel that?"

And she leaned against him and allowed him to wrap his arms around her.

"Don't mistake that for not feeling sad about it, Evie."

"But you felt something though. You said so."

"I felt overwhelmed, that's what I felt."

"Is that what this is then? Am I so overwhelmed I can't feel anything?"

"It's whatever you need it to be, Evie. Don't think too much. Just let it come."

It was then she remembered the flowers she had plucked from the roadside that morning. When she pulled them out of her backpack, they were crushed and wilted, and she wished she had taken more time to buy a proper wreath or something.

"God," she said as she held them. "It's almost an insult to leave these here. I mean, look at them, they're pathetic."

"Come on," her dad said. "Don't be so harsh on yourself. You picked them yourself. That means something. More than any fancy bouquet or wreath."

She looked at the wilted flowers and sighed before placing them on the ground.

"We should say something, I suppose," Andrew said.

"I don't know if I can. Will you do it?"

"Okay."

They stood there for a moment waiting for Andrew to find the right words. And while he hesitated, she made a little speech in her head. A brief, sad eulogy for someone she still loved and missed deeply.

Until then, his absence had been an abstract sort of thing. There was just this emptiness. A space where Michael had once been. The space she was waiting for him to fill again. But there was no filling it and she needed to accept that now, with all her being.

She also found herself silently pleading. "He didn't mean to hurt you, Michael. Please believe me when I say that."

And then, a voice, or perhaps it was the screech of a bird as it flew overhead, or the rush of wind brushing past her ears.

Or a ghost after all, deep inside her, in that black space they kept telling her was empty. Only it wasn't, was it? It contained something. It contained the voice of a dead boy. A dead boy who was confronting her with a question.

If you believe he couldn't do it, she heard him say, *then you know what that means, Evie. You know what that means.*

But who else could have done this to you? she thought. *Who could have been so cruel?*

There was a menacing tone to the reply. A tone that made her stomach clench and her heart skip a beat.

Oh, you know who, Evie. You know.

CHAPTER THIRTY-TWO

March 2015

Commemoration.

All day that word lingered. Carole and Ethan's conversation on repeat in her head, the drum of it something physical. It throbbed in her temple, behind her eyes, a pressure from which there was no relief. Eyes closed, eyes opened, it made no difference. It was like a reflex she could neither stop nor control.

She sat alone in her room and tried to remember. Something, anything. She had run. Run to the forest. And she smelled it then, the sharp smell of pine, the damp mossy smell of earth. And when she looked at her hands, she saw the dirt there, under her fingernails. Dirt from digging.

The box, she thought. She smelled the dirt under her fingernails again. Yesterday, she had been there, back in the clearing. She had retrieved the box and its contents, worn now and most of it disintegrated to the point where it was impossible to recognize the objects. And the sight of all those damaged things, those precious things her father had taken so much care over, had filled her with overwhelming sadness.

Finding the box and objects again, feeling them, brought back something else. In the blackness, emptied of everything, there was a tiny speck of light now. A memory? She couldn't quite grasp it. But that light, that tiny speck, was illuminating something, and it was giving shape and form to all the things that had been hiding in the darkness. And now she had to choose.

Give it air to grow or snuff the flame between finger and thumb and let in the darkness in forever.

*

The house was quiet, and Ethan and her mom were still sleeping when Evie made her way downstairs. Outside, the sky was only just beginning to brighten, and the darkness made everything seem calmer than it was.

For an instant, she allowed herself to imagine the morning was just like any other before her father had died, and before Ethan had returned. She could make herself coffee and sit by the window watching the sunlight fill the sky, and think about all the small, mundane things that needed to be done, enjoying how uncomplicated life could be.

She now wanted those days to return, for her mother and brother to be gone, for the past to retreat to that dark corner of her memory where she never shone a light. She would snuff out the flame. She had to.

Most of all, she wanted the chance to grieve for her father, and to think about the things she missed about him, the small ways she loved him. She wanted to go to his graveside and set down some flowers, then sit there for a while and talk to him, tell him what had happened and what she thought about it all.

She wanted time to think about the future and who she wanted in it. Her mother? Her brother? Did she want them around? Did she need them? The natural answer should be yes, but she felt the hesitation there, the doubt, and wondered if, in her case, life would be easier if she spent it alone.

When the coffee was made, she poured herself a cup and headed to the living room. Things may have changed, but she could still sit in the window and watch the day begin.

From the hallway window, she saw the mailbox flag was raised, and she went outside and emptied it and took the letters with her into the living room, then sat in the window seat and shuffled through them, sorting out the junk from the bills.

She wasn't prepared to see her father's handwriting and had to read it twice to be sure what she was seeing was real. The handwriting, the familiar rushed slant, there was no mistaking it. But what confused her was that it was addressed to Ethan.

She couldn't figure it out. A letter for Ethan, it made no sense. How could Andrew have known Ethan would be here? When she looked at the date stamp, she saw it was from a few days ago.

Someone else must have posted it for him, she thought. But when she tried to think why he would do such a thing, and who would agree to post a letter on his behalf, she drew a blank.

Open it, she said to herself.

Ethan was asleep still, and he would not be expecting a letter. She could open it, read it, re-seal it and he would never know.

But her hands trembled at the thought. Not because it felt wrong to open a letter which wasn't hers, but at the thought of what might be written there. Something she was not supposed to be privy to.

No, she thought. *This is your house and you have a right to know what's going on.*

She took a few sips of coffee and waited for her hands to steady, then opened the envelope and pulled out the letter and started to read.

Dear Ethan,

By the time you read this, I'll be dead. I asked Tony at the post office to post it for me if you came home. So if you're reading this now, it means you came home after all and I can only assume it's because you plan to go through with it. And you know what I think about that. You know I can't face it.

All I can do is ask you again: please don't do it. Please just let it lie. There's nothing to be gained from any of it. It won't make up for the past. It won't make you feel better. You'll gain no peace of mind from any of this, despite what you may think. That's the lesson I've learned from all of this. There is no peace to be had. What happened to Michael, what we did to him, will always haunt us. But there is no need to hurt anyone else now. Not after all this time. So let my death be enough for you. Let that be the end of it all. Please Ethan, I'm begging you. Do it for Evie.

She leaned her head against the cool of the windowpane and let the words sink.

"*What we did to him?*" she whispered. "What do you mean?"

Outside, beyond the glass, she watched as a glimmer of light caught the ridge of the mountains and saw their shadowed shape take form as the sky brightened. And as the sun illuminated the valley, she thought she heard her father whispering a reply.

This letter was not written for you, Evie. Put it back in the envelope and leave it for Ethan.

"No!" she cried, her voice louder than she anticipated, and she gritted her teeth and listened, hoping she had not woken Ethan and Carole. But the house was silent.

"No," she whispered. "You have no say in things now."

And she lifted the letter and carried on reading.

I know you think she needs to know the truth, but I know what the truth will do to her, and if I'm right then it's something you will have already seen for yourself. Because your return will have upset the balance she's achieved, I'm sure of it. So she'll have started to lose days again, and to fall into whatever strange place it is she goes to when things become too much for her. Blackouts is what most people call them. Though it's more than that with Evie. Much more.

She'll have taken to wandering again too. Into the forest. Back to where it all started. You'll have found her there a few times now, no doubt. You'll have found her, just as I used to find her, curled up in the clearing and oblivious, and you'll think she is asleep when you first look at her, until you notice her eyes are open, until you hear her whispering. But she's not there. She may as well be asleep. You can call her name, shake her, look her in the eye, but she will not see you. All you can do is wait for her to come back to you. All you can do is carry her home, back to safety, and wait.

And when she returns, she'll have no explanation, she won't be able to tell you where she's been or who she saw or what happened to her. Though she'll be scared. Terrified even. And she has every reason to be.

Because the place she went to is the past. The place she went to is real. It existed. It happened. And we have spent years trying to forget it. Years trying to create a different history, another time and place where none of this ever happened.

And, while you were away, we were successful. I persuaded her, you see, and she trusted me, she believed me. But now that you are home again, I can only assume the edifice we built so carefully has started to crumble, and that soon, if it hasn't happened already, it will all come crashing down. Is that what you want, Ethan? Is that what you want to do to her? You told me you want to help her. But this isn't the way. It really isn't.

And once again, her father's words stopped her in her tracks. She couldn't read on. What he had written made no sense. There was no edifice, there was nothing he needed to persuade her of. Unless…

You lied to me, didn't you? About what happened that day, what I saw. You lied.

But ever since Ethan's return she had felt it coming, some sort of reckoning. And now, here it was, and it was not what she was expecting. Her father, calmly stating that she was standing on the precipice and predicting she would fall. Begging Ethan to save her. Ethan, the man her father had always insisted was something close to evil. The brother she had been told to forget and had been forced to abandon.

What did you do to me? What did you do?

I tried to keep you safe, Evie. I tried to save you.

But this didn't feel like salvation. An edifice about to crumble was not safe. And again, she asked him, her voice faltering as she spoke, the slight burning taste of bile catching in her throat and making her gag.

What did you do to me?

No answer. Save for the words on the page. Words she now had to read to the end, because she had to know. The truth. It was there, written down and she had to read it.

. . . the edifice is built on the promise we made twenty years ago, a promise you vowed you would always keep and a promise from which I have never wavered. It's a fragile foundation but until now it has stood the test of time. All Evie knows about that day is what I have told her. And if you love her the way you say you love her then this is what you will tell her too:

Michael was found in the cabin. She witnessed a fight between you and Michael, and she ran away because when she saw Michael battered and bloodied, she thought he was dead, and the trauma caused her to black out and forget everything that happened. In her mind, she created a false truth—that she had seen Michael in the forest, lying on the ground, the wound to his stomach bleeding profusely. "Like a deer," she used to say to me. "He looked like a deer." And I told her that was what it was. She was remembering the deer a cougar had killed and left there. Her mind was playing tricks on her. I made her believe that this was what she had seen that day in the woods. It was nothing more than a mistake. Different events, coming together to form one mistaken whole.

It took years for her to accept that you killed him. To really believe it, I mean. I think a piece of her has always doubted it. And yes, my reason for telling you this is simple: I want you to know that she loved you, that she trusted you; that this doubt was always there, and it persisted because she cares about you. In the end, you will always be her brother.

She remembers I found her in the clearing and brought her home. And she saw you, sitting in the kitchen with blood on your hands and there is only one way it could have got there: you killed Michael.

Over the years she has come to accept you are guilty.

I know you think that we are only guilty of protecting her, and that is true. But we are not entirely innocent either and you can't deny that Ethan, no matter how much you may want to. We lied and we covered things up. We're not so innocent.

She had to pause again and let it sink in. *We are only guilty of protecting her.* How was that possible, she thought? She shook her head, then read it again and again, but could make no sense of it. Her dad had always been so resolute, so insistent of the fact Ethan was guilty and there could be no doubt about it, and this was the story she had believed all these years. This was the only truth she recognized, and it was her dad who had made sure she believed it.

Only, it was not the truth. The story was a fabrication. A lie.

You lied to me? You lied?

No, Evie, that's not how it is.

"Shut up! Just shut up!" She closed her eyes and tried to empty her head of the noise which now threatened to overwhelm her, a buzzing growing louder and louder.

"Breathe and wait, Evie," she whispered. "Breathe and wait."

She had to read on, she knew that, but the fear of what she might learn was momentarily paralyzing. If Andrew knew, with so much certainty, that Ethan was innocent, then there could be only one explanation. It was because he knew the truth. The real truth. He knew who killed Michael. And if her father had kept that truth hidden from her for all these years, if he had preferred to go to his grave rather than reveal it, then Evie shuddered to think what it meant.

When she opened her eyes and looked down at the letter in her lap, the words were blurred and skittered across the page, and she needed to stare closely before they came back into focus. She didn't want to read what was there, but she had come so far now, and she knew she had to.

You want to know the truth, don't you? she told herself. *Then keep reading.*

You remember the state she was in when you found her in the woods, how terrified she was. The shock was so deep she barely registered your presence, as if she was in a trance, that was what you told me when you rushed home to find me. And when we returned to help her, she hadn't moved. She was just sitting there staring at her hands and rocking back and forth and neither of us could reach her.

And I know you think that what we did was wrong and believe me, there have been many times, through the years, when I have felt it too, the weight of that regret, the doubt. It came close to breaking me so many times.

But then I would remember why we did it. We did it for her. Because she didn't mean to kill him and you, more than anyone know that. That was the first thing you told me, when you saw him lying there on the ground with the wound in the side of his head, you didn't understand and you asked her:

*"What did you do, Evie?" And what was it she told you? "I
thought he would take me with him."*

And she saw a drop of blood. Michael's hair stuck to the side
of his skull as the open wound bleeds. And she remembered
something. A rock. A thud. The weight of it in her hand, the
terrible sensation of the energy as it transferred from her arm to
his head. The crack. The sound of him as he fell.

And then it rushed at her. That whole day accelerating toward
her. The sun shining and both of them baking hot.

He had asked her on the phone to meet him and she had not
been able to resist. She had disobeyed her father and sneaked
down to the lake to meet him. The days spent without him had
felt interminable and empty. She had needed to see him, needed
to touch him, to talk to him and see his smile.

She had wanted to tell him about the decision she had made
during those long days without him. She had sat in her room and
thought about all those dreams they had. To be together in California, away from the cruel, critical gaze of everyone here and free to
do what they wanted and be who they wanted. They would leave
together, that was what she had decided and that was what she told
him as they sat by the lakeshore, warm in the sun and happy again.

"Let's go," she said. "Let's go, today. You and me. Make that
trip round California and then see where life takes us."

And he had looked at her and smiled and said, "Uh-huh."

"No, I'm serious. Why not? What you said on the phone about
people freaking out here about nothing. You're right. It's crazy,
they have no right to laugh like that. So let's do it."

And he turned to face her and leaned on his elbow, still
smiling, but with a little crease there on his brow, a little wrinkle
of uncertainty. "Are you serious?"

"Yes. Deadly serious," she told him. "Honestly, Michael, I can't
stand it here anymore. Those photos, the way people look at me

now, their chattering and their laughter. It's never going to stop. They're always going to look at me that way, as a girl gone wrong. Mason did a good job of convincing them."

"Oh come on, Evie. It's not that bad. It's just a few photos. I swear, in a few weeks from now everyone will have forgotten it."

And she had looked at him and not known what to say. Because how could he not understand that it wasn't just their cruel reactions that hurt her? It was the knowledge that she would never get over the shame and embarrassment. She would be reminded of it every time she spoke to them, that glint of ridicule would always be there in their eyes. She didn't want to have to face that humiliation day after day and why should she?

"But if it's something we were going to do anyway, then why not now? Why wait?"

"What? What do you mean? What were we planning on doing?"

"The two of us, together. Our trip around California."

And she saw it then, the pity in his eyes, and understood her need for him would not be reciprocated. She had dreamed, but he had not dreamed with her.

"Evie, I'm sorry, I didn't realize that you... I mean..."

But she didn't stop to hear what he had to say. "Fuck, Michael. I thought you... I thought..."

Then she stood up and ran, the humiliation too great for her now. The need to get away from him too strong. The hurt too unfathomable.

"Evie! Please, come on!" she heard him shout. And when she turned, she saw he was running after her and she turned and ran as fast as she could. Ran to the mountain. Ran to the place where she always felt safe. Her legs burning as she pushed up the hillside.

In the clearing, she sought out the granite rock and climbed onto it and sat there, her head in her hands, and wept. She didn't hear him coming, just felt him touch her shoulder and say, "Evie,

I'm sorry. I'm so sorry." And she looked up at him and saw it there in his eyes still, that pity, that disbelief.

"No you're not, Michael. No you're not."

"Of come on, please, Evie. Don't be so… so…"

"What? Melodramatic? Foolish?"

He leaned toward her and tried to embrace her and as she pulled away, she felt the sharp edge of a rock press against her thigh and she lifted it, without thinking. Clutching it tight, because she didn't want him to touch her, she didn't want him near her. She would push him away, if she needed to.

But he didn't notice her. "That's not what I meant, Evie," he said. And again he moved toward her and she felt his hand on her shoulder, felt his breath upon her face as he leaned in closer, that smile on his face taunting her, as if he thought that was all it would take. One smile, one touch, one kiss and she would do whatever he wanted again.

"Come on," he said, his hand stroking her thigh, rising up to her hip, then her belly. "Let's just forget about it and have some fun while we still can, huh, Evie, what do you say?"

No, she thought. *Not this time, Michael.*

And she felt the weight of the rock in her hand, felt the press of his hand on her shoulder and she lifted her arm and… A dull thud to the head, the force of it rippling through the muscles in her forearm. She saw him lean back, saw his head flop to one side and his eyes roll back, before he slumped and then fell to the ground.

"Shit, Michael!" she cried. "Michael! Are you okay?"

But when she looked over the edge, he was lying on the forest floor and she called to him again and again, but there was no reply. She slid off the boulder and leaned over him, wiped the hair from his forehead and saw the blood there on his cheek, on his hands. She saw his eyes. That beautiful pale blue, bright still, for an instant, before that terrible empty black began to fill it.

And the room presses back into view as she tries to force the memory away and she sees she is there in the living room, feels the weight of the letter in her hand.

Breathe, she thinks. *Slowly. Close your eyes and take your time. Just breathe.* And she remembers the metronome and tries to catch its rhythm. *Push it all away. Forget. Forget.*

But when she opens her eyes, the letter is still there in her hand. Relentless and refusing to let her forget. Her father's handwriting drawing her in. So she has to finish reading it.

And what is it you want, Ethan? To punish her for that? For defending herself?

Because what we did was worse, far worse. And don't you forget it.

She let you lift her up and sit her down on that rock and she watched me as I stood there and thought about what to do. And, God help me, but it was a quick decision to move from thought to action. And you agreed with me. You helped me bundle him up and carry him back to the cabin. You poured on the gasoline and lit the match.

It was true, she remembered. When she saw her father hoist the body over his shoulder and prepare to take him away, she had screamed at him, "No! Don't!" and they had looked at her as if they only then remembered she was there, watching them and taking it all in. Not blind to it at all. And Ethan begging Andrew to stop.

"This is crazy, Dad. Please, stop. No one will believe it. We need to get help. Get the police."

And her father had swung round then and struck a blow so hard it had sent Ethan reeling to the ground.

"No, you listen to me. Do as you're told. This is all your fault. You should never have let her near him. I told you that. I told you!"

And then… then he was gone. They must have taken him to the cabin. Set it alight and left him there to burn. The evidence of what she had done incinerated.

She looked at the letter and tried her best to read on.

There were times when she came close to remembering. I'd see her hesitate because she'd see me, standing over him in the forest. She'd think, for one moment that she was remembering something else. Not a father trying to help his daughter, but a man inflicting damage and pain on a boy who didn't deserve it. And it would take all my energy to calm her and tell her to forget it all. To accept the judgment of those who knew better. All those people who told her there was nothing there for her remember.

And now, here we are. And I have only one thing to ask you. Keep our secret, Ethan.

And if you can't, then let me take the blame for what I did.

There's a film in the studio. An envelope with an SD card inside. Watch it and show it to whoever needs to see it. Ryan or someone like that.

And burn this letter for me, please Ethan. I'm gone now so what does it matter? And you're free to live your life. And Evie, what good would it do to harm her anymore? She's suffered enough, we all have.

So find that film and finish this. Do it for me. Do it for Evie.

Your father,
Andrew

She closed her eyes and tried to do what she had learned, to breathe slowly and regularly, to focus on that alone and wait for calm.

But it did not come. Her father's words rattled through her head and pushed away her attempts to clear her mind. The words in the letter seemed to be banging against her skull, their truth imperative and growing louder.

She repeated the truth to herself, *You did this, Evie. You did this.*

Then, the disbelief. *No! It can't be true*, she thought. *It can't be.*

It was impossible for a person to do what her father claimed she had done and then erase it from their life so comprehensively. But she could not fight the memory now. It was there, sharp and clear and inescapable—the trickle of blood, the look in Michael's eyes, that cool blue emptiness. When she had looked at him, she had thought she was going to die from heartache.

"You liar!" she said. "You liar!"

But again she caught a flash of it. What he had written there, she had come close to remembering it sometimes but she had always been so good at pushing away: her father and brother standing over Michael. A flash of red, yes, she did sometimes see that, and her father's voice soothing her, she heard that too, but she could never quite place it. Had he comforted her there in the forest? Or only later, back home? She could never get the sequencing right. Sometimes he was there with her and sometimes he was not.

And yet, there was something filtering through. A sense somewhere in her arms, in her legs, in her head that she had witnessed something in the forest that day. Something so terrible her body had needed to push it away. To hold it down and keep it from rising to the surface. She had never really needed her father to help her keep it at bay. She had always possessed the power to suppress it. Her survival had depended on it.

But whatever was on that film, she couldn't let anyone see it. *Let me take the blame for what I did.* No, she wouldn't let that happen. *Why*, she thought. *Why do you need to do this, Dad?*

Before she could catch it, she felt the bile burn in her throat and rise, then pour from her mouth and dribble down her pajamas.

"Shit! Shit!"

She wiped her mouth and headed upstairs to the bathroom and quietly washed away the vomit, then got dressed. She could hear her mother stirring and wanted to be gone before Carole woke up and went downstairs.

She wanted to go over to the studio and find that film and understand what her father was trying to do and why.

She would burn the letter. Before Ethan ever got the chance to read it. And she felt something new replace her shock and disbelief. Anger and resolve. That her father could write such a thing. No, he was wrong. He had to be wrong. And she would make sure no one ever saw that film.

CHAPTER THIRTY-THREE

March 2015

When Evie opened the door to the studio and stepped inside, she was hit by the fuggy smell of stale, heavy air. She coughed as she breathed it in and walked over to the small window at the back of the room and opened it, then fetched a hook and cranked open the skylight window too.

She could feel her father's presence in every nook and cranny. He existed there still, in the unfinished projects and the splatters of paint on the floor.

She looked at it all and, despite herself, thought of him crumpled and broken on the mountain, and was surprised at the pain she felt when she remembered it as she looked round the room.

The shelves stacked with art books. The piles of newspapers and magazines he had accumulated over the years, the glass pots filled with turpentine and paint brushes, the tubes of paint stacked in boxes and trays, the dried out and encrusted palette. And the floor, the paint-splashed floor, a multicolored, indecipherable homage to Jackson Pollock.

Everything was a testament to who her dad was.

And somewhere among it all was the film. She felt her limbs slacken with despondency as the impossibility of finding it overwhelmed her.

"Goddammit, Evie," she said. "Just take your time. It's in here somewhere."

Or you can listen to me, Evie and leave well alone.

"No! Enough!"

The sound of her voice echoed around the room and into the corners, up to the ceiling and filled the space, as if she was claiming it for herself. It made her less afraid and made her feel that perhaps she could do it after all.

She walked over to a stack of paintings lined up against the wall. Most of them were canvases left unfinished or discarded, no doubt with a view to painting over them and re-using them.

She flipped through them and smiled at the recognizable scenes and colors. It was amazing to see her dad's whole artistic life there, propped against the studio wall, and it surprised her how lonely it made her feel.

But she wasn't here for nostalgia. She wasn't here to grieve for her father and contemplate his life or his death. She should clear it all out, she realized. Have Ethan help her. They could make a bonfire of it all in the yard outback and be done with it all. And the idea soothed her, and she turned around meaning to yell it out loud so he would hear it.

"Do you hear that, Dad? We'll burn the lot."

That was when she saw it, set in the easel, as if it was waiting for her. As if her father knew how to torment her.

A whirl of sweeping red brushstrokes, ferocious still even after all these years. She felt her skin prickle, saw the goosebumps rise, and again she tasted the sharp tang of something acidic burn the back of her throat again. The old familiar taste of panic.

The painting had lost none of its power to shock. She had forgotten all about it and was amazed by its size. It was unlike anything else her father had ever created.

She remembered him painting it and as she closed her eyes and tried to push the memory away, she heard someone call out her name.

What do you remember, Evie?

The question asked a long time ago. She was sitting in a chair, in that cold non-descript interview room, the light filtering through, the curtains weak and gray, the day closing in. The police officer asking her question after question. But she had no answers. And whenever she replied they just started all over again.

"Can you tell us what you remember?"

And she gave them the same reply, every time.

"Nothing. I remember nothing. There's nothing there."

But that's a lie though, isn't it, Evie? There is something there, she thought.

She stared at the painting. At the fiery red and felt the blood rush to her head. Then she turned and ran. She ran over the road, felt the cold in the air as she moved. One thought in her head.

Keep running. Keep running.

She needed to get away from all that red. The red of blood, the red of fire, the red of paint.

The words, a rhythm she could repeat and that her feet could move to. A beat that kept her pace steady as she took the bend in the road and began to climb. Up to the forest path, up to the hills. Up there to find him again on the summit of Mount Saxon.

Evie? Evie?

It was her dad calling to her.

Evie? Evie?

Growing louder, closer. Coming down from the mountain. Until she could stand it no longer. She ran.

"I'm coming," she called to him. "I'm coming."

CHAPTER THIRTY-FOUR

March 2015

The studio door was ajar.

So she came over here after all, Ethan thought. And he decided to check she was okay because it must have cost her a lot of energy to get up the nerve to go inside. Every time he'd suggested they go over and maybe make a start on clearing things away, Evie had hesitated and told him she wasn't ready to face seeing the way Andrew's life had been cut short.

"There's so much of him in there," she had explained. "It would feel as though he was still alive."

So he had never pushed it. She would have to come to terms with Andrew's death in her own time, he figured. But something had apparently changed; she had felt ready to confront whatever it was she imagined was there, inside the studio. And he felt hopeful, for the first time since he'd come home, that maybe he would be able to help her after all. That he could clear things up, and she would understand why he had needed to do so.

He called out to her as he pushed open the door and stepped inside.

"Hey, Evie. Everything okay?"

But there was no reply and in the weak winter light he couldn't make anything out.

"Evie?" he called.

There was a light switch by the door, and he flipped it on. Overhead, four rows of florescent tube lights buzzed to life and flooded the room with a nasty white glare that reminded him of prison. It was a light that drove you mad because it left you no room to retreat from yourself.

He had never understood how his dad could stand to work under such a harsh unforgiving glare, and he remembered the affect it could sometimes have on his mood. How he would come home after a long stretch in the studio and look tormented, as if the intense scrutiny of that bright, white glare had left him in need of further solitude and quiet. They all knew to keep out of his way on such days. To whisper around him, and not look him in the eye. To pretend he wasn't in the room.

"He's had a long day," Carole would say to them. And they knew what she meant. *Stay out of his way.* An unspoken instruction they were always careful to follow.

"Evie?" Ethan called out again, just to be sure, though it was clear now that she wasn't there. She'd left in a rush, it seemed, without closing the door behind her. Whatever it was she had feared confronting here had driven her away after all, and looking around the studio, he couldn't blame her. He wanted to run away himself. Because their dad was there in that room in ways he hadn't expected. It wasn't just the stuffy air and the oppressive glare of the overhead lights. It was more an uneasy feeling that his dad was still alive in some way, contained in every object in the room. And he wasn't ready to confront his dad's ghost.

As he turned to leave, he saw it. A large red canvas propped up on an easel. It stopped him in his tracks, the size, the color so startling it made him gasp. Because there was something shocking about it. Something unsettling. Even from a distance he could see there was something not quite right about it.

Because he remembered his father's style. That calm, romantic palette he always preferred. A *naturalist,* was always how he described himself. Someone who felt and understood the beauty around them and could communicate it to others and leave them awed.

But this? This was an abstract inferno that spoke of emotions and thoughts beyond the romantic or the sublime. And the voice was not his father's.

He walked over to the easel, so he could take a closer look.

It was too abstract to make sense of. There was none of his father's usual precision and delicacy. Close up, it resembled nothing, in fact. The energy of it was the only thing apparent. He could feel it, the rage that was there, and he could see how his father had apparently attacked the canvas. In one corner there was even a puncture mark where his palette knife had pierced the canvas.

He took a few paces backward to see if he could make more sense of it with a different perspective.

It was a forest, he could see it now, the elongated stretch of the pine trees as they reached for the sky. The densely packed proximity of the trees creating shadows and depths that felt oppressive, as if the trees had some sort of sinister motive – they wanted to draw you into those dark corners and then abandon you to get lost there, unaware that something was raging around you. The accelerating flames of a forest fire.

There was something so strange about the violence of it all, and the melancholy that seemed to have found its way in there too, as if his dad couldn't really bear to see this place he loved damaged like this. It was as if the painting was something he had needed to set down on the canvas as a way of saying to the viewer: "Look! Look at this terrible thing which has happened."

When Ethan looked closer he could just make them out. Words, printed and bold. It took him a second before he saw what they were. The brash headlines that had tormented them all during the trial and long afterward, the whole tabloid saga their lives had become.

Michael. The cabin up in flames. It was a testimony.

"My God," he whispered. "My God."

He sat down on the battered old sofa pushed up against the wall to catch his breath. He didn't dare look at the painting again.

Is this what happened to you? he thought. *Is this what it did to you?*

But he knew the answer to that. He could see it there in every brushstroke: the guilt, the regret, the years of torment and rage and sorrow. He had felt it all too. For years, while his dad painted by the florescent lights of the studio, far away under the bright glare of the prison lights, Ethan had tried to come to terms with those same feelings, the slow realization that maybe they had not done the right thing.

But he hadn't realized until now, when he first looked at that painting, how close to the edge his dad had been all the while. Only ever one step away from the abyss. For the first time, he felt a sharp pang of remorse.

But it's too late now, he thought.

"Hello?"

"Geez, Mom! You scared the hell out of me."

"Oh, sorry. I saw the light on and thought I'd check in. Are you okay?"

"Yeah… I…"

"You look like you've seen a ghost."

"It feels like I have."

"Why, what happened?"

"I was looking for Evie. The door was open, and I thought she was in here. And then I saw that." He pointed at the easel and Carole looked around and saw the painting. For a long while she stared at it, then asked, "Did your dad paint that?"

"He must have," Ethan replied.

He watched as Carole walked slowly toward it. She seemed wary of it, as if it was something she didn't want to look at.

"It isn't his usual sort of thing," she said.

He didn't know how to explain it to her, to tell her what he thought and so he waited for her to figure it out herself and watched as she cocked her head at different angles, as if taking it in from various perspectives would allow her to appreciate it better.

"I'm not sure what I'm supposed to make of it," she said.

Ethan got up from the sofa and walked over to where she was standing. "Look at the words there. Don't you remember them? Those headlines?"

And she saw it too then. Remembered she had seen this canvas years ago. And understood.

"Oh," she said. She walked over to the sofa where he had been sitting and slumped down in it, stared at the painting and looked at Ethan, waiting for him to articulate what it was she was feeling: the shock, the confusion, the anger.

His dad had had no right to commit all the pain and suffering, all the horror Michael had endured to canvas, as if pain and suffering of that kind could be turned into art. He felt a rage toward his father swell in him then.

"The whole time, he felt the damage it did to keep everything in. To never talk about it. But he never thought about me and that I might have being going through exactly the same pain as he was. Why did he think it was only Evie who needed to be protected from it? Why did I believe him when he said I needed to protect her? What about me? Why did he never think about me?"

Carole pulled him close and kissed his head. "I don't know, Ethan. I don't know. But it was wrong, that's all I can say. It was wrong of him."

He stood up, grabbed the painting and tried to lift it from the wooden frame.

"Fuck him," he yelled. "Fuck him."

"Ethan, what are you doing!"

"I'm going to burn it," he said.

The idea took hold and the more Ethan looked at that painting, the more he wanted to do it and to do it immediately.

"Come on," he said. "Give me a hand with this will you?" He stood by one side of the painting and grabbed a hold of it. "Mom? Grab your end."

"Don't you think you should talk to Evie about this first?"

"Why?"

She hesitated. "Ethan, you can't just burn all this art, I mean—"

"Fine, then I'll do it myself."

But as he tried to lever the canvas from the easel, he felt the weight of it and the cumbersome, awkward shape of the thing, and it slipped from his grasp as he failed to gain purchase and it fell to the ground.

"Careful!" she cried.

When they looked down, they saw the back of the frame exposed, and an envelope dislodged by the fall.

"What's that?" Ethan asked as he bent down to look at it.

The writing on the envelope was clear: *To my family.*

He recognized his father's handwriting immediately, and when he opened it, inside was a letter, and folded within it, an SD card.

They read the letter side by side, their eyes slowly scanning the page.

To my family,

By now you will know what has happened. You'll have found me and buried me and now you will have set about clearing away my things.

When I say I hope my death was not too much of a shock for you all, please believe me. It was my choice and, I believe, it was the right one.

I thought I could face Ethan when he came home. I thought the past would stay behind us. That it would no longer come between us.

I was wrong about that. The past is always there and there is only one way to escape it.

But this is not a goodbye. I am gone, and that's how it is. And I had my reasons. It's all here in the film. Put the card in your computer and play it. Show it to whoever you feel you need to. Make of it what you will.

An explanation. A confession. An admission of regret.

It's all of this if you need it to be.

But I am not asking you for forgiveness. It is too late for that now. It was too late years ago.

Yours,
Andrew

The sad resignation in Andrew's tone subdued them and Ethan took hold of his mom's had and squeezed it as he tried to absorb the news. When he turned to face her, she was staring at their hands. She looked hopeless, defeated, as if Andrew's final act had emptied her of purpose.

"You okay?" Ethan asked her.

"I don't know if I can really take it in. I mean, he walked up that mountain, he…" She slumped against his shoulder as if she needed his support before she could speak. "What are we going to do?" she asked him.

Ethan wrapped his arm around her shoulder and took a deep breath.

"We need to watch the film. We need to see what he had planned."

Carole sighed and tilted her face toward him, looking him in the eye and taking strength it seemed from his presence.

"Evie has a computer at the house," she said. "We can watch it there."

CHAPTER THIRTY-FIVE

March 2015

In the cramped room Evie used as an office, they sat at the desk and waited for the computer to fire up.

"Does this thing need a password?" he asked Carole.

"I don't think so."

They waited for the screen to flicker to life and Ethan breathed a sigh of relief when he saw it was password free.

"Thank God for that," he said as he inserted the SD card and waited.

It took a while for the system to start and they sat and stared at the screen, waiting. When the SD files eventually popped up on the screen Ethan noticed his mom hesitate; she was shaking.

"Are you sure you want to watch this?" she asked him.

"I don't know," he replied.

"How about we get a drink first?" she suggested. "Coffee?"

"Let's just get this over with. I don't think I can wait much longer."

He fumbled with the mouse and they both stared at the screen as the cursor hovered over the file name, *To whom it may concern.*

"You ready?" he asked her.

Carole nodded and he clicked open the file, then pressed play.

And there was his dad, sitting at the table in his studio. For a man who knew he was about to die, he seemed disturbingly composed. He looked straight at the camera and had a peaceful air about him.

His voice was steady. No wavering, no nerves, no coughs or trace of doubt. He had clearly thought through what he wanted to say, and his calmness shook them both. It was as if what he was telling them was not something he considered shocking or terrible.

These were simply the facts, he seemed to suggest. This is what happened. It was like watching someone read the news, and it then also surprised Ethan how calm he felt watching him. He wasn't shocked or horrified or upset. But hearing his dad's words was not a relief or a vindication. It was simply the sad climax to years of pain and sorrow.

They listened and watched as Andrew calmly told his story, a story they both knew was a lie. He explained how he had followed Michael to the cabin that day, not because he wanted to hurt him. All he wanted to do was warn him. Tell him he needed to leave and let him know that he wasn't to jeopardize his children's future with his hedonism and his wild ways.

All he wanted to do was send Michael away. But Michael had other ideas and grew angry at Andrew's suggestion that what he had done was wrong.

"He insisted they were doing nothing wrong," Andrew explained. "He told me I needed to stop interfering in my children's lives. That I needed to 'butt out' as he put it. He told me Evie didn't need me telling her what to do."

Carole looked away then and stifled a sob. "Stop it, please," she said.

And he reached over for the mouse and pressed pause.

"I know what he's going to say," Carole said. "But I'm just not sure I'm able to hear it. I mean, that he thinks that *this* was the right thing to do. That *this* was the solution?"

"I know," Ethan replied. "But let's watch it. Let's just watch it. I need to hear it."

He clicked the mouse and Andrew came back to life again on the screen.

There was an argument. Then a fight. The knife was something he always carried with him. Sheathed and hung from the belt around his waist.

"I could lie and say I acted without thinking," Andrew said. "I could say that anger and instinct made me reach for that knife. That I was blinded by rage or some such thing. But that's not the truth of it. I pulled that knife deliberately. I thought it through. I watched him turn and walk away. He thought he was done with me. He had said his piece and now he was walking away, and he was so contemptuous.

"If you know what you're doing—if you are used to a knife and if you've killed and gutted and skinned a deer, then it's easy. You know how to lunge. You know where to jam in the blade and how to twist it. You know how it feels to stick a blade into flesh, and it doesn't make you shudder or recoil. An older man can deal with a younger one if he needs to.

"I didn't know that Evie was there. She saw it all. That blood she talked about, she did see it. That wasn't something she imagined. But she was in a strange state. It was more than alcohol. Her pupils were so large. She walked over to Michael and touched him, and then looked at me, but I could see she wasn't there, that her brain was someplace else. So I told her to run. I told her to get away. I knew where she would run to. The place she always ran to. And when she left, I set the cabin on fire, leaving no trace of what had happened there."

Ethan stopped the film then, and tried to process what they had watched. It wasn't what he had hoped for or expected. His father sitting there, calmly trying to take the blame. Trying to undo a terrible wrong with yet another lie. Ethan had come home, looking for the truth, but now his dad was offering up another lie and daring him, again, to defy him.

"You know, maybe he's right," Ethan said. His mom looked at him, one eyebrow raised, unsure what he meant. "What I mean," he continued, "is he knew what this was going to do to Evie. He knew how bad it could get for her if she was confronted with the truth."

"That still doesn't justify what he—"

"No, Mom, please, let me finish." And she nodded, though he could see she didn't agree with him. "We should have thought it through more clearly before we came back. I thought Evie would understand if I told her I had only agreed to Dad's plan because I was so horrified at what we had done. We'd covered up what happened, and that was wrong. I thought it would be easy to convince her, because she'd remember how scared I was of Dad and how impossible it was to stand up to him. I was just a kid then."

"He should never have asked you to take the blame for it. He should never have used your shame and your guilt against you."

"But I was ashamed. What we did was wrong. And I did think I deserved to get locked up for what I did. I'm not trying to excuse what Dad did. But maybe he's right. Because if we tell her we found Michael dead in the forest and that we tried to hide what really happened, she's going to want to know how Michael died. We can't pretend that we found him lying there and didn't know what had happened—another lie. We can't pretend we didn't know what she did. She'll ask us about it. She'll start to remember."

"So what do we do?"

He looked at the computer screen and sighed. "Maybe this is the solution after all? Maybe Dad understood it better than we did. Maybe we have to go along with it."

"With another lie?"

"Is it really so different to what we were planning on doing?"

"We weren't going to lie to her Ethan," she protested.

"No, but we weren't going to tell her everything, were we? And that's as good as a lie, if you ask me."

His mom sat in silence, then she looked up at the ceiling and sighed. "Is that why he walked up there then, do you think?" she asked him. "Up to Mount Saxon."

"Maybe, I don't know. Do you really think he would do that?"

"It's possible. He tried it before, remember? And I never understood how he could have done that, why he wanted to cause us all even more pain, but maybe this is why. The guilt, maybe it did overwhelm him. Maybe he needed these lies because he could never face the truth."

"So it wasn't an accident then? His fall?"

"Why don't we let him answer that. Turn it back on and let's see what he has to say."

But there was no explanation. Just a plea from Andrew that they show the film to whomever they thought needed to see it.

When they finished it, Ethan sighed, and said, "So what am I supposed to do with this? I mean it's not really proof of my innocence, is it? The confession of a dead man? If I show it to anyone will they believe him?"

"I think he wanted you to choose. For what it's worth, I actually think he believed you'd never show this to anyone. I think he's just setting the record straight for Evie. He thought that would be enough. That this was all he owed you. No plea for forgiveness, no explanation, just his warped version of the truth. All the rest of it, all the things you really want from him, I don't think he thought about it."

"He's leaving it up to me to decide."

"Yes, I think he is."

"Goddammit. What the fuck does he want from me? He's dead and he's still doing it. He's still causing hurt and harm and pain."

On the screen Andrew's face, paused at the end of the film, flickered in grainy pixels, and he couldn't bear to look at him any longer. When he leaned over to turn it off, he thought he saw the trace of a smile on his dad's lips, as if he was pleased with this choice he had bequeathed them all.

Ethan stared at the face for a moment then whispered, "You son of a bitch. But fine, if this is what you want, then so be it. I'm going to let the whole world believe this is what you did." Then he snapped the laptop shut.

"Listen, we're going to have to show this to Evie," he said.

Carole nodded. "She must be upstairs, asleep still."

He could see how tired she was, as if the film had sapped her of all her energy. "Do you want me to go and get her?" he asked.

"Could you?"

He nodded then headed upstairs wondering how he was going to explain it all to her.

CHAPTER THIRTY-SIX

March 2015

The early morning light was still faint, but she knew the way. This was her place, every corner of it. Even blindfolded, she could walk this path. She stumbled forward, upward, the destination unseen, but known. Up the hillside. Into the forest. Safe again, beneath the trees. But there on the breeze, rustling through the branches, came a voice.

Look what you've done. Look what you've done.

"Dad?" she cried out.

No reply.

"Dad!"

And again, silence.

She kept walking. Her legs were burning with the exertion but she did not slow down.

And then, there it was. The clearing. The granite rock. The pine trees. And she stopped and leaned forward, hands on her knees, gasping for breath. The burn and tang of vomit squeezing up her throat again. She could not contain it and she let the contents spill to the forest floor. Smelled it and remembered. The same smell that day. She was sick then too. Made sick by the sight of that trickle of blood and the seeping blackness as it consumed the blue of his eyes.

She tried to scream, but no sound emerged. There was only the grip around her throat. And as she tried to catch her breath, from the corner of her eye she saw something move and take shape, and when she looked up, there he was.

Michael.

No, that can't be right, she thought. *It can't be him. Because the shape that was lying there did not look human. No, it couldn't be.*

It's just a deer, Evie. The voice clear and emphatic even though those words had been spoken decades ago. *It's just a deer, Evie. It's just a deer.*

She stepped forward, wanting to believe it. Just a deer, it was just a deer. One step. Two. She walked closer, closer. Saw the blood spilling to the forest floor. Saw eyes looking up to the sky, through the trees and into the open space, searching for an escape route. But there was none, the way out was blocked. She saw blood, so much blood. Dripping and dripping to the forest floor. She looked down and saw the pine needles seeped in it. Wet and glossy and red.

She walked toward it but couldn't look at it. The deer. That thing. Whatever it was. Just moments before he had been there. She was sure of it. The eyes she had looked into were not animal. They were blue. Dilated. Terrified. And she knew them.

She had bent down and touched his hair, felt the warmth of him. Then a drop of blood. She had seen it on his cheek, sliding down his face.

She touched his cheek and tried to wipe it away. Saw it smudge, red across his skin. Felt his warmth too. Death something new. Moments ago, he was alive. A boy still. Human still. Until that crack, that thud. And the gash to the side of his head. His eyes so blue, then the pupils dilating and filling his eyes with a hollow, black stare.

Look at me, Evie. Look at me. His eyes. Demanding. Insisting. *Look at what you have done.*

Death was the same no matter how it occurred. An animal, a boy. A tooth, a claw. A rock. Hunted or by accident. The horror was the same however it happened. The carcass abandoned on the forest floor. The boy, lying there, waiting to be burned. The memories once jumbled, now becoming clearer. There was Michael. There was the deer.

Then, she heard a voice again. *Look what you've done. Look what you did to me, Evie.*

She turned and looked through the trees to where the sound came from. But there was no one there. Only the rustle of the trees and the sound of her breath rising and falling. Fast at first, then slowing until it could barely be heard.

She was alone. And the memories were separating. The dreams from the reality. The lies from the truth. The confusion from the clarity.

The rock was there in her hand. The weight of it, familiar. And she looked at him. Saw the dead black dilation of his eyes, the faint rim of blue there. She saw the head, crooked, tilted at an angle as if he was asking her a question. *Why did you do this to me, Evie?*

Death, fresh still. New still. A moment ago…

And she screamed, she wailed, "No! No!" and then dropped the rock, turned and ran and ran and ran.

*

At the door to her bedroom, Ethan hesitated. The space beyond still felt out of bounds, though when he tried to explain it to himself, tried to figure out why he needed to stop at the threshold as if he was waiting for permission to step inside, he couldn't find an answer.

Instead he found himself knocking gently on the door and calling out her name again, "Evie? You in there?" then waiting, counting to ten, before turning the handle and stepping inside and flicking on the light switch.

The room was monastically empty. A bed, a small table with a lamp, a wardrobe and chest of drawers. No mirror. No decoration to speak of, not even a painting on the wall or a rug on the floor. Even the curtains were a pale, monotone gray.

He was surprised by how sad it made him feel to see the bareness of her room. There was something extremely lonely about it.

And it was almost like a prison cell, he thought. As if she wanted to erase herself from the space and insist that it wasn't her own, as if she was waiting for something or someone to take her away.

He stood paralyzed and unsettled by the sight of the room, until his mom called up to him and roused him from his thoughts.

"Is she there?" she asked.

"No," he replied.

He turned off the light, closed the door and headed back downstairs and tried not to think about what he had just seen.

"Later," he thought. "You can think about it later."

"Maybe she went over to Andrew's?" Carole continued. "We were talking about making a start on clearing things away. Maybe she's over there sorting through things."

"Yeah, maybe…"

"Ethan, is everything okay?"

"Something doesn't feel right is all. That painting. Evie was in there this morning, she must have been, that's why the door was open. She'd have seen that painting too and—"

"What?"

"You saw that painting, you saw what it was. If Evie saw it, she would have understood that it was Michael there in that painting, in all that red, and…"

"We need to find her, before she does something stupid."

They both understood where to find her. Where she always went.

*

They saw her immediately. A figure in the distance, heading to the path that led to the summit of Mount Saxon, her yellow jacket flapping. She stumbled as she ran, and Carole called out to her, "Evie! Evie!" But she either didn't hear her or she decided to pay no attention. "Evie," she called out to her again, more in despair than hope. "Evie."

But again, Evie paid no heed. She just ran and ran and didn't look back, propelled by a fear that defied gravity. And then she slowed down, and then suddenly stopped. She was by the outcrop, that edging closer to the drop, to the very place where Andrew had gone over.

Carole told Ethan to go then. "You have to go! Don't wait for me. Go and help her."

Evie was heading back to her father, and if they didn't stop her now, she would follow him, over the edge.

*

They were there that day. They saw everything. They saw her. They saw what she did.

She had seen them too, standing there beside Michael's bloodied body, deciding what to do. She had seen her father pick up the bloodied rock and drop it into his pocket, then call her name. But she hadn't been able to move. All she saw were those blue eyes staring up at the sky.

When she looked again, her father was gone, disappeared as swift as a wisp of fog, and she wondered if she had really seen him at all, or if he was an apparition, a figment of her imagination, a ghost of some sort.

She will never know why she walked toward what was left of Michael. To check it really was him? To comfort him? To try to save him or help him? Perhaps that is what she hoped, but he was gone. She had reached out and touched him just to be sure. Had felt his skin, warm still.

And then...

The years of it. The blackness, the hole where her memory had been. And her dad beside her all those years, watching her and waiting for her to remember. Telling her to forget. But knowing that one day it would resurface. Ethan would return, and Evie would remember the three of them in the forest that day, creating lies upon lies. Inflicting pain upon pain. And what for?

She screamed then, the agony of it all bursting through her. "Why? Why?"

A voice somewhere called her name, tried to calm her.

"Evie, don't move. Please, don't move."

*

He had seen her like this before, that panic in her eyes, that primal fear. It was a fear driven by the need to survive, by the need to flee something awful and dangerous.

"Evie!" he called out to her.

A mistake to shock her like that. She saw him and took a step backward, closer to the edge, and when he stepped toward her, she took another step back and cried out to him, "No, go away! Go away!"

He had to fight the urge to rush toward her and pull her away from the edge. He knew exactly what was running through her mind: *jump*, that was what she was thinking.

So he stood still and held her gaze. As long as she didn't look away from him, as long as he could become the focus of her attention, then there was a chance. For a minute or two they faced one another, silent and unmoving. Just the rush of air as it flowed over the mountainside. From below, he could hear their mom making her way up the path, the gravel slipping under her feet.

For a moment she seemed to recognize him. "Ethan?"

"It's okay, Evie. Everything's okay."

"No, it's not," she replied.

He dared to take a small step forward, reaching out his hand toward her, but she screamed, "No! Stay away from me! Stay away!"

Then Carole's voice came from behind. "Evie, please, come here. Please, we have to tell you something. It's important."

And it was all or nothing now, Ethan realized. His mother had pushed it too soon, but what choice did he have now but to follow through on it.

"Evie," he said, "we know what happened that day. We know Dad was in the forest, and—"

"He thought he could protect me. He thought I would never remember. He thought—"

"It's okay, Evie," Carole said. "We know what he did, and we'll help you through this. We can help you."

"Why? I don't deserve your help. All that blood, all that pain. You can't help me. You can't undo that. Look…" She held out her hands to them and turned them over palms upward. "Look," she said again. "Look at the blood. Look at what I did."

"Evie," Carole said. "There's no blood there."

"Yes! Look at it! How can you not see it? Michael's blood. Look!"

And she walked toward them, hands out, showing them her palms, her dirtied palms, covered in grit and mud.

"It's dirt, Evie," Carole pleaded with her. "It's just dirt."

Evie looked down at her hands then shook her head, not noticing how he approached with quiet steady steps. He was within reach now, two more strides and he could reach out and touch her, pull her back from the edge.

But the movement made her look up, then jump back, and she saw him then, so close to her as he lunged to grab her, knowing he could do nothing else now, and she jumped back then turned.

"No, Evie, don't" Carole cried.

But she didn't hear them, she didn't turn to face them, or stop. She simply ran, a sound coming from her chest that was guttural and wordless and agonized.

And at the edge, she didn't stop, she kept on running, away from them and toward something unknown.

"Evie!" they both screamed.

But it was too late. At the edge, she fell forward, her yellow coat flapping around her like a pair of broken wings. Then she was gone.

CHAPTER THIRTY-SEVEN

March 2015

It made the news again, the papers all over it. A story like theirs was too sensational to ignore. Ethan knew they would seek him out eventually and thought, naïvely perhaps, that he could fend them off for a while with a brief quote, asking that his privacy be respected. But it was more a hope than anything. Deep down, he knew someone would come knocking on the door. He had been here before and knew what to expect. Though when the phone started ringing at all hours of the day, he felt under siege and unprepared for it. It would be just a matter of days before they came to his door, he figured.

"Let's just go home," Carole had offered. "At least in Boulder, you won't be so visible. This place is too small for anyone to hide away and expect some privacy."

She was right, but he wasn't ready to leave.

"We need to be here for Evie," he told her. "The funeral, the arrangements…"

"We can do that in Boulder. And Ashley has said she'll help."

"I know, but I don't really want to leave her here alone, do you?"

"No, but we need to come through this as well, Ethan."

"Okay… If it gets too much, we'll head home. But for now, let's stay, for Evie."

They had left it at that and in the intervening days he had made a conscious effort to avoid the news as much as possible.

No television, no newspapers, no email. But isolation was only possible for so long. In the end, it was Ryan who broke through. He was standing at the door one morning, and when Ethan saw the figure behind the glass, he panicked.

"What's happened?" he asked Ryan as he opened the door.

"Nothing. I just wanted to check you were okay."

"Oh, right, thanks. I'm fine."

He waited for Ryan to leave it at that, but instead of walking away, he hovered there on the doorstep, waiting to be invited in.

"What is it Ryan?"

"Is it okay if I come in?"

Ethan nodded and opened the door wide and Ryan stepped inside and headed to the living room.

"I was just worried all this nonsense in the papers might have upset you."

"What nonsense in the papers?"

And he saw it then, the paper in Ryan's hand. Not a tabloid at least, and for that he was grateful, though the headline was jarring enough. A photo of his father, staring out at the world, right there on the front page, beneath a headline that was biblical and judgmental: *The Sins of the Father.*

He was speechless.

"Sorry," Ryan apologized. "I thought you'd already seen it."

"No, I've been trying to avoid the news."

"Right. I guess that makes sense."

They sat in the armchairs in the living room and Ryan set the paper on the coffee table.

Ethan looked at his father's face in the photo, and noticed it was a still from the video, though how they had managed to get a hold of it, he wasn't sure. The police must have released it, he supposed.

He looked so calm, so forthright. There was no need to try and second-guess what he was saying: "I am guilty."

There was a trash can in the corner of the room and Ryan spotted it and got up, taking the paper with him.

"No, don't," Ethan told him. "I might as well read it."

"Are you sure?"

"The headline, I assume, is the worst of it."

And Ryan laughed at that. "It is actually. The rest of it is just talking about the case. They're saying you can clear your name. A miscarriage of justice."

"Yeah? Well I don't know about that. A confession from a dead man, would a thing like that hold up in court?"

"I don't know. Maybe. The papers seem to think so."

Ryan put the newspaper back down on the table, and Ethan pulled it toward him and tried to read it. But the words seemed to merge into one incoherent babble. Ryan had not been entirely honest. The main story dealt with the legal aspects of the case, but there was more. Any newspaper editor knew the story always lay in the people rather than the facts and so the journalist had tried to imagine the impact all of this was having on the family. How it must feel to *"be so betrayed by your own father."*

If any journalist had been sitting there beside him now, he could have answered that question quickly and unequivocally. It could pretty much be summed up in one word.

Heartbreaking, he would tell them. *You never recover from it.*

"Here," Ryan interrupted him. "Give me that, I don't know why I brought it over, now I think of it. I guess I thought it was good news."

Ethan looked again at his dad's photo. "It is, I suppose. I just can't think that far ahead. We've got Evie to take care of."

Ryan nodded, and Ethan saw him swallow and blink away his emotions, then he folded the paper over so that his dad's face disappeared and was replaced by the sports pages.

"You know, the terrible thing is that all those years I was inside," he told Ryan, "there was a part of me that always wondered if he'd ever admit it." He shook his head. "Ach, I don't know. None of it makes sense, does it?"

"No, it doesn't," Ryan agreed.

Ethan could see the question there in Ryan's eyes. The way he held back from asking it, because he was scared to ask it, scared of what the answer might be.

"You want to ask why I confessed, don't you?" Ethan broke the silence. "You want to understand, because it makes no sense."

Ryan shuffled in his seat, then gathered his composure and looked him in the eye. "Why did you confess then?"

"I don't know if I can answer that. Not yet. I think Dad put a whole lifetime of pressure on me to look after her. I always thought she was my responsibility. If any harm came to her, then it was my fault. And when I think back to that summer, to the crazy things we did, I mean, I was young, we were in trouble, and I really did think I was the one who had put Evie in that situation and so…"

"Hey, it's okay. We don't have to go into it all right now. You did what you thought was right."

"Did I? I don't know if I did. What a mess, all of this. I… Dammit, Ryan, why didn't she let us tell her? Why did she run like that?"

"She figured it out, is what I think," Ryan said. "She knew what Andrew had done, and it broke her. The one person she loved and trusted had betrayed her. And she was too frail to cope with something like that, Ethan. It was too much."

"I was so close to catching her. I could have reached out. Just one step that was all, just one step."

"Don't Ethan. This wasn't your fault. If she'd seen that film, if you'd shown her what Andrew had done to her, do you think she would have survived that?"

Ethan thought about the letter he'd found crumpled in the living room, the pages torn and thrown on the floor. He thought about Evie, how she must have felt when she read it.

No, she hadn't been able to cope with it.

But it was a truth she needed to hear. He'd had twenty years to think about it. Twenty years to understand that the truth, in the end, was more important than anything else. Even family. Even loyalty. Even love.

He'd tried to make her understand that. He'd really tried. But she wouldn't listen. She would never remember.

"We would have helped her get through it," he told Ryan. "God knows how, but we would have helped her somehow."

Ryan smiled and draped an arm around Ethan's shoulder to comfort and console him. "I know you would, Ethan."

*

The small group stood in silence near the summit of Mount Saxon and looked out over the valley.

Ethan closed his eyes and felt his mom squeeze his hand. Even with his eyes closed he saw it still, the sweep of the land, the glint of the lake, home, a place he had learned to carry within him all these years. A comfort and a constant which had sustained him.

And now, there they were, waiting to leave. Just one final task before they went.

"Should we say something?" Ryan asked.

Ethan opened his eyes and looked at Carole and Ashley. "I don't know what to say," he admitted.

"Me neither," Ashley said.

Ethan eased the backpack from his shoulder and unzipped it, then lifted out the urn and placed it on the ground, and as if by instinct they gathered around it and looked down, heads bent in a solemn silence. No words were needed. Theirs was a grief that couldn't be articulated. Evie should still be there with them, that was all they knew, and that was what their silence meant—this unobtainable longing to have her with them still.

His mom bent down and lifted the urn, then turned to face Ethan. "Are you ready?"

He nodded and watched as she unscrewed the lid. Then a voice, quiet and uncertain. Ryan's.

"Could I say something?" he asked.

"Yes," they all whispered, relieved that one of them could find the words to say goodbye to Evie.

"I don't have much to say, Evie, but I just wanted you to know that you will always be here in this place you loved. You'll be here, all around us, in these mountains and when we look at them, it's you we'll see, it's you we'll hear, it's you we'll always think of and always love."

Ethan looked out over the valley and watched the sky. In the distance, clouds were rolling in, black and thunderous, the sun breaking through now and again in shafts of dirty yellow, illuminating the side of the hill and glancing off the dark glassy surface of the lake.

He wanted to sit there and wait for the rain. Have it drench them and leave them shivering and soaked to the bone. And cleansed.

Carole lifted the lid and they watched as a layer of ash floated into the air and was carried by the wind. Then she lifted it higher and tilted it toward the mountain, into the wind and they watched as the gray cloud merged with the air then headed out to the pines and moss and the lake. Evie everywhere then, and nowhere.

He thought he heard her, a voice on the wind that was carried away, whispering goodbye, and he took hold of his mom's hand and squeezed it tight, then said, "Come on, let's go."

*

It was dark as they drove over the bridge and turned onto the road. The quiet dark of an early spring morning, even the birds asleep still in the trees.

His mom drove slowly through town and tried not to look back.

On the road, in the darkness, he sensed it, looming: Mount Saxon. His father. His sister. The past. And as if she could feel the pull of it too, she squeezed the accelerator gently, and the car thrust forward. But he knew if he was to look in the rear-view mirror, he would see it there, its vast imposing form distinct and unwavering, even in the darkness.

But he did not look. He kept his eyes on the road and focused on the white of the line that marked the edges. Saw it illuminated, pointing the way forward. Away from the past and onward to the future.

A LETTER FROM JENNIFER

Dear reader,

I want to say a huge thank you for choosing to read *All the Lies We Told*. I hope you enjoyed reading it as much as I enjoyed writing it.

For an author, there is nothing more inspiring than knowing there are readers out there in the world reading, and hopefully enjoying, your work. If you want to keep up to date with all my latest releases please sign up at the following link. Your email address will never be shared, and you can unsubscribe at any time.

www.bookouture.com/jennifer-harvey

If you did enjoy reading *All the Lies We Told*, I would be very grateful if you could write a review. I'd love to hear what you think, and it makes such a difference helping new readers to discover one of my books for the first time. Thank you!

I love hearing from my readers—you can get in touch through Twitter, Goodreads or my website.

Thank you,
Jennifer Harvey

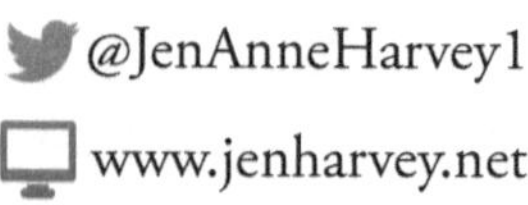